"Compelling. . . . An exploration of the quiet desperation of teenagers on the edge of adulthood. . . ."   – *Globe and Mail*

"David Bergen sounds nary a false note in his latest precise, challenging novel."   – *Toronto Star*

"Bergen's story of 16-year-old Mason Crowe explores the mystery of coming of age: how it happens and, equally important, what happens when the process goes awry."   – *Hamilton Spectator*

"Bergen's psychological portraits are accurate and passionately observed."   – Jury citation, Governor General's Award

"His excellent writing [has] piquancy and nuance. . . ."   – *Quill & Quire*

"Spare, lucid, haunting and overlaid with melancholy. . . . It's a terrific performance. . . . Bergen is simply too good and too clear-eyed a writer to ever circle around the truth of his subject. His subject here, the emotional and physical lives of teenagers, is revealed as both sad and perplexing. . . . A deeply beautiful book."   – *Edmonton Journal*

"Goes well beyond the traditional coming-of-age chronicle to pose problems of loss and rejection and to set these questions against the uncertainties of young adulthood. . . . The book is well written and insightful and captures the clamour, chaos and fractured idiom of youth as it passes into adulthood. As a commentary on the priorities of the young, *The Case of Lena S.* ranks high indeed."   – *London Free Press*

"Bergen's language flows and his descriptions are tantalizing."   – *FFWD*

BOOKS BY DAVID BERGEN

Sitting Opposite My Brother (1993)
A Year of Lesser (1996)
See the Child (1999)
The Case of Lena S. (2002)

DAVID BERGEN

THE

CASE

OF

LENA S.

EMBLEM EDITIONS
Published by McClelland & Stewart Ltd.

Cloth edition published 2002
First Emblem Editions publication 2003

National Library of Canada Cataloguing in Publication

Bergen, David, 1957–
The case of Lena S. / David Bergen.

ISBN 0-7710-1187-3

I. Title.

PS8553.E665C38 2004   C813'.54   C2003-901806-7
PR9199.3.B413C38 2004

We acknowledge the financial support of the Government of Canada through the Book Publishing Industry Development Program and that of the Government of Ontario through the Ontario Media Development Corporation's Ontario Book Initiative. We further acknowledge the support of the Canada Council for the Arts and the Ontario Arts Council for our publishing program.

The author gratefully acknowledges the support of the Manitoba Arts Council and the Canada Council for the Arts.

An excerpt from this novel appeared in a slightly different form in *Toronto Life* magazine.

SERIES EDITOR: ELLEN SELIGMAN

Cover design: Brian Bean
Cover image: © Lisa Spindler/Graphistock
Series logo design: Brian Bean

Typeset in Bembo by M&S
Printed and bound in Canada

EMBLEM EDITIONS
McClelland & Stewart Ltd.
The Canadian Publishers
481 University Avenue
Toronto, Ontario
M5G 2E9
www.mcclelland.com/emblem

1   2   3   4   5   07   06   05   04   03

For Mary

"The greatest danger, that of losing one's own self, may pass off as quietly as if it were nothing; every other loss, that of an arm, a leg, five dollars, a wife, etc., is sure to be noticed."

— Søren Kierkegaard

1

The year he turned sixteen, Mason Crowe met Seeta Chahal, a girl who was to be married in late summer to a man she had never met. They were in the same gym class where one of their blocks was tennis. She was not very good. He was. She asked him one day if he could teach her because her future husband, Ajit Dhaliwal from the Punjab, had requested, if not competence, than at least a little knowledge about tennis, English poetry, and philosophy. And so Mason became Seeta's tennis tutor, and almost immediately introduced her to Keats and Donne. About philosophy, he knew nothing.

They met twice a week in the late afternoon. Seeta wore low white runners and black jeans and a white flowing shirt that could have been her father's. She implied, through their conversations, that she had chosen Mason because he was two years younger than she and ought not to have been seen as a threat to Ajit's territory. She pronounced "territory" quickly, with clipped vowels. She said she liked the name Mason Crowe. Though crow ate carrion, she said, she admired their sleek blackness. She added that he looked sporty and his large forearms seemed tennis-y. He explained that his arms were strong because, on Saturdays, he was a bricklayer's helper. He said he worked for two Portuguese brothers who were crude and cheap. They were so hard up they sculpted nudes in their mortar. Seeta ignored this detail; she heard it and smiled slightly, but still, she ignored it.

By the second lesson Seeta had configured the velocity of a tennis ball to the straight-armed swing of a racquet but still, after half an hour, she fell breathless at the sidelines, the court littered with errant balls, the net her principle enemy. Mason had arrived with a head full of freshly acquired English verse that he threw in Seeta's direction, usually just before a serve. He held the ball between his fingers and cradled the sweaty racquet. Beyond the haze of brilliant sunshine, Seeta bounced on her thin white treads. The seven bracelets on her right wrist jangled. "Love is beauty and beauty is love," he sang out and lobbed the ball her way like a missive that contained an ode to her, the urn. He also memorized bits of Yeats and discovered that she liked the rhythm and language. He quoted "The Stolen Child" one afternoon and she tilted her head, paused, and said, "That, I like. Though it's sad."

They were never alone. Seeta always brought her sister Sadia along, who would sit on a bench by the chain-link fence and read romance novels, lifting her head whenever Seeta squealed with delight, then looking away, returning to her book, a solitary sentinel.

After one session, the three of them sat on benches in the shade and drank water and Seeta talked about "Nietzsche," the man she was going to marry. She called him Nietzsche because he was a philosopher and she knew that the first Nietzsche, the real one, had said God was dead, and these days she felt that that was true. She spoke about her future husband as if this were not her life, as if she were describing an object that was passing by in the distance. When she finished, she held Mason's hand, traced his knuckles, and said, "Do you think I am mad?"

"Not if you don't," he said. "Obviously this was planned long ago. When you were three or four or something like that."

"Last year," she said, "My grandfather chose him."

"Can you get out of it?" Mason asked, made bold by their arms touching and Seeta noting his knuckles, however absent-mindedly.

"I'm not sure I want to." The side of her mouth went up, a subtle smile. "I was offered several," she continued. "A doctor, a shoe factory owner, and Ajit, the philosopher. I chose Ajit."

"You met them?"

"No, I saw pictures of them. Along with biographies, family details, all."

"Shoes would have been nice," Mason said. He made a motion with his hand at her runners and she pulled her legs away, as if he had violated some space. Perhaps the feet were sacred, he thought.

"How about you?" he asked Sadia, who, though her book was still open, was obviously aware of the conversation.

"Hah," she cried out, "Never."

"Daddy will insist," Seeta told her sister.

Sadia shrugged. Compared to Seeta she was plain. Mason thought then that no man, being allowed to choose, would want her.

It was May. They lived on Academy, a good distance from Seeta's place. There were four of them in the house, mother, brother, Mason, and father, who was usually off seeking customers for unwanted sets of encyclopedias in Southeastern Manitoba and Northwest Ontario, around Rainy River, an area he frequented not for the local people's willingness to buy, but because in the late afternoons, along the shore of Lake of the Woods, he could fish. Danny, the older brother, was rarely home. He was a head chef in a fancy restaurant and he dated girls who were very good-looking and he drove a red Mazda and was generally not very bright.

Their house was small but it looked backwards toward the mansions of Wellington Crescent, and on warm evenings the sound of laughter and music came to them like signals from a faraway and unapproachable place. One evening there was a fight, with raised voices and the breaking of glass. A woman sobbed. Mason's mother was pleased. She said, "Listen," and she lifted her head and moved it back and forth like some kind of small bird. She was reading a thick book that sat in her lap and her legs parted slightly so that the spine of the book dipped between her thighs. The book was too heavy to hold up so she had to lean forward, neck bent, and this made her look childlike. She looked over her glasses and said, "Being rich does not make you smart or beautiful."

Mason didn't answer. This was one of the typical puzzling statements his mother liked to make, as if by throwing out nonsense she herself sounded smart. He was eating toast and standing by the screen door, listening to the night noises and thinking about Seeta. Earlier, he had looked up a recipe for chapatti and he planned to try making it that evening, after his mother was sleeping or had gone out. When Mason's father was away she sometimes dressed up in a nice top and a skirt and pantyhose and dark high-heeled shoes and went out dancing with her friend Rhonda. Or someone.

The rich cries had subsided, but the night noises continued – sirens, revving engines, the clatter of motorcycles. Mrs. Crowe rose and walked to the bathroom. When she came back Mason's father telephoned to say that he was near the American border. He'd been chased by two dogs, been thrown off of one farmer's land, but finally shared a meal with a family called Menke to whom he'd sold a set of encyclopedias. He was spending the night there. Mason's mother told him this after his father hung up. When she had first answered the phone she did not seem happy. She listened and looked at her nails and at one point she said, "Good. Good. Don't let them kill you in your sleep."

Mason imagined that his father chuckled then and said something provocative because his mother's eyebrows went up and her face softened. Her tongue touched a top tooth and then pulled away. She bit a nail. She was wearing a white short-sleeved top, and a pale-green skirt. Her feet were bare. She said, "He's okay," and then she said, "Mason, it's your dad," and she put the phone down and walked away from it.

Mason took the receiver. He could smell his mother on it, the same smell of the perfume he'd bought for her at the Bay. A little bottle that said *Iliad*. Mason waited a bit, then said, "Hello."

"Mason, how're you doing?"

"Fine." The phone creaked in his father's hand, like he was trying to crush it. "Where are you?" Mason asked. He was a polite boy.

"Sprague, near the border. I found a buyer. Now we can eat steak."

"Good," Mason said.

"You take care of your mother, okay?"

"I am."

"I'll be there this weekend. We'll do the family thing."

Mason said that that was nice. He said that Danny could cook and they'd all eat well. "Mom'll be happy," he said.

His father laughed and asked if he was still working for Jack Costa. Mason said he was, though it wasn't much fun and Mr. Costa was mean.

"Whaddya mean, mean?"

"He's cheap," Mason said. "That makes him mean."

"Huh," Mr. Crowe went. Then he said, "It's just Saturdays. It can't harm you." And then he said goodbye and hung up.

Mason's mother came back into the room holding a drink. She sat down and put her feet on the footstool. Mason looked at her heels, her insteps, the fine lines through the milkiness. She opened a bottle of clear nail polish and drew one foot up and leaned over it. The bare calf now and the blue bone of her shin. The little brush flashed and painted. A seed from the raspberry jam was stuck between his teeth. He sucked at it.

"Don't do that. It makes you sound simple."

Mason closed his mouth.

"Your father is always so happy when he's gone."

"He made a sale," Mason said.

"Even when he hasn't sold anything, and we all know that's common, even then he's happy. Help me here."

Mason took the bottle and closed it and set it on the mantel. His mother had retrieved her glass of gin and water. He looked down at her and saw that one day he would be her age. He said, "If you like someone and you know that they might like you but can't because there's someone else, someone from another place, someone coming to take them away, what do you do?"

"Is this true?" his mother asked. She seemed about to smile and Mason thought if he made this into a funny story it wouldn't be as dangerous.

"Her grandfather has chosen a man and he's a philosopher and his name's Ajit but she's never met him. I told her it wasn't fair because my name was never in the lottery and how can you win if your ticket's not in the hat."

"Who's *she*?"

"Seeta."

"Have I met Seeta?"

"She's the girl I play tennis with."

"And you like her?"

"I don't know. I think so."

"And she encourages you?"

"I don't know. How do you know?"

"Oh, Mason. Come here." She patted the couch beside her and Mason sat and she took his head and looked at him and then pulled his face towards her shoulder and neck and he felt her heat and smelled the *Iliad*. "That's not fair. You want me to call up her mother and put in a bid? Or ask her over. This weekend. When your father's here."

"She wouldn't come."

"She might. Ask her. She might." She let go of his head and neck and looked at him and said there was always danger in love. She said that he was young and though his heart was swollen now it might not be next week. "The vagaries of love," she said. "Distance does not make the heart grow fonder. I can't imagine loving a man who arrives from a distance, like this Ajit. Isn't there someone else? A girl your age?"

Mason thought of Lena Schellendal, a girl he'd admired from a distance.[1] He said, "I'm not interested in anybody else."

"I just don't want your heart broken," Mrs. Crowe said. She touched Mason's face and he saw the underside of her arm and the crease of her blouse and he thought how he'd seen his mother naked just last week. She'd been changing her top and she wasn't wearing a bra and he'd come into the

---

[1] He sometimes eats breakfast at The Nook, where Lena works, and he has noticed her polishing the counter or has overheard her taking orders: "Would you like rye, brown, or white toast with that?" He likes her voice.

bedroom and looked at her and she'd looked at him and she hadn't tried to cover up, just said, "Maybe you should knock." Her assurance had surprised him and the beauty of her breasts had surprised him; it was as if assurance and beauty were two halves of the same circle.

The next morning Mason phoned Seeta. Her mother answered.

"Mrs. Chahal," Mason said, "it's Charlie from Charlie's. Seeta's boss. Is Seeta there?" Mrs. Chahal responded with a yes and disappeared, and for a few minutes Mason heard scuffling and dark whispers and then, finally, Seeta said, "Hello?"

"Seeta, this is Mason."

"Really?"

"You said I could call there. I thought maybe you or your sister would answer."

"Really? My mother thinks you're funny. 'It's that Mason boy,' she says. Wouldn't let me come near the phone. I had to wrestle her for it. Why don't you at least lower your voice if you're going to be Charlie. She knows Charlie. Likes Charlie. You she sees as a horny sixteen-year-old. You know that."

"My father's coming up here for the weekend," Mason said. "Would you come for supper Saturday night?"

"I could."

"You wouldn't have to be my date."

"I could be. If you like."

"I just thought, with everyone there, you know. My brother'll cook. He's a chef." Mason could hear a jangle of bracelets as Seeta's hand moved. He heard a quick breath and she said, "I'll come. I'd like to meet your family, though I might have to bring my sister."

They talked some more, about Sadia, whom Seeta claimed was shy but seductive, about Mason's mother, who was a math teacher, about Ajit and the food he would eat and what it would be like to sleep with a stranger. "At least he isn't a doctor," Seeta said. "Doctors have a funny smell. Ajit will smell like books."

"Is he rich?"

"He has an inheritance. Not large. My uncle in Vancouver owns a community newspaper, he expects Ajit to work for him."

Listening to the rise and fall of Seeta's voice, the intake of breath after each sentence, Mason concluded, after hanging up, that he knew nothing about love other than the desire to hear Seeta call out his name.

Over the following days Mason thought about Seeta. Her willingness to come to his house had surprised him and though he anticipated her visit the possibilities for failure were enormous. His father could be especially tactless. He liked to ask lots of questions and tell bad jokes and show off his limited knowledge of pop culture.

The evening of the dinner there were seven people sitting around the table. They ate spaghetti squash and steak and baked potatoes and salad and they drank beer with the meal. Seeta had arrived halfway through the meal, her younger sister Sadia in tow. They'd come by bus and then walked the last distance and Seeta, especially, had been slightly out of breath. Her hair was wind-tossed. She didn't apologize for being late, just sat down and after introductions and hellos accepted a steak and potato. Sadia said she wasn't very hungry and took only squash. She drank water and lifted her chin and pointed it at each speaker and her thin mouth moved occasionally as if she were carrying on her own conversation. Her hair was in two braids tied with white ribbons. She was more angular than Seeta; her coldness, her distance, made her an enigma. Danny had brought his girl-friend, Maryann. They were sitting side by side, across from Seeta and Mason, and Mason was both proud and jealous of his brother, who was twenty-four years old and had a beautiful girlfriend and his own good looks. "He's swarthy," Mason would tell Seeta later, and she wouldn't disagree.

When Seeta arrived Mr. Crowe pulled out her chair for her and then he did the same for Sadia. "Voila," he said.

"Jesus, Dad," Mason said.

His father ignored him. He studied Seeta and asked her where she was from.

"Give her a break, Dad," Mason said. "Besides, that's such a stupid question."

"That's okay," Seeta said. "I'm from Winnipeg."

Mason's father seemed unfazed. He asked, "I mean, your parents. What country do they come from?"

"The Punjab. That's in India. I'm Sikh."

Mason's father nodded. His mother asked, "Do you have family there?"

"My future husband, he's from there."

"Your husband?" Danny asked. He looked at Mason, at Seeta.

"You thought I was Mason's girlfriend."

"Yeah."

"I am," Seeta said, and she took Mason's hand and smiled. "I'm a polyandrist."

"Son of a bitch," Danny said.

Mason felt the smoothness of Seeta's palm and held her little finger.

"What's a polyandrist?" Maryann asked.

"The female version of a polygamist," Mason said.

"You're joking," Danny said. He was looking at Mason, who shrugged. The attention was nice. Seeta was lovely. Mason liked her very much, even though she was eighteen and would, in several months, leave him, and he knew that she wasn't now and never would be his girlfriend. She liked older men, someone like Danny, who was eyeing her now.

"Love is not a joke," Seeta said.

"That's a fact," Maryann said, placing a hand on Danny's neck. "What's the problem?" she asked him. Her nails were streaks of neon. "Are you jealous?"

Danny laughed.

Mrs. Crowe said, "I take it this is an arranged marriage, Seeta?"

"Yes, Mrs. Crowe."

"And you don't mind talking about it? It's not too intimate?"

"It's just different. Not intimate. At least, not yet." Her small shoulders went up and down. The vertebrae moved in her neck. "I'm used to it," she said.

"That polyandry part, that was a joke," Danny said.

"Of course." Seeta let go of Mason and placed her own hands back on the table. "People feel sorry for me. I hate that part."

Danny asked, "You have no choice?"

"Of course I have choice."

"Yes, yes, about who. I understand that. But whether to do this or not. Ultimately, I mean. Can you choose, finally?"

"I believe in free will."

"She believes in free will," Danny announced.

Mason said to Seeta, "Ignore him. He thinks he knows something about everything. Tonight it's philosophy."

"It's okay," she said. Her eyes were bright. She didn't seem to mind Danny's mockery.

"My husband studies philosophy," Seeta said. "My future husband, I mean. That's why I call him Nietzsche. When I'm talking to Mason." She was moving her hands, trying to locate her enthusiasm. Her bracelets banged.

"Live dangerously, that's what he said." Danny smiled at Seeta when he said this.

"Who?" Maryann asked.

"Nietzsche," Danny said.

"Christ," Mason said.

"That's what *we* do, isn't it, Silas?" Mrs. Crowe said, and she looked at her husband and smiled, though it was not a happy smile.

"Did he?" Seeta asked Danny. She sat up expectantly and said, "I'm trying to find out anything I can about philosophy." She smiled. "Possible pillow talk. Practice."

"Will your sister marry a stranger as well?" Mrs. Crowe asked, looking at Sadia, who was leaning on her elbows.

Sadia smiled and shook her head.

"Yes, she will," Seeta said.

"Arranged marriages fascinate me," Mrs. Crowe said. "Don't more of them last?"

"Sure they do," Danny said, "But look at their origin. Submission. The whole idea is based on submission."

"That's terrible," Maryann said. "You're calling Seeta submissive."

"That's okay," Seeta said. "Maybe I am."

"No, you're not," Mason said. The conversation, the dinner, was out of control. It was Danny who said, "And *you* know?"

Mason hated him right then. Danny's chin was long, his eyebrows thick. In fact, everything about him was thicker, as if he'd been drinking too much. He liked to drink.

"What's wrong with submission," Mr. Crowe asked. "You talk as if it were a poison."

"Could be," Mrs. Crowe said. She looked at her husband and then turned away.

"Who knows," Danny said, right at Seeta. "Maybe it's a good thing."

"Oh God." Maryann rolled her eyes. She had a long neck and thin shoulders. She was a model. Danny had explained that. She flew to New York and Paris and Italy and was famous. Danny had said, "There aren't many international models from Manitoba, and Maryann's one." He was quite proud, as if it were his accomplishment. Mason imagined that Maryann spent a lot of time taking care of herself. She had small breasts, no hips, a long neck. He wondered if she liked Danny. It didn't seem so at the moment. She had a big mouth, bigger than Seeta's and her lips were bigger, too. She said, "You're full of shit, Danny."

Mr. Crowe lifted a hand and looked at Maryann. He waved and said, "Enough." They all returned to their food and the cutlery scraped across plates and Mason heard Seeta chewing her steak, a faint rolling of her molars around the meat, and this filled him with immense joy and, surprising himself, he pressed the back of his hand against her leg. Her thigh.

Seeta neither responded nor pulled away. She said, addressing Mr. Crowe, "This is why, you see. It's the pity." She looked at Danny and said, "You don't have to marry my future husband, but you do seem concerned, and for that, I thank you. I may only be eighteen, but I'm not stupid."

"Of course you're not, dear," Mrs. Crowe said. "We should be celebrating. Silas, get that bottle of champagne from the fridge."

Mason's father rose and from the kitchen came the crack of the cork. He returned and filled the glasses and Mrs. Crowe said, "To Seeta and her husband," and the glasses were raised and as they banged together gently Seeta reached down and held Mason's hand. Didn't let go until her glass was empty. And, later, when he drove her home in his father's Parisienne, which smelled of naphtha from the Coleman stove in the trunk, they held hands again, Seeta asking, "Do you mind?" and Mason said, "I don't." Sadia sat in the back and Mason could feel her presence, the mouselike lightness of her. She said nothing, just as she had said nothing throughout the evening save for a brief and feverish comment on a movie that the group had been discussing. At that point Seeta had whispered in Mason's ear, "Sadia's mad about movies."

Mason drove with his left hand, down Wellington to Waverley and then all the way up past Corydon. Seeta said that Danny was handsome and Maryann was a thin doll with small beautiful breasts. "Didn't you think?" she asked and Mason said he'd never noticed and Seeta said, "Sure."

"Danny gets what he wants," Mason said.

"I can see that."

Seeta's house, when they arrived, offered one rectangle of light from a front window.

"My mother's waiting."

Sadia got out, said, "Thank you," and walked into the house.

"I'm sorry about my brother," Mason said. "He's aggressive. Thinks he owns the world."

"He was nice," Seeta said.

"Don't be fooled. He's a drunk." Mason turned on the radio. He didn't want Seeta to leave. The small space of the car was like a cocoon, dark and warm. For a brief moment Mason imagined himself as Nietzsche and he would lie beside Seeta every night, watch her bathe, undress, dress, sit across from her at meals. Side by side, they would brush their teeth.

"Your mother is unhappy," Seeta said.

This surprised Mason. He nodded as if he'd known this all along.

"She's beautiful."

"Too beautiful," Mason said. "I walk down the street with her and men are always hitting on her. I mean, she's my mother."

"Maybe that's why she's unhappy."

"No. No. She likes the attention. What did you see? Did she say something?"

"I don't know. It's just whenever your father spoke she'd cut him off or she wouldn't listen to him. It was like she was tired of him."

Mason said that that wasn't a surprise. His mother was happiest when his father wasn't home. "Maybe that's what happens when you marry," he said.

"Is that a warning?" Seeta asked and then she laughed, a little chirrup that filled Mason with hope. She climbed out then and Mason walked around to join her and she went up on tiptoes and kissed him on the temple and said, "Funny boy." She slipped away and Mason climbed back into the Parisienne and sat and waited, watching the house until the lights went out, then on again and finally out, a signal sent from a foreign place.

၅

"She was pretty," Mrs. Crowe said. "You wouldn't be able to tell they were sisters. Sadia was so quiet. Almost scared. Though I liked her."

It was the following night and Mason was at home with his mother. His father had left on a road trip to Kenora and Danny was working at the restaurant. Mason and his mother sat in the dim light of the study, and she offered this information quietly, as if it were something to be treated with care.

"She's like that," Mason said. "Just sits and watches. Still, she's not scared."

Mrs. Crowe asked then what Mason thought would come of him and Seeta. What did he imagine could be gained by spending time with a girl who was engaged?

"She's not my girlfriend," Mason said.

"I guess not. What is she?"

"I don't know. She's a girl I like to be with."

"I felt sorry for you."

"Don't. I didn't."

"I don't get it."

"Nothing to get, Mom. She's not my girlfriend. I don't need a girlfriend. Anyways, she felt sorry for *you*."

"She did? Oh, my."

"She thinks you're unhappy."

"Really? What did you say?"

"Not much. I told her that Dad was often gone and that you didn't mind that."

"Huh." His mother touched her knee and tilted her head and said, "Is that what you think?" Before Mason could answer, she announced, "Lots of adults are unhappy. That happens."

"But are you?"

"Actually, there are times when I'm very happy."

"And Dad? Is he happy?"

"Sometimes I think that he isn't smart enough to be unhappy." She stood and walked to the sink and washed a glass. She was wearing a short red skirt and black tights and a black top. She said she was going out with Rhonda, and when she spoke, her back was to Mason and he didn't know if she was telling the truth. He wondered who she danced with, if the men were young or old, and he wondered why a woman would fall into the arms of a strange man, a man who could hit and hurt her.

His English class had just been reading Turgenev's *First Love*, about a boy who falls in love with a girl who ends up loving the boy's father. Not actually *loving* the father, but there was adoration and a hint of sexual perversion, and this interested Mason and the rest of the class. It was a short book and the teacher, Ms. Abendschade, got excited about the possibilities, especially near the end, when the father hits the girl and she opens her arms to him. Ms. Abendschade asked, "Do you understand what is happening here? This is a young boy whose first love has been taken from him by his father. And then, when the father treats the girl badly and hits her with his riding crop, all of which the boy witnesses, the girl falls into the father's arms, only the boy believes his father is still beating her." Ms. Abendschade paused. "Why does she run back to the father? What power is this that makes her want to go to him, to be with him, to lose herself with him there in the darkness of the garden, with the rustling of the trees and the murmur of the fountain? What should a boy of sixteen believe?" she asked, and she looked at Mason, or perhaps Mason believed she looked at him.

They read another story which, Ms. Abendschade said, "ambled arm in arm" with *First Love*. It was a short story by Joyce called "Araby." Ms. Abendschade read it out loud to the class and when she was done she did not speak for what seemed like five minutes, though it was certainly shorter, and when she finally did talk, her voice was husky and she asked, "What makes this story so sad?" And then, not waiting for an answer, because the answer offered would have been wrong, she said, "It's the hope, the expectation, and ultimately the failure. And not simply the failure, but the awareness of the failure and then the anguish. With love, hope is a voice crying out, 'If only.' Vladimir waits for Zinaida. In "Araby" the boy waits for Mangan's sister, watching as the soft rope of her hair tosses from side to side. We all wait. The person waiting could wait forever. That is passion. Vladimir is not waiting for a taxi, or a haircut, or a meal in a restaurant. He is waiting for something unnamed." And then she reread the passage from "Araby" in which the young boy spies on Mangan's sister.

Every morning I lay on the floor in the front parlour watching her door. The blind was pulled down to within an inch of the sash so that I could not be seen. When she came out on the doorstep my heart leaped. I ran to the hall, seized my books and followed her. I kept her brown figure always in my eye and, when we came near the point at which our ways diverged, I quickened my pace and passed her. This happened morning after morning. I had never spoken to her, except for a few casual words, and yet her name was like a summons to all my foolish blood.

When Ms. Abendschade talked her face became both serious and excited. She had a long neck. Sometimes Mason imagined that he and Ms. Abendschade were lovers. She was thirty-four. He was sixteen. He reasoned that this was not a wide gap until Lena Schellendal pointed out, with cold-hearted math, that that would be like him dating someone who wasn't born yet.[2] They were talking about this outside during class break. Lena was smoking and leaning against the fence. Mason was looking around for Seeta, hoping to catch a glimpse. He said, "You think Abendschade has a boyfriend? She gets so excited about Zinaida and Vladimir. Like it was her own life."

"She's a prude," Lena said. "Bet she just goes for the straight-ahead fuck."

Mason didn't pursue this. Lena was bright and haughty and all-knowing. She leaned into her answers and seemed so sure. When a test was given on *First Love* she got a perfect mark. Mason failed. A paragraph was offered and analysis required. The passage arrived from out of nowhere, oblique and eso-teric, and on one of the pages, a previous student had written in bold black letters, TRENT MEDLAND FUCKED ME UP THE

---

[2] Lena has been aware of Mason for a long time. She is interested in the erotic, in Mason Crowe as a possibility. Sometimes they eat lunch together and once they had coffee at the Bagel Shop, where Lena said that she both loved and hated her father. If Mason weren't so infatu-ated by Seeta, an impossible goal, he would concentrate on Lena, whom he finds mystical and odd. Perhaps Lena knows this and is simply waiting. She is single-minded and patient. Last night she wrote in her journal, "It is either him or no one at all."

ASS, and, more demandingly, STICK YOUR COCK IN MY BELLY BUTTON. These were not new images for Mason but they seemed hard and cold on the pages of Turgenev. Mason lost interest in discussing the question and proceeded instead to write a poem titled "Belly Button Kissing." After class, he showed the poem to Lena and described the phrases in his book. She sighed and said that kids were stupid. "How can you not love Turgenev? I predict that the boy who wrote that will end up in prison."

"How do you know it was a boy?" Mason had imagined a girl, wan like Lena, who was secretly wild.

"Because it's perverted shit."

In the distance Seeta approached. Her shoulders swayed. Mason said, "See there?" but no one heard him.[3]

They still played tennis through the last weeks of May and into June. Seeta had taken to wearing shorts and her legs criss-crossed like dark twigs and she began to charge the net, her runners emitting little barks as they bit the tarmac. Sadia, for her part, had stopped reading, and now sat on the bench and observed her sister flail about. Seeta astonished Mason. She was so bright about everything, so willing to try, and her frailty, the

---

[3] Lena heard him. She ignored it. She wrote in her journal later, "Mason Crowe read me a poem today. He has the lightest loveliest lisp and a twisted mind. He thinks he likes Seeta Chahal. Patience!"

inconsequence of her small body with the sharp elbows and thin ankles, seemed to require attention. In the moments when they sat, resting and drinking water, he took to touching her shoulder with a finger, or patting her on the back, or wiping the sweat from a slash of eyebrow. He was a hesitant swimmer testing the water with a toe.

One Saturday evening Seeta, Mason, and Sadia went to a house party in Charleswood. Seeta suggested it. Mason had his mom's car and they were driving around and Seeta said, "There's a party at Lonnie Finkle's," so they went. The house was all lit up. In the back there was a pool and some kids were swimming and others were dancing on the lawn. Mason looked around. Seeta had disappeared. He wandered into the house and Sadia followed. In the kitchen he poured rye into glasses and added ice.

"Did you see Seeta?" Mason asked.

"See Seeta," Sadia said. "See Seeta walk. See Seeta run. Poor Mason."

In the front room, a cavernous space with a centre fire-place, couples were dancing. Sadia and Mason sat against the far wall and watched and drank and Mason refilled their glasses and they drank some more.

"You surprise me," Mason said.

Sadia looked at him. She shrugged. She took out a ciga-rette and lit it and blew the smoke up above his head. Mason watched her. He asked, "How old are you?"

"Fifteen."

"Does Seeta talk to you?"

"Sometimes."

"Does she say anything? About me?" Mason felt that he was walking out into a dangerous lake, but the alcohol had made him both brave and foolish.

"Never."

"Never?"

"That's right."

Mason surveyed the dancers. He said, "You wanna dance?"

Sadia put out her cigarette and shrugged. "I'm not very good," she said.

"Look around, you don't have to be good."

They stood and walked out into the crowd and faced each other. Mason moved his feet and watched Sadia. Her arms were folded across her chest and she stood, unmoving.

"Go like this," Mason called out, and he shuffled a foot sideways and back and then dipped his knees.

"Dancing's stupid," Sadia said.

"Sure it is. Here." Mason took her hands and pulled her arms outwards. He liked the idea of teaching Sadia something. Her hesitance, the first faltering step that led to another, pleased him. She had a cold sore on her lip.

"There," he said. He let her go and closed his eyes. The rye had left him woozy. When he opened his eyes again Sadia was leaning against the wall, watching him. He went over to her and sat down.

When Lena Schellendal walked by he saw her shoes and her ankles and he looked up at her face and she nodded at him and then kept walking. He said to Sadia, "That girl there, see her? Her name's Lena," Mason said. "She's in my English class and thinks she's smart. Which she is. It's just she likes to show off." He paused and watched Lena dance with a short boy. Lena put her hands on the boy's shoulders and the boy talked up at Lena's chin. She was very composed.[4]

After a bit, Mason walked around looking for Seeta. She was squatting in a corner, talking to an older boy. He might have been a man. Mason stood beside her while Seeta talked and smiled and touched the man's arm. He was squatting too and their knees were touching and they were both smoking and laughing.

"We're gonna go," Mason said.

Seeta ignored him. The man looked up.

"Sadia wants to go," Mason said.

The man wore an eyebrow ring and he had an odd mouth, too wide on one side.

Seeta looked up and said, "I'm staying." She waved a hand, dismissing him.

He went back and found Sadia sitting beside the patio doors and looking out towards the pool where kids were taking off their clothes and jumping in.

---

[4] And very aware of Mason watching her. She was dancing with Callum Thom, a boy she had no interest in but had chosen because he was in Mason's vicinity. He was talking to her about hockey and she was nodding and thinking, "You stupid boy, I could crush you." She saw, beyond Callum's small head, Mason exit the room with Sadia Chahal in his wake. Much later in the evening she saw Seeta dancing with an older boy, not Mason, and this pleased her. She did not look for Mason again. She saw no need to pursue a phantom.

"Look at them," Sadia said.

"Seeta's staying," Mason said.

"This is depressing," Sadia said. She took Mason's hand and pulled him out to the car where they sat and looked back at the house. The din had lessened, though the occasional cry floated upwards. Sadia reached over, turned the key in the ignition, and said, "Let's go."

They drove around town slowly without talking. They went to a Tim Hortons Drive-Thru and had three doughnuts each and a Coke. Sadia ate quickly and licked her fingers. She had a small jaw and when she bent her head and put her fingers in her mouth she looked like a monkey. Mason wondered if she shaved her armpits.

They smoked cigarettes and ashed through the open window and Mason thought about Seeta and the man. He said, "I don't know what she wants."

Sadia snorted. She said, "I don't want to talk about her. She's perfect. She's skinny and she's beautiful. You should see her naked."

Like a dare, these words washed over Mason and he shouldered them and looked away and then back at Sadia, who was smoking and looking matter-of-fact, as if discussions about her naked sister were commonplace.

They were out along the Perimeter. Mason turned onto the Number 3 and said, "Sometimes I come out here with my brother and we drive fast."

Sadia's face was shadowed. The nearest half caught the green glow of the dash lights. She was wearing her seat belt and it crossed between her breasts like a bandolier. "Go ahead," she said.

The wind rushed in through the window and snapped at Sadia's hair so that she had to take a hand and hold it back and Mason saw the underside of her arm and he saw that she had her own tough dark beauty.

"Faster," she called and he obeyed, and the car shuddered around a curve. They passed through a darkened town without slowing and Mason called out "Fuck," and Sadia grinned briefly.

He slowed finally and pulled onto a side road and put the car in park and looked at Sadia. She leaned over and kissed him. Her mouth was soft and her tongue was interested in his. When she pulled away she looked at him as if waiting for him to say something. He didn't. He turned away and lit a cigarette.

"I'm not Seeta," she said.

"I know that."

"I don't fool around. I know what I want. Does that frighten you?"

"Does that *frighten* me? Jesus. What's weird is that I wanted to kiss Seeta, which I never have, and I end up kissing her sister. You know?" He looked over at her to see if something was wrong. She was turned away from him, shaking her head.

He started the car and pulled it back onto the highway and drove slowly, returning through the town, which lay sleepy and silent, on past the Perimeter and towards the centre of the city where Sadia and Seeta's house lay waiting, their parents awake and worried. Sadia, just before Mason dropped her off, said, "Right about now my dad's going crazy. He'll be calling the cops and getting in his car to find his daughters."

"I'm sorry," Mason said.

"Why?"

"I don't know. About what happened. You won't tell Seeta?"

Sadia breathed through her nose quickly and said, "Ha." She seemed suddenly childish and helpless and Mason realized that the evening had gone wrong. He looked over at Sadia and thought he should say something but there was nothing to say. He dropped her off and she climbed from the car and paused, her hand on the door, but then she turned and she was gone.

About this time, Mason quit working as a bricklayer's helper. Saying goodbye to the Portuguese brothers was a pleasure but Mason was short of spending money, and so he was looking for work. One night his brother Danny said he had a good job for him. It was late and they were in the kitchen. Mason was eating cereal and Danny had poured himself a beer and was standing and leaning against the counter and talking about a man called Mr. Ferry, the neighbour to the back of them, who sometimes ate in the restaurant where Danny worked. He was blind and needed someone to read to him. "He's an eccentric son of a bitch who comes in, cane swinging, full of bluster, and expects the finest service. I talk to him once in a while and he's odd. He asks lots of questions. Likes discussing things, not a dumb man. He's a retired professor. Anyway, he told me that he needs a reader." He paused and looked at Mason and said, "What do you think?"

"I'm not a social worker," Mason said.

"He pays."

"How much?"

"I don't know. Ask him."

"Can he go to the bathroom on his own? Do I have to feed him?"

"He's blind, he's not an invalid."

"How'd he get blind?"

"His wife poked his eyes out. Her name was Delilah."

"Shit."

"I hear she was beautiful. Those are the ones you have to look out for. I don't know. Diabetes?"

Mason said he would think about it. The next day he walked past Mr. Ferry's house. It was a brick three-storey. The grass was trimmed, there were flowers in the beds. In the back-yard there was a beat-up garage and inside sat an old car. Late seventies. A table and umbrella on the patio.

On Saturday Danny and Mason walked over to the house. As they turned onto Wellington Crescent, Danny asked, "How's Seeta?"

"Seeta's fine," Mason said.

"Still playing tennis?"

"Yeah, once a week."

"That all you see her?"

Mason shrugged.

"If you're gonna get anywhere you gotta work for it."

"Maybe *it* isn't what I want."

"Okay. Fine. You were at Finkle's party with her?"

Mason looked quickly at Danny. "How do you know?"

"You told me."

"No, I didn't."

"Well, I don't know, maybe I dreamed it." He stopped talking. They walked on. He said, "She's gorgeous. You know that? That night at our house. Even Maryann thought she was beautiful."

"That's good," Mason said. "Maybe you two'd like to ask her out. Take pictures of her."

Danny laughed. "It was an observation." Then he said, "Seeta," and as the *t* dropped off his top teeth into the *a* Mason said, "Leave her alone. She's not like us."

"Is that right? Because she has a trousseau full of saris and wears bindi dots and has a mother who yells at her in Hindi and a strange man called Ajit is coming to take her away?"

Mason stopped. He said, "How do you know Ajit's name? She never said his name."

"Relax, Mason. She called one time and I answered and we got to talking and as we were talking there it was, the guy's name, Ajit. You can't forget that name."

When they had arrived at Mr. Ferry's, Danny said, "Be polite. He likes that."

"I always am."

The man who came to the door held a pair of dark glasses in one hand. There was no evidence of a cane. He did not look blind.

Danny said, "Mr. Ferry, it's me, Danny Crowe. I'm here with my brother, Mason. Remember I told you about him?"

Mr. Ferry reached out a hand and said, "Hi, Mason," and Mason took his hand and he could smell the house and Mr. Ferry and it wasn't a bad smell, somewhat dry and clean, and as they entered they passed a machine running in the hallway, a dehumidifier, and they sat, the three of them, in the library, where the walls were shelves full of books and the light fell in through two large windows. Mr. Ferry told Danny to fetch some beer from the fridge. Danny left and the sound of him working in the kitchen was comforting to Mason, who had no idea what to say to the man sitting beside him. Mr. Ferry cleared his throat and stabbed a hand out at the room and drew it back in and said, "Your brother's quite an artist in the kitchen. I've eaten at the restaurant where he's a chef and he does a fine job. He told me he had a brother and I guess he wasn't lying." Mr. Ferry chuckled.

Mason looked around. He didn't think he should laugh too but he smiled and then realized that a smile meant nothing to Mr. Ferry and so he laughed and the laugh was forced and much too late.

Mr. Ferry didn't seem to notice. He said, "And you? Do you have a penchant for that sort of thing? For cooking?"

"No," Mason said. "I don't. I'm a terrible cook." He wondered how long it would take for Danny to rejoin them. Mr. Ferry's eyebrows were very thick. He raised them now and said, "I see," and crossed his legs. Smoothed his grey pants. Said, "What's your favourite book?"

Mason did not have a ready answer. He thought about books he had read recently but considered them – *Junky*, for example – too unseemly for Mr. Ferry. The silence stretched out and Mason panicked and he said, "*First Love*."[5]

"Turgenev."

"Yes." Mr. Ferry's hands were old but his face looked younger. His hair was greying. Mason had no idea of his age. He thought Mr. Ferry might be older than his mother but there was no guarantee. To keep the silence away, Mason said that *First Love* wasn't really his favourite, it was just that he'd been reading it for a class. "It was easy to read," he said.

"Hmmm. Well, it's certainly a thin book, isn't it?"

Mason said that it was. Very thin.

"Though thin is not bad, is it?"

Mason said that it wasn't.

"The thing is," Mr. Ferry said, "to ask how long a book is seems a bit of an insult. Rather like asking how big someone's penis is."

Mason looked at Mr. Ferry. He looked towards the kitchen where Danny was clinking bottles.

"Don't you think?"

---

[5] This was *not* Mason's favourite book. In fact, it was an indifferent choice. What he most liked about it was Ms. Abendschade's relation to the book; more specifically, the movement of Abendschade's mouth as she spoke, the fervour of her love for Turgenev, the passion, him dreaming of lifting up Abendschade's skirt. About all of this, of course, Mr. Ferry had no inkling.

"I don't know. I guess."

Mr. Ferry said, "I'm frightening you. It's a tough question. A stupid question. *What's your favourite?* Like asking a parent if he has a favourite child. Danny's your brother."

Mason didn't know if this was a question but he said, "Yes. He is."

"Does your mother love him more than she loves you?"

"She's never said that."

"Does she love you more than she loves him?"

"I don't think so."

"Ahh, so there's a possibility."

"Danny's older, he's hardly home. I'm usually home so I guess that makes me easier to love. You know?"

Danny finally came back. He was balancing three bottles of beer on a tray. Mr. Ferry called out, "Your mother, Danny, how old is she?"

Danny set the tray down. Passed a beer to Mr. Ferry, who said, "Thank you." Handed a beer to Mason and took one himself and sat down. "Forty-three, I think."

"Four," Mason said.

"See?" Mr. Ferry lifted his bottle and said, "Cheers," and he drank and when he was finished he placed the bottle on the table beside him and turned his head towards Mason and said, "Why would a boy your age want to read to an old man like me?"

Mason looked at Danny, who motioned for him to answer.

Mason said, "I was working for Jack and Jim Costa, they're bricklayers, and now I'm not and I need a job."

"A job?" Mr. Ferry said. "That's all?"

"He likes to read," Danny said. "He reads all the time. I told him that you were a big reader and so was he and that this made sense. Didn't I tell you that, Mason?"

Mr. Ferry swivelled. "Did he?"

"Yeah, he did. And it's true, I do like to read. I'm just not sure if I like what you like."

"Does that matter?" Mr. Ferry asked.

Mason said he wasn't sure, though he guessed maybe it didn't matter. He said he'd be quite happy reading whatever Mr. Ferry wanted.

Mr. Ferry nodded his head at this as if Mason had said something important. Then he said that Mason would read to him twice a week in the evening for two hours each time, on Tuesday and Thursday, and that he was to enter the house without knocking and he was to make sure that the cats did not escape – "I have two of them, Minnie and Albert, and they are precious" – and he was to come in after he'd taken his shoes off and he was to sit to his right and he was to read until he was asked to stop. "Do you understand?" Mr. Ferry asked.

Mason said that that would be fine and then Mr. Ferry said he would see Mason on Tuesday. They finished their beer then and Mr. Ferry and Danny talked about food while Mason walked over to the shelves and studied the spines of the many books.

So Mason read to Mr. Ferry, sometimes coming on Saturday as well when he was invited. Mr. Ferry sat in an armchair and

Mason sat on a wooden chair to his right, as requested. A collection of books lay on the small table at his side, and from this pile Mason read *Memoirs of an Egotist*; a short book on being modern; various philosophers, Hume included; and most of Kierkegaard. "Good depressing stuff," Mr. Ferry said. "Especially Kierkegaard. He did all his wild living as a university student and then repented and thought we all should repent with him. He loved a girl named Regine and watched her from a distance, rather like Terence's Phaedria, who fell in love with a cither player and followed her to and from school. Kierkegaard asked Regine to marry him and then broke off the engagement two weeks later. He felt he had to decide between Regine and a higher calling. Regine said she would die. But then she up and married another man. This is what happens, isn't it? We are betrayed and then we move on."

Mason said he wasn't sure. And he wasn't. When Mason read Kierkegaard he did not understand what he was reading and Mr. Ferry did not explain. Much was made of nothing. One day he read the parable of the girl who is in despair over love because she was betrayed.

When Mason had finished reading, Mr. Ferry held up a hand and said, "Have you ever been in love?"

Mr. Ferry's question was not unexpected. During the readings he liked to lecture for a time and then ask Mason personal questions, and Mason had become used to this.

Mason thought about Seeta. She seemed, at that moment, a speck in the distance and he said, as if she had already disappeared, "There's a girl called Seeta. She doesn't know, though. Anyways, she's getting married." He explained that the marriage was planned and that Seeta was quite willing to be married to a stranger.

"How old is she?" Mr. Ferry asked.

"Eighteen."

"And you?"

"Sixteen."

Mr. Ferry felt for his glass of water. Mason slipped it into his hand. He drank and put the glass back. He lifted his head. "What does she look like?"

Mason said he wasn't sure how to describe her. He said she had thin legs. They played tennis together and she had a terrible backhand but she was enthusiastic. "Her body's like a spring. She's pretty. She's got dark skin." And then he said, and he wasn't sure why, because it seemed an unnecessary observation, that she had a hollow on the outside of her knee when she sat. "Between the ligaments and the muscle," he said. "On both knees."

Mr. Ferry's head was turned to the light that fell through the circular window of the far wall. "My wife played tennis," he said. "She wore a white skirt and white shoes. She was as light as a bird, as bold as a thought. She left me.[6] Have I ever shown you a picture of her?"

"No." Mason could see Mr. Ferry's eyes and he imagined his wife in her white skirt and shoes, light as a bird, poking his eyes out.

---

[6] What he doesn't tell Mason is that his wife left him for another man. Later, during their readings, he will describe this in greater detail.

Mr. Ferry said he would show Mason the photo another time. "In any case, pictures are deceiving, they don't tell the truth." He rested and lifted a hand to his temple. Then he asked, "And what will you do with Seeta?"

The question seemed suddenly perverse and made Mason pause. He said, "Can we talk about something else?"

"That's fine," Mr. Ferry said. "Absolutely. Be wary of the blind pervert."

"I didn't mean it that way."

"Of course you didn't. Yesterday I was trying to recall my life at sixteen. I was very ignorant. More concerned with poetry than girls. Your mother called me the other day to find out who I was. She told me you write poetry."

"She did? She thinks I'm Wordsworth."

"Perhaps you could read some of your poetry to me some time."

"I don't think so."

"Only if you like."

"Should I read on?" Mason asked, holding up the book.

"Of course."

And so Mason continued and eventually the old man slept, his hands twitching. And on Mason read, till his two hours were up, his voice floating around the large room, the slim book opened in his lap like a cipher.

༄

In his Creative Writing class, taught by a man who resembled a young John Cleese, Mason had been befriended by a vain and dreamy boy named Turbine, who believed that movies were the most important thing in the world. Turbine spent his evenings at home eating and watching movies. He was a big boy, fat some might say, who thought he was a genius and believed that one day he would live in Hollywood and write film scripts. He liked to read his work to the class and was usually full of opinions. Mason spent time with him; thought he was all bluster and bulk, but didn't mind Turbine's presence.

Turbine called Mason "My pristine poet," or "Dylan," or, in more mocking moments, "Sylvia." He said he liked Mason's poetry. "You aren't sheepish and sentimental. Or vague. I hate vague. If there's a frying pan on the stove, just call it a goddam frying pan."

Mason didn't like Turbine's scripts. They were bloody and too full of "fuck's." He didn't say so; instead he complimented him on his long poems that were, he said, like Ginsberg.

One day after school Mason walked home with Turbine. They cut through the grounds of St. Mary's Academy, walking along the sidewalk of the west side where the windows of the main hall allowed a view of girls bending over books and beakers. In one classroom a tall girl with long black hair was making a presentation. Turbine sighed and said that there was something very carnal about a private girl's school. Mason agreed. He said that in the mornings the girls huddled together and smoked in the park across the street and on cold days some of them wore jeans under their skirts. "You wouldn't think it," he said, "but it's quite erotic. It's like you know that the girl isn't going to keep both the jeans and the skirt on and that it'll be the jeans that she'll slip out of and that's what makes it erotic."

Turbine looked up at the sky and grinned and said that Mason might want to teach at a girl's school some day. Or, failing that, be a janitor.

They passed along the curving drive of the school grounds and down the street through the park to Turbine's parents' condominium. There was an electric gate and cameras and a guard at the main entrance who said hello to Turbine. Up in the condo Mason lay down on the leather couch in the family room and stared at the art on the wall. Turbine stepped out through the French doors that looked out onto a small green space. He smoked a joint and came back inside. "There we go," he said.

"All inspired then?" Mason asked. Turbine grinned.

"That's such horseshit," Mason said. "You know Jackie, that girl who was in our Bio class last year? She claims it frees her mind, makes her write things she'd never think of otherwise."

"Possible," Turbine said. He lay down on the rug, looking up at the ceiling through his spread fingers. "Love that stipple." He sat up and said, "An ugly invention but a great word. Stipple."

"Why don't you write a bad poem about it?"

Turbine said, "I was at a party the other night, Brent Knight's place, and there was this guy in the basement shooting up. I was looking for the bathroom and I stumbled across him. His girlfriend was helping him. There was the belt and the wild-eyed guy and the needle and the smell of sulphur and I thought, Whoaa, this is a Tarantino film. The girl told me to go away. So I did."

"Who was the guy? Did you know him?" Mason asked.

"I didn't. But the girl was Crystal. You've seen her around. The thing is, most people don't think. You ever noticed that? They care about zits or hair or abs or fucking or the football team. Really important stuff. I took a survey at that party and asked each kid who Baudelaire was. Only one person knew and that was, guess? Yes, that's right, Nurse Crystal. She was standing by the dry bar, her addict boyfriend nowhere to be seen, and I approached her and asked her the question and she looked at me as if I were way too fat and said, 'I'm *reading* Baudelaire.' She took this book out of her purse and waved it in my face. It was Baudelaire, all right. *Flowers of Evil.* I fell in love with her. Even though she's probably got tracks running up her forearm and is sure to have full-blown something. I mean how often does that happen? It was sublime." He sat up and reached for his backpack by the couch, took a book out, and held it up. "Here it is. She left it on the table and I picked it up and later I couldn't find her." He opened it and read, "To Crystal, Love Dad."

Mason held out his hand and Turbine passed it on. The inscription inside the front cover was faded and smudged. Mason fanned the pages. He said, "Jesus, Turbine, you took it."

"I'll return it to her. I will." He stood and asked, "You hungry?"

"No," Mason said. Turbine went into the kitchen and Mason could hear him going through the fridge and the cupboards. When he returned he was eating a salami sandwich and holding a can of root beer. He sat back down on the floor and said, "I saw Seeta Chahal at that party. You still seeing her?"

Mason shrugged.

"What a great name," Turbine said. "Chahal. Sounds like a steam engine getting ready to go."

The book was still clamped in Mason's hand. "Was she at the party by herself?"

"I don't know."

Mason saw that he was lying. A resignation settled in. He said, "Her sister Sadia," and then he stopped.

"What about Sadia?"

"She's okay," Mason said. He was remembering her smell but he didn't want Turbine to know that.

Later that night he and Turbine went to the belfry, a small room in the gable of the Rehabilitation Centre for Children. The hospital was on Wellington Crescent and gave onto the river and the room was accessible by a metal ladder attached to the rear wall. They climbed the ladder and sat on the flat-tarred roof and looked out over the river. An ambulance passed over the bridge. A dog barked. Turbine was going on about the film *Down by Law*, which he said got better with every viewing. "Seen it sixteen times," Turbine said. "And each time I expect the dance scene at the end, with Waits and Barkin, to get sentimental and wrong, but it doesn't. I think it's her. Barkin. She's very sexy."

"Anybody with breasts is sexy to you," Mason said.

Turbine agreed. He was smoking a joint again. Holding the smoke and closing his eyes. His face was wide and empty. He said, "I get desperate. I mean, who'd want to have sex with a fat guy like me?"

"You're not that fat."

"Fuck off. I can't even see my dick when I'm naked and standing. Gotta use my mom's compact to see what's there." He looked out into the darkness. "Don't worry." Then he said, "I could have a party. My parents are off on one of their jaunts. Gone for two weeks, all kinds of depravity down in Barbados. I could call up some girls and we could party. You, me, and the girls."

Mason said, "Girls. A few weeks ago I was at Lonnie Finkle's party with Seeta. And she ignored me. She left with someone else. It's as if I'm this extra arm she notices once in a while. Oh, hey, hi there, arm, why don't you come out of the dark and scratch my back."

"Did she ever say she liked you?"

"Not exactly. But she held my hand and we kissed."

"No shit. You kissed. I figure you're in deep water."

Mason didn't answer. He heard the traffic on the bridge, the call of a child, a boat splashing by. He saw himself as a fool, as having offended against propriety, decency, and modesty. This was the definition of shame. He'd looked it up the day before in class.

The following Wednesday, the day he was supposed to play tennis with Seeta, she didn't show, and then the next Wednesday Sadia came alone. She was on the bench and Mason sat beside her. "Where's Seeta?" he asked.

"Out."

"Oh. So, she sent you?"

"No, I just came."

"Out where?"

She looked at Mason, eyes black like Seeta's. "My father says you're birdshit."

"He does?"

"He finds things out."

"Is that why Seeta didn't come today?"

Sadia looked away and shrugged, and in that brief shrug Mason saw her sister, the slight movement of her clavicle, the pushing away of all worries. "No," she said, and then she said, "She likes your brother."

"I know," Mason said, too quickly, for he didn't really know, though he had sensed something. He asked, "How long?"

"About a month now. Right after that dinner at your house. She goes out with Danny. Not every night, but enough. My father is going mad." She paused, considered, then said, "Seeta's a lot older than you."

"Only a year."

"Two. Anyway, that's not what I meant." She had slipped out of her sandals; three silver toe rings and her left ankle hennaed with what resembled a figure eight. "Your brother went after her. Brought her flowers, took her to dinner, bought her things. What'd you ever do for her?"

"We played tennis," Mason said. "I didn't know she wanted anything else."

Sadia smiled and said, "Girls always want more. Achy-breaky heart. Don't you hate that?"

Mason said, "Danny can't be trusted."

Sadia said she had an uncle in Vancouver and that her Dad was going to send Seeta to live there until Nietzsche showed up. She said the name Nietzsche as if he were real, like he deserved being named after a famous philosopher, like he'd done something special and lived only for pessimism and passion.

Mason said it didn't matter. "Anyway, I'm seeing another girl."

Sadia was surprised and hurt. "Who?" she asked.

"Lena Schellendal,[7] you don't know her."

"Oh."

"It's very casual," Mason said.

"So, not serious."

"Well, sort of serious. You can tell Seeta if you want."

"You'd like that, then, wouldn't you?"

---

[7] This is absolutely true. In the last while Mason has been sitting in the Bagel Shop on Academy and waiting for Lena to pass by on her way to music lessons. A few weeks earlier, in a brief conversation, she had mentioned that she took voice lessons and he had asked her where, and she had told him. When? he asked. Every Monday, she said. So, now he watches her walk by and then waits to observe her on her return. He does this once a week. He doesn't speak to Lena and he believes she doesn't know he's watching her, though she does. She wrote in her journal, the night before, "He watches me as I walk by on my way to voice lessons. There is something both sweet and sick about it. Though if he wasn't watching I would be disappointed. Last week I stood and waited outside the café window, just long enough for him to look me up and down, and then I moved on. How amazing."

Sadia looked so small, so helpless, sitting beside him. He said, "Yeah, tell her."

The following week Mason saw Seeta only once, a brief encounter at the checkout at Charlie's, he holding a loaf of bread and asking her when she was leaving for Vancouver while an old man wheezed impatiently behind him. The man smelled of cigarette smoke and jingled his change in his pocket and Mason wanted to hit him.

"Saturday," Seeta said. She smiled, but the smile meant nothing.

"This?"

"No, next."

"Are you in love with Danny?" he asked.

Seeta slipped two quarters and a dime into Mason's hand. She shook her head. She sighed. "Oh, Mason."

He went up on tiptoes expectantly. "I've been calling. Did your mother say?"

"You shouldn't, it just makes my mother upset and then she tells my father and he threatens to shoot people."

"Tell him to shoot Danny."

Seeta lifted an eyebrow. It was thick and black and there didn't exist in the world an eyebrow more beautiful.

"I'm more interesting than him," Mason said. "He's not as smart."

"Oh, is that right? Remember you said you were going to teach me English poetry? Well, it turns out Yeats is Irish, not

English. Danny told me that." She passed a hand like a dark leaf through the air. "Anyways, Sadia says you have someone else."

Mason was pleased that Sadia would have passed this fact on. "Yes. Yes, I do."

"Congratulations. I'm happy for you." She motioned for the next customer. "Bye, Mason," she said, and she turned away.

That same day after supper Maryann came by the house and sat with Mason on the front porch. They watched the traffic on Academy, and Maryann talked about Paris. She had just come back. Her eyes were tired and dark and her lips were dry, as if she was sick. Mason liked sitting beside her; it gave him a place above the world. She was wearing new jeans and she slouched in her chair and rocked one leg back and forth.

She said that she was still interested in seeing Danny, though Danny seemed to have other things to do. "Even when I'm out of the country I call him but he's never home and then when I come home I can't find him. I wish he was more like you." She took Mason's hand and held it and said, "Sweet and kind and careful. Danny likes to gobble things up and then spit them out."

Mason said nothing. Maryann's fingertips were ragged and raw. This went against the fact of her beauty and Mason liked it.

She said, "We should go play pool. Would you like that? I've got my car. Are you doing anything?"

They went to Pockets on Bannatyne. Mason thought there might be a problem with his age but Maryann said that he should just act older than he looked and she would buy the beer. When she said this they were walking from their car towards the bar. Maryann was the same height as Mason and he was aware of the shape of her jaw and her wide mouth. As they passed other people Mason wondered if they would notice Maryann's beauty. She took his arm at one point and this encouraged him to move closer to her just to show possession and she didn't mind. She knew she was being watched but she was smart enough to pretend she didn't know and this gave her an aloof and intelligent air and it was this confidence that Mason borrowed from. She was wearing a short leather jacket and she carried a leather purse that, when opened, smelled of Dentyne.

They played two games of pool. Maryann called all her shots. She bent at the waist, her legs straight, and eyed the lay of the balls. Mason thought that his brother was a fool and that there would be no reason to treat Maryann badly.

When they were done, Maryann bought them each another beer and they sat looking out at the street. She asked him about Seeta and the way she asked indicated she knew nothing about Danny and Seeta.

Mason said, "Seeta's fine."

Maryann crossed her legs and swung her foot, banging it gently against Mason's shin as if to remind him of her presence. She said, "If I were a boy I'd go for Sadia." Mason tried to recall Sadia's face but all he could see was Seeta and then Maryann and then Seeta again. Sadia didn't exist. "Sometimes," Maryann said, "You have to be happy with what you get." Then she said, "Your brother's a pervert. You know that?"

Mason picked up his glass of beer and then put it down. Maryann was looking upwards to stop from crying. "Oh, Christ," she said.

"Did he hurt you?" Mason asked. It wouldn't have surprised him.

"No," she said. "It's not like I didn't enjoy everything. He's very inventive. But you don't want to hear about that. The thing is, he's just a chef, he's nothing, and what do I do, I go crawling around after him." She lit a cigarette and then bit at her finger. "He's a zero. I'm grovelling in front of a zero."

"Guys are like that," Mason said. As he said this, an image arrived, fluent and bright, of Maryann undressing. He wondered how small her breasts were and what exactly she meant by inventive, and if she was so willing, *what* was she so willing to do?

She said, "It makes no sense for you to spend time with a girl who's about to be married." Then she wondered aloud where Danny was tonight and she stood and put out her cigarette and said she would phone him. "Do you think he's at home?"

Mason said he didn't know. "I'm not my brother's keeper."

Maryann lifted her eyebrows. She touched Mason's knee as she stood. She went off to find a pay phone and when she returned she sat and clasped her hands between her thighs and said that she wanted to go dancing. Over at the Royal Albert just down the street. She said that the bands were sometimes good and she'd like to take a chance but most of all she'd like to get drunk and dance. She took Mason's arm as they walked the two blocks over. In one of the store windows Mason saw a boy walking with a girl and for a moment he did not understand that it was him and Maryann. His own existence surprised him. At the bar, Maryann ordered drinks and brought them back, swaying between the chairs. She held the bottles away from her body, her elbows slightly bent.

"Here," she said.

They stayed an hour, listening to a band of young girls while Maryann drank quickly and ferociously. When they left she had trouble walking so Mason held her arm. "I think," she said, and looked around. Outside the bar she paused and pushed against Mason and said, "Danny."

"I'm not Danny," Mason said. He held her arm and could feel the slight weight of her. Everything was clear to him. The slope of her shoulders and the softness of her hair.

"No way."

Her elbow in his hand. Feet stepping on his. There was nothing to her.

"Do you think I'm talented?" she asked. "Or am I just a beautiful body?"

"You're beautiful. That's a talent."

"No. It isn't, Mason. I have the genes for skinny. And long legs. It's like blue eyes. What colour are your eyes?"

"Brown."

"Same as Danny."

They'd reached the car. Maryann dumped the contents of her purse out onto the sidewalk. She raked at the pile, searching for her keys. She held them up and Mason took them. "I'll drive," he said. She began to pick up the pieces. Tampons, lipstick, cinnamon gum, a marble-green compact, Band-Aids, tweezers, wallet, change, credit card, mints, cigarettes. "Oh,

God," she said. She sat down and hugged her legs, put her face into her knees. She rocked and wept and Mason picked up her belongings. When he was finished he handed her the purse. "Thank you," she said.

In the car she sighed and closed her eyes. She appeared helpless. He drove through the empty city, a chauffeur returning a child to her bed. The street lamps glowed yellow and the evening, the darkness, was suddenly magical. He was alone and in charge, happy in the moment.

✺

Mr. Ferry told Mason that when he wrote he shouldn't worry about physical appearance. "Name things, yes, be concrete, but don't go on and on with appearances. That's unnecessary. Do we know what K. in *The Castle* looks like? If he has big ears? Rotten teeth?" Then Mr. Ferry said that he should read French writers. Rimbaud, Flaubert. The mud on Emma's boots after her tryst with Leon. He recited a poem.

Jenny kissed me when we met,
Jumping from the chair she sat in;
Time, you thief, who love to get
Sweets into your list, put that in!
Say I'm weary, say I'm sad,
Say that health and wealth have missed me,
Say I'm growing old, but add,
Jenny kissed me.

"Life can be full of regrets," he said. "But you don't want to hear that. You're only sixteen and you have no regrets. Not yet." He said that unrequited love wasn't a bad thing. "Kierkegaard loved Regine, Stendhal loved Methilde." He pronounced Methilde as a French person would. They were walking along the boulevard on Wellington. People passed, women with dogs, children on bikes, and Mason wondered when the man would shut up about dead writers.

They walked on in silence with Mr. Ferry grasping Mason's elbow and swinging his head back and forth until he asked, "And Seeta? How is she?"

Mason didn't answer. He thought about his brother. About Mr. Chahal threatening to shoot people. He recalled the joy in Seeta's voice as she told him about Yeats. He said, "Seeta's gone."

Mr. Ferry nodded. He said, "I remember the first girl I liked. She was slightly older and took me to a play. After, she wanted to discuss the play but I had no knowledge of the play or the writer and by the end of the evening her voice was full of disappointment and disdain. I liked her and had failed miserably. She died the following spring. Appendicitis."

"Seeta won't die."

The corner of Mr. Ferry's mouth lifted. "Do you wish that she would?"

"No," Mason said. He looked at Mr. Ferry and perhaps it was the man's blindness, the fact that he could not look at Mason's face as he spoke, that allowed him to say, "I think my brother stole her."

"I see. How did he steal her?"

"He's very persuasive. He's got a girlfriend. Maryann."

Mr. Ferry said, "It sounds like melodrama." He held up his hand. "That doesn't mean it's not real or that you shouldn't feel anything. You can feel whatever you feel. Is Seeta treacherous, do you think?"

"What do you mean?"

"Does she go out of the way to harm you? Is she unreliable?"

"I don't know. I don't think so."

"Maybe she doesn't know. Maybe she just acts, does things and regrets them later."

They had turned to go back. The group of girls jogged by, a flicker of limbs. Mason wondered how it happened that someone could just act without considering the consequences. Then he said that his brother Danny was like an animal that would eat until it was sick. He liked to stuff himself with girls and the strangest thing was that the girls allowed this. He didn't even love them and that didn't seem to matter. "Everyone loves my brother," he said.

They did not talk after this and when they reached the house they entered and Mr. Ferry went to the kitchen to prepare something to drink and Mason sat in the reading room. When Mr. Ferry returned with coffee and a glass of water and had seated himself, he said, "The Danny you described is not the Danny I know."

"He's good at fooling people."

"But I'm not easily fooled," Mr. Ferry said. "Maybe it's not true, about him and Seeta. Have you actually asked him?"

"It's true. He went after Seeta. Bought her things. Took her out to dinner. That sort of thing. That's what her sister Sadia told me."

"I suppose her sister would know." He paused, then said, "Perhaps in the case of Seeta, treachery loves company."

Mason did not respond to this statement and after a while Mr. Ferry said, "That's fine, Mason. Do you feel bad for telling me what you did?"

Mason shrugged. He looked at Mr. Ferry's hands and said that no, he didn't feel bad.

They read then, Mr. Ferry's head dropping almost immediately, snapping back up once in a while as if a thought had arrived, but it was simply the reaction of a man who is unconscious becoming briefly aware and then falling asleep again.

It was Sunday afternoon and Danny was home. He and Mason were digging up the garden for their mother and Danny had taken off his shirt and the hair at his belly was dark and thick. They took turns with the one shovel. When it was Mason's turn, Danny said, "Put more weight on it, cut through the shit and stuff."

"You're so good, *you* do it," Mason said.

"I'm offering help here."

Mason stopped digging, leaned on his shovel, and looked at Danny. He said, "When you work, when you cook at those fancy places where all the fancy people eat, do you tell everybody what to do?"

"I'm the head chef, that's my job."

"So you like being the boss."

"I don't know if I like it. I do it because I'm paid to do it."

"Must be lots of pretty women who eat there. All dressed up."

Danny sat down on the steps of the porch. "Some," he said.

"I was thinking," Mason said, "that if we were sitting at a table and eating, you would want what was on my plate even though you had something pretty good on your own."

"What are you talking about?"

"Well, wouldn't you?"

"Stop with the bullshit."

"Why do you want Seeta?" Mason asked. "You've got Maryann." He said this as he turned to dig again, not looking at Danny.

"Who says I want her? She say that?"

"No, she said you were a piece of birdshit. Sadia told me."

"Seeta wouldn't have said that." He grinned.

"You're my brother," Mason said.

"That's true. Whatever I did though, she did worse. She's too much for you, Mason. She's too much for me. I can't figure out what she wants. She likes to talk about Nietzsche and Confucius and duty, but she's not saving herself for that Ajit philosopher guy. I'd say she's verging on being a slut. A very good-looking one, but still a slut."

Mason let the shovel fall. He could see his brother's face where the sun fell onto it and he could see his own shadow that was foreshortened and his head looked small.

"I went out with Maryann," Mason said. "To a movie. Then we went for drinks and danced and I drove her home. She said you loved yourself too much."

Danny stood without saying anything and went into the house and then he came back with a beer and he sat down and opened it and drank a third, tipping his head back and closing his eyes, and when he'd pulled the bottle away he looked at Mason and said, "And you told her about Seeta."

"No. I didn't."

Danny pointed his beer bottle at Mason and said, "The problem is you think you're better than me. That might be true some of the time. But not all of the time. There's nothing wrong with liking yourself. Maybe if you were more like me Seeta would still be playing tennis with you." He paused, then said, "Pock, pock."

"What is that?" Mason asked.

"A tennis ball. Maybe she wanted more than tennis and you were too slow."

"You think everything is fucking, Danny. I don't. And that makes me better than you more than 50 per cent of the time. Mom'd agree with that. Sadia. Maryann. Seeta. Any girl who's got some brains would think that."

"What makes you think I fucked her?"

"That's what you do, isn't it?"

Danny said, "Mason, Mason. The girls, they love you. Seeta does, she said so. 'Sweet Mason,' she said. I can't figure it out. She said you were a watcher and that there was something curious about a watcher, that if you got close enough to a watcher certain things would be revealed. I didn't know what the hell she was talking about. But there you go." He lifted his empty bottle. "You wanna beer?"

Mason picked up the shovel and said, "She's leaving on Saturday. She's going up to Vancouver to live with her uncle. To wait for Nietzsche." Mason said Nietzsche with some emphasis, as if it were a word that required work.

This surprised Danny. He pondered a bit and then he said, "I was looking back to see, if you were looking back to see, if I was looking back to see, if you were looking back at me." He smiled at Mason.

"You're full of shit," Mason said.

"Things happen, decisions are made, you'll find out," he said, and he left and walked up the porch stairs. And before he went into the house Mason could see his broad back and the shape of him cut out against the light.

෨

Late Friday night Danny brought Seeta home. Mason knew it was her by the tinkle of bracelets. Danny said something and Seeta laughed. Mason was in his room but he came up and stood at the edge of the doorway where they could have seen him if they wanted. They didn't. Seeta was sitting at the kitchen table and throwing popcorn into Danny's mouth. "Oops," she said, each time she missed. Whenever she got one in, Danny leaned across the table and kissed her. Seeta closed her eyes and one time Danny touched her breasts with his hands. He looked like a blind man feeling his way through a strange house. The bowl of popcorn spilled but they didn't notice. Seeta placed her hands on Danny's forehead as if she were checking for fever. They pulled away and looked at each other.

The telephone rang and Mason walked down the hall and lay down on his mother's bed. He waited for Danny to answer but he didn't. Mrs. Crowe had gone up to Rainy River with Mason's dad so Danny and Mason were alone. It was one in the morning. The phone rang on, then stopped. Mason could hear what was going on in the kitchen. Danny was talking and Seeta was going, "Hmmm," and one time she said, "No, no, no, no," quite carefully as if she were refusing a generous but impossible offer.

Mason suffered their voices a little longer and then the phone rang again and this time he picked it up. It was Seeta's father.

"Seeta," he said, "I'm looking for Seeta Chahal. Who are you?"

"Mason."

"Do you have her? Is she there?"

"She's here with my brother," Mason said.

Mr. Chahal covered the phone and there was some muffled yelling and then he came back and said, "What's your address?"

And Mason told him. He practically drew him a map. Academy, close to Stafford, and gave him the house number and told him to come over. "Do," Mason said, "the door is open."

Mason waited a bit and then he walked out of the bedroom and went into the kitchen where Seeta was sitting on Danny's lap and said, "Your father's coming to pick you up. He phoned."

Seeta got up off of Danny and started to pull her hair up into a bun.

Danny said. "You *told* him she was here."

"He asked."

"He'll kill me," Seeta said. She was fumbling with a bobby pin. Her arms were like wings, the smooth underside, the elbows sticking out.

"He won't," Danny said.

"Or you," she said, "He'll kill you." She turned and asked, "Could you take me home, Mason?"

"I can't," Mason said, though he badly wanted to say Yes, yes.

Seeta walked past him, her shoulder touching his. He could smell the popcorn and he saw the pins in her hair and her ears and the back of her neck. Her arms were bare and thin. She went to the door and opened it and looked out at the night. She came back and said, "Okay," as if seeking solace or resolve, and then she said, "The Crowe boys," and she stood with her bum against the counter and waited.

When Mr. Chahal arrived he banged and entered and Seeta went, "Who, who, who?" and Mr. Chahal called out, "What for?" and Danny swung his big feet off the table.

Mr. Chahal was in the foyer, holding a rake.

"Daddy-jee," Seeta said.

"Birdshit," Mr. Chahal said. "You are birdshit." He said this to Danny, who was standing by the table, behind Seeta. Then he saw Mason and he said it again, "Birdshit." He looked frightened. "Come here," he said to Seeta. She stepped towards him and he reached out with his free hand and slapped her. The glint of a silver watch, the snap of the palm, the bounce of Seeta's hair as her head was pushed sideways and her bun fell apart.

"Hey," Danny called out.

Mr. Chahal lifted the rake like a baseball bat and aimed it at Danny's head.

"Daddy-jee," Seeta said, and stepped up beside her father and hugged his one arm. "Let's go," she said. Her voice was shaky. She wouldn't look at Mason or Danny.

Mr. Chahal took her chin in his hand and asked, "Have they hurt you?"

Seeta shook her head.

"Do you love these boys? Do you want to marry one? Which one? Him?" He pointed at Danny. "Or him?" The tines of the rake swung towards Mason. "They are nothing. They have nothing. Hah!" He shook a finger at Danny. "You know nothing. You think everything is sex, sex, sex. It isn't. There is more to this world than sex."

"I don't think that," Danny said.

"Don't speak while I am speaking," Mr. Chahal cried out. "Of course you do. You both do. You want to rape my daughter."

"I didn't," Danny said.

"He didn't say you did. He said you wanted to." This was Seeta, suddenly and calmly, a translator. She shrugged her small shoulders. She was still holding her father's arm and now she pulled and said, "Come," and then they were gone, too quickly, and Mason wanted to call out that they should stay, should threaten them some more, make them ask for forgiveness, anything to prolong her presence.

Danny left. He said, "Unbelievable," and then he said, "Fuck it," and then he walked outside, got in his car, and drove away.

Mason went into the kitchen and saw the popcorn bowl and the kernels on the floor and the chairs askew. Seeta's sweater was folded on the kitchen counter. It was dark green with bone-coloured buttons. He smelled it and then searched it. In the pockets he found matches, cigarettes, a bus ticket, a tube of lipstick, and a note written in the characters of a foreign language. He threw out the matches and ticket. He put the note on his dresser and hung the sweater in his closet. Months later it would disappear.

*O*nce a week she went to her singing lessons. He knew her route and liked to seat himself in a coffee shop in order to see her as she walked by. He sat and watched and waited for her to come back. One time she stopped before the shop to speak to an older man and she held her books to her chest and shifted from foot to foot. She was wearing a red turtleneck sweater and her hair was dark and long. Inside, he leaned back in his chair, worried that he would be seen. She knew him from school and parties and hanging out. They had taken a class together and they had talked of Turgenev and Ms. Abendschade, and once she had asked, "Are you going to the dance?" and he said he wasn't. In the last days of the school year they had eaten lunch together, sitting on the stands that looked out onto the football field. There had always been other people in their group and so it was never clear if they were sitting by themselves or with a crowd. He had no reason to hide from her; the pleasure was in the waiting and the longing, in seeing her without being seen.

The summer passed and one Friday, in fall, he arranged it so that he met her on the street just outside her house. She said his name, Mason, and then said that there was no one at home. He took this as an invitation and went in with her. They stood in the front room. The piano was by the window and he asked if she could play something. "A little concert then?" she asked, and said she would play one of her favourite pieces. She sat and played "Adoration," by Borowski, her right foot depressing the pedal. The music was simple and sombre. When she was finished she turned to him and said that she'd quit school, he must have noticed, and was working as a waitress at The Nook. "I'm throwing my life away," she said. "My father worries that I am preoccupied with sad things. He's making me take correspondence. I read textbooks, write the tests, and send them away in the mail, and then they come back. I imagine some little old lady bending over and correcting my work." She got up and walked into the kitchen. He followed her. She opened the fridge and took out two pears and gave him one. They sat in the room where the piano was and she folded her feet under her thighs. It was like they were husband and wife and were sitting down to discuss the day. It was that easy. She said, "I remember that English course we took together. You were in love with Abendschade. I saw you watching me this summer. Every time I went to voice lessons you were in the Bagel Shop. Am I embarrassing you?"

Mason shrugged and said, "I was there a couple of times. Okay, maybe more. But at first it was by chance and then it was kinda regular and then, because you went to voice lessons every week at the same time, it was every time. I admit it. You knew, though, and you didn't do anything about it. It wasn't like I was stalking you."

"I know everything. You read to a man called Mr. Ferry. You have a brother. His name's Danny. You hang out with a guy called Turbine and you like to write poetry. You used to play tennis with Seeta Chahal, but that's old news. She's left. You're alone. How's that?"

"You have spies."

"I have sisters." She took a quick breath. "I was waiting and waiting. I said, Lena, wait till August 15. Then September. So, today, suddenly, there you were and I was surprised. That was nice. To be surprised. You're very slow, do you know that? That's not bad, it's just some guys when they like a girl they tell the girl but you'd rather sit in a coffee shop and spy. It's kind of weird, but it's interesting. Much more interesting than boys who just wanna get laid. Quickly."

Mason hadn't eaten his pear. Lena had finished hers. She stood and went to the kitchen and when she came back she said that she drove out to the country twice a week for eggs and milk. "The Nook likes farm-fresh," she said. She asked if he wanted to come along some time and he said he would like that.

On Wednesday afternoon, the first time she picked him up, she was dressed in boots and jeans and a flannel shirt and the sun fell through the windshield and caught her left forearm, revealing a single blue vein winding down to her wrist. He looked at her and said that this ride was the best thing that had happened in a long time. At the farm he helped her load the flats of eggs while she paid Mr. Koop, writing out a cheque on the hood of the van.

A week later Mason gave her a piece of paper on which he had written,

At the Koops'
Leaning into the light
Like two eggs
I saw your shoulders all white.

"White rhymes with light," he said. "And Koops' ends like eggs." He smiled. "I wanted to keep the word Koops' because it's a great name for a chicken farmer. Don't you think?"

"That's so sweet," she said.

He imagined touching her head, running his palm along the top and down her crown, the hardness of her skull, smooth, marmoreal, her brain a jumble of ideas and possibilities.

"Was I wearing my white vest that day?" she asked.

"What day?"

"The day the poem comes out of. That day. Was I wearing my white down vest?"

"It's not true, what I wrote. It didn't really happen. I mean, you leaned into the light, but I didn't see your shoulders. I imagined them. It's just a poem."

"I've never had one written for me." She took it and folded it into the front pocket of her shirt.

And so it happened that every Wednesday and Friday when she went for eggs, Mason joined her. She picked him up at the edge of the school grounds. One afternoon she announced that her father had caught wind of Mason. "He wants to meet you. He has four daughters so he's a bit protective."

She drove with her left hand and her right hand lay on her thigh. She wore jeans with a zipper up the back and an embroidery of flowers and dragons on one leg. There was a gap between her short top and her jeans; her belly button, a hipbone, the ridge of her vertebrae.

"My father has tests. Three of them. Supper at our house, a quiz on some historical figure – the last time, it was Galileo – and you'll have to memorize a Bible passage. My father asked if you were a Christian and I said yes, but I don't think he believed me." She glanced at him. "You are, aren't you?"

"I guess so. If I have to be."

She reached over and took his hand. Didn't ask, just took it and held it, and Mason looked out at the road. He wanted to look down at their hands but he didn't.

"You have to be," she said.

At the library he did a search on famous people throughout history, and he found a commentary on original sin and the infallibility of Scripture and Christ's sojourn in the wilderness, all topics Lena had invited him to prepare for. The last time coming back from the Koops' she had pulled the van onto a narrow road and stopped and said, "Let's go into the back."

They sat amongst the cartons of eggs and kissed. Lena unbuttoned her shirt. "This is my shirt," she said. She removed her tank top. "This is my undershirt." Then she unclasped her bra and said, "This is my bra. You can touch."

She had dark hair and her skin was alabaster.

"Are you cold?" he asked.

She said she wasn't.

They kissed some more and Lena touched Mason's face and his neck and then her hands dropped to her sides as Mason put his mouth on a breast.

"That's nice," she said. Then she asked, "What do you want me to do for you?"

"It doesn't matter," he said. He was aware of her looking down at him and the slight heat of her breath against his forehead. He closed his eyes and opened them again. She was still there.

"You're a spring chicken," she said. She loosened his belt and tugged at his jeans. Then she removed her own and slipped out of her panties. She climbed back into the front for her purse and Mason saw her from behind. He turned away and then back to look again. His hands shook.

When she came back she lay on the floor of the van. "We can have sex," she said. "Just be careful of the eggs."

"Are you sure?" he asked.

"Yes." She took a condom from her purse, opened it, and slipped it onto Mason. "There," she said.

She helped him get inside her and then she wrapped her arms around his neck and head and breathed in his ear until he was finished. "Okay," she said. "Stay like that."

He obeyed.

They didn't talk for a long time and Mason, his head pressed into Lena's neck, wondered if she had fallen asleep. "Are you all right?" he asked.

She said she was. She said that she was not aware of how other people experienced sex but that this wasn't bad. It was kind of quick, she said, but that could be improved upon. She held Mason's head and pressed her nose against his and said that the way they were lying right now was quite nice, "Our feet, our legs, our hips, our bellies, our mouths. That's all good."

Mason moved and slipped out of her.

She touched his face. Pressed her thumbs against his eyes and said, "I like you, Mason Crowe. You don't scare me."

Driving home later the van was hot and Mason was sleepy. He closed his eyes and then opened them. He saw Lena's hand on the wheel and her bare arm. Her flannel shirt lying loosely across her shoulders. Mason looked out the window and they drove on and later, coming into the edge of the city, he said, "What great arms you have."

One Saturday, Mason went with his mother to a Mexican restaurant for lunch. Mrs. Crowe ate half her meal and then smoked and drank Mexican beer while Mason cut up his food into neat bits and chewed slowly.

"You're happier," his mother said. "I can see that. What's up?"

"Nothing."

"Rhonda saw you with someone the other day. She wondered if you had a girlfriend. I said I didn't know. My boys don't talk to me."

"I talk to you."

"So, what's her name?"

"Lena."

"Lena. That sounds old-fashioned. Nice. Is she?"

"She's nice. I don't know if she's old-fashioned."

"Is she from school?"

"She was. She quit."

"I see. You like her." This was a statement, as if this fact were to be feared.

"I think so."

"You're still young, Mason. At your age I hung around with a bunch of friends. There were eight of us. We never had the inclination to pair off or get too serious. *Are* you serious?"

"I like her a lot. She's interesting, she sees things in a different way."

"Are you having sex?"

"Mom." An image of Lena crawling into the front of the van to fetch the condom. The shape of her from behind. Her lack of shame.

"Rhonda said that lots of kids are. But I said they weren't. Not necessarily. It's so dangerous these days." She lit another cigarette. "You hate talking about this, don't you? It's just that I don't want you hurt. Remember what happened with that other girl. Seeta. Okay?"

Mason shrugged. There were two men in suits at the next table. They were watching his mother. Perhaps she noticed, because she became more animated.

"Those guys are jerks," he said to his mother.

"What guys?"

"The ones beside us."

His mother snuck a look and then turned back to Mason and said, "You know them personally, then, you know what they're thinking, what they believe?"

"I can tell," Mason said. "They either sell real estate or cars and they live for making a big sale and they like looking at women. They're so obvious. They don't care if you're smart or not, Mom."

She laughed. "That's great, Mason. You just keep on being my little knight." She called for another beer. Her arm went up and he saw the underside and the men at the other table were looking and they too must have seen her bare arm and the white smudge of deodorant on the underarm of her black top. She folded her hands and rested her chin on them. Her hair was dyed black with copper streaks. It made her look either cheap or attractive. Mason couldn't tell.

His mother said, "Your father's coming home on the weekend. He comes back with the road all over him. Full of stories about hitchhikers and freaks. It used to be fun, when we were younger. Now it's tiresome." She paused and looked under the table and crossed her legs and said, "I shouldn't be telling you this."

Mason didn't say anything. He reached for his mother's beer and poured some into his glass.

"Careful," she said. Her fingers circled his wrist and pulled the beer back.

"Dad's not stupid," Mason said. "Sometimes he just seems sad. You know? He comes home and he doesn't know what to do. He walks around the house and tries to talk to my friends as if he were still a teenager. It's embarrassing. But I wouldn't call him stupid."

"I didn't mean to make it sound like that. I'm sorry." She drank and her throat moved as she swallowed and Mason watched this. She put the glass down. "How old am I? Do you know?"

"Sure. You're forty-four."

"That must seem ancient." She touched her face, her hair.

"Not that ancient, Mom. Eric Lozowy thinks you're hot. Mrs. Robinson. That's what he calls you." Mason rolled his eyes.

"Ha. Really?" She was pleased. She looked over at the next table. Said, "Your father's fifty." She called for the bill then, as if this fact were a reason to move on. She said, "I want to meet Lena. I want you to bring her over." Then she added, nodding at the distant waiter, "I like to meet these girls that my sons are friends with. You know?" And, not waiting for a response, she stood and paid and then took his arm as they left the restaurant.

When his father came home he stayed two days and two nights. On the second evening Mason's parents went out to a play. Danny had moved out of the house and was living in a small apartment downtown. Mason was alone. He wanted to call Lena but she'd told him she'd be out with the family for the evening, so he did his homework and he was still studying when his parents came home. He could hear his mother banging things around in the kitchen and asking why she should work and pay for everything. "Why is that, Silas?"

Then she said, "What about Mason? Do you spend time with him? No. Why don't you take him on a trip with you? God knows you don't spend a lot of time in people's kitchens selling things."

There were muttered noises and voices and then his father said, "You tell me. When's the last time we had sex?"

"You want to? Let's do it right now then. How do you want me?"

"I'm talking about closeness, Penny. About you touching me. About you wanting to be with me."

"I don't mind being with you. I just don't want to have sex right now."

"When, then? I figure if you love someone you should want to have sex with them."

"I love Rhonda. I don't want to have sex with her."

"Well, that's good. It's certainly nice to know you don't lean that way."

There was silence and then the kettle whistled and Mason figured his mother was making tea. She usually drank Earl Grey with a shot of something on the side. Two kinds of warmth, she said. The sound of the kettle disappeared and spoons tapped against mugs and his mother asked his father, "When you're out there, Silas, and you run into a good-looking woman, do you ever think, Oh, my, she's beautiful and easy and I'm all alone and what the hell. You know?"

"Road pussy?"

"Don't, Silas. Mason might hear you."

"Never."

"Never?"

"Never. I've got a Cadillac at home. It's pretty simple."

"But a Cadillac that doesn't always start." And then his mother said, "Hey," and their voices floated away and Mason listened but silence had fallen and when he passed through the kitchen later their mugs were on the table, half-full, and they weren't in the living room or the den. In the morning his father came into his room and sat down on his bed and said he was leaving again. He said there was work to be done. Then he said, "Your mother's in a better mood when I'm not here."

"That's not true," Mason said. "Maybe she misses you."

"Maybe."

"Or she thinks you're happier out there," Mason said.

"Sometimes I am. Though I miss you, Mason. We don't talk much, do we? I don't know if you have a girlfriend, or if you're playing basketball, or if you're still working for the Costa brothers."

"I'm not working for them any more and I've never played basketball," Mason said. He was watching his father's mouth and thinking about road pussy. The words made his father new, as if a light had been focused on him to reveal some flaw. His father was sitting on the edge of the bed. He had his hand on Mason's leg, which was under the blanket. He had small hands. A small head. He was wide across the chest and his mouth was soft. Mason felt sorry for him.

His father said, "You could come with me some time. I'm selling encyclopedias on CD-ROM now. Our world is a strange place. Everything's changing. Soon we'll have headless chickens and pigs that produce no shit. My own grandchildren, should I ever have them, probably won't need legs and arms." He said, "I was sitting in a restaurant in Sprague eating pumpkin pie and I saw this young boy and girl in the back booth and the boy reminded me of you. He didn't look like you, it was just the way he looked at the girl and said something. That's when

I thought of you and that girl you had here for dinner one night. Seeta. How'd that work out?"

"It didn't work out. She's married," Mason said.

"Already? I knew that was in the plans but I didn't know it was so soon." He pondered this. Then he asked if there were any other fish in the sea and at this Mason shrugged. His father leaned forward to hug Mason, who hugged him back. Mason could smell his father's clean hair. His face was smooth and his back was broad and strong.

Later, when Mason went downstairs, his mother was eating breakfast and she nodded at an empty chair and said he should sit with her. She drank coffee and he ate toast and she talked about the play the night before. "Your dad loved it," she said. "But then he's fond of anything dark and hopeless. 'What a dump.' That's the first line. 'What a dump.' And that summed up the play." She said that she was too much of a mathematician and had a hard time moving past the acting. "The actors are acting," she said, and her hand went to her bangs and she pushed at her hair.

She said that during the third act she felt claustrophobic and she left and sat in the lobby. She could hear the actors yelling at each other and that depressed her. "Then the play was over," she said. "And all these people came out and they were strangers walking by, talking and smiling, and I couldn't hear them, it was like I was on the other side of a glass wall, and then I saw your dad and he said, 'Are you ill?' I said I wasn't and then he got angry. Did you hear us last night?" she asked.

Mason shook his head. "Not really."

"That's good," his mother said. She looked at him, tilted her head. "The other day, after our lunch, I was thinking about boys and how they are with girls. Probably because I have two boys. I was thinking that what girls want is kindness and attention and I was hoping my boys offer that. That you give that to Lena. You know?"

"You can count Danny out," Mason said.

His mother sighed. "You know I won't take sides with you and Danny. I'm aware of how he is, but it's not as simple as 'He's bad and you're good.' He bought me this the other day. Did you see?" She held up her wrist and showed Mason a thin silver bracelet. He thought of Seeta and the bang of her bracelets as she swung her tennis racquet. He said, "So, he's got money to buy you things."

"Oh, Mason. That's not what I meant. You're terribly sweet and if I had a daughter I'd want her to be with a boy like you. That's why when I talked about kindness and attention I was thinking more of you. When you look at Lena what do you see?"

"Jesus, Mom."

"Do you see Lena or do you see Lena's body?"

"What do you think? I see Lena, okay?"

"Well, it's a fair question. Lots of guys see the body."

"I like Lena. She's got a brain. She's not just a body."

"That's good." His mother put her arm around his neck and squeezed and brushed her lips across his head.

Only later did Mason think about Lena's boldness, especially around sex. How matter-of-fact she was. "What's the big deal," she said once, and to this Mason had said nothing, for he was the amazed recipient. The fact was, Lena Schellendal – daughter of a bank manager, sister of three girls, bright precocious quoter of Old Testament prophets – broke Mason's heart. Because in her brazenness she seemed innocent, lost. But she sensed his pity and she pushed it away as she leaned forward and kissed him and said, "Let's fuck, Mason Crowe."

℘

When Mason told Lena about Mr. Ferry, she said, "Maybe when he dies you'll be rich."

"I don't think so," Mason said. "He wants me to introduce you to him some time."

"He knows about us?"

"He asks."

"That's creepy."

Still, one time Lena came with Mason to the house. She stood before Mr. Ferry and he said, "You've brought Lena." He held out his hand and Lena grasped it and then pulled back.

"Sit down," he said. He offered beer. He said, "Do you like beer, Lena?" He smiled in her direction.

"Sure. Yeah," Lena said. "I could do that."

Mr. Ferry stood and walked towards the kitchen. He touched the wall occasionally but he walked with the assurance of a man who saw.

"He's not blind," Lena whispered.

"Yes, he is."

"He doesn't act like it." She went over to the shelves and studied the books. "Everything's in alphabetical order." She turned back to face Mason and said, in a low voice, "We must have order."

Mr. Ferry returned then carrying a tray with three glasses and three bottles of beer set on it.

"Will your mother object to you drinking some beer? Mason?" he asked shifting his head in the direction of Lena, who held a book in her hand.

Mason said that it didn't matter. His mother didn't care. Mr. Ferry sat and looked directly at Lena. Lena looked at Mason. Mr. Ferry folded his hands. He looked happy. He said, "This is wonderful that you had time to come visit, Lena. I guess you know Mason reads to me."

"Yes, he told me," Lena said. "This is a very nice house, Mr. Ferry."

"Is it? That's good. Tell me about yourself, Lena."

Lena blinked. "Really?" she asked. "Why?"

Mr. Ferry lifted his hand and held it in mid-air. "Because I'm blind and I don't know you. I like to have a mental image of the person I'm talking to. Little things are important. The shape of your nose. A crooked tooth. Colour is important to me, as well. What colour is your hair?"

"Dark. Brown."

"You mean walnut, like this?" His knuckle tapped the small dark table to his right. The glasses of beer sat, untouched. Mason took a glass for himself and motioned for Lena to come get hers. She did this, stepping up and reaching over Mason's lap.

"Please, do help yourself," Mr. Ferry said. He reached out for the final glass of beer and said, "And your eyes, Lena?"

"Oh, they're dark too, and wide."

"Wide. Do you mean large eyes, or set far apart? Or maybe you mean startled."

Lena shook her head. "No, not that." She paused, then said, "Far apart."

"That's nice. Some of the most beautiful women in the world have eyes like that." He sipped carefully from his beer and then asked, "Are you pretty?"

Lena looked at Mason. "I'm a boot, Mr. Ferry. *Très* ugly."

"Really? Is that true, Mason?"

Lena made a face and leaned forward. Her hair fell across her face.

"No," Mason said. "She's very pretty."

"I thought so." Mr. Ferry paused. He said, "You play piano, Mason tells me."

Lena nodded and said, "True."

"I play the harp," he said, and then waved a hand at Lena, as if tired of her. "Why don't you look around while Mason reads?"

And so she did. Mason heard her walking around on the main floor and then she climbed the stairs and the noises she made were distant and muffled and at times he heard nothing at all. After a while, she came down and sat and drank her beer while Mason read aloud. She watched Mason and Mason was aware of her watching him. He looked up now and then and when he did she grinned at him and one time she blew him a kiss. He was reading about a man who came to the city with lots of money and bought new shoes and socks and then went out to get drunk. On his way home the man lay down in the road and fell asleep. Along came a wagon and the driver shouted to him to move or he would drive over his legs. The drunken man woke, looked at his legs, didn't recognize the shoes, and said to the driver, "Drive on, those are not my legs."

Mr. Ferry chuckled and said, "Drive on."

Lena stood and came over to Mason and bit his neck. He pushed her away. She wandered about until he was finished reading and Mr. Ferry had looked up and said, "Lena, are you there?"

She came over to her chair and sat down. Mr. Ferry held out his hand. "Here," he said.

Lena looked at Mason and then gave Mr. Ferry her own hand. He touched her knuckles with a finger. "How old are you, Lena?" he asked.

"Seventeen." She shifted and crossed her legs, as if hoping that this movement would release her hand, but Mr. Ferry held on.

"A good age," he said. "What did you find upstairs?"

Lena shrugged.

Mason said, "She was just wandering around."

Mr. Ferry answered too quickly. "Was she?" He looked over at Lena.

"You have cats," Lena said.

"Did you see my cats?"

"Yes," Lena said. "I did."

"The tabby is Albert. The fat calico is Minnie. Do you like cats?" He appeared to be studying Lena.

"I guess so."

"You prefer dogs."

"Not really. Cats are okay."

"You have one?"

"We did," Lena said, "It died." She looked at Mason and

wrinkled her nose. "It was sick. My dad killed it because it was suffering."

Mr. Ferry seemed surprised. He still held Lena's hand. He asked, "When you were upstairs, did you look in my dresser drawers? In my closet?"

"No," she said. "I didn't."

"Why not? Weren't you curious? It's quite natural to want to search through people's cupboards or read their mail. Don't you think?"

Lena pulled her hand away and turned to Mason and mouthed silently that she wanted to go.

"What about you, Mason? Are you curious in that way?"

"I don't know." Then he said that they had to go, that Lena worked and she had to get ready.

"Oh. Where do you work?" Mr. Ferry asked Lena.

"The Nook."

"Is that right? I'll have to come in and have breakfast some day."

Mason nodded at Lena and said, "Is it okay, Mr. Ferry, if we go?"

"Of course, of course. This isn't a prison. Does it feel like a prison, Lena?"

Lena shook her head.

"That's a no, then?" Mr. Ferry asked.

"Yes," Lena said, "It's just that it's late."

Outside, they stood on the sidewalk and when Lena let out a breath and said, "Whoaa."

Mason said, "Don't do that."

"What?"

"Act like he doesn't exist."

"When?"

"He knows everything."

"Ohhhh. He's god now."

"He knows when you smile. He knows whether you're watching him."

"Shoot me before I end up like that." She took Mason's hand and said, "I was looking at him and wondering if it would matter if he was alive or dead. I imagined taking a hammer and hitting him on the head. Does that ever happen to you?"

Mason didn't answer, though he turned his head away.

Lena said, "I wouldn't do it. But are you ever standing beside someone and holding a knife, like when you're cutting onions or something, and you imagine stabbing that person?" She did a quick pirouette, her face all bright, and shrugged, "We could kill his cat, Albert."

Mason said, "*Did* you look in his drawers?"

Lena squealed and grabbed Mason's arm. "Holy shit, Mason. He's got everything in packages still. Underwear, socks. Never been worn. In his closet there are rows of suits and shoes all lined up and I thought, does he ever go out? That man is anal and rich."

"See, he knew."

"He was guessing."

"He knew."

"He wanted me to look. He probably gets off on it. Like asking me if I'm pretty. Does he always want to know the colour of someone's eyes and hair?"

"He asks weird stuff, like my shoe size or if my shirt is cotton or polyester. You get used to it."

"What about Seeta? Did he ever ask about her?"

"Come on, Lena."

Lena said, "I can tell that he's not dumb. He's just very odd. He's an old man, Mason. That's all. A lonely old man who's probably beating off right now. Oh, man, that's so sick."

Mason didn't answer. He pulled Lena in towards him. They walked on until they arrived at Mason's house. They went inside and Mason called out to see if anybody was home but it was silent and he took Lena's hand and said, "We're alone." They stood in the blue light of the open fridge and each drank a glass of milk. Later, in Mason's bedroom, Lena sat on the bed, leaned back against a pillow, and said, "You wanna do something?"

Mason lay down beside her. He put his head on her breast, on top of her sweater, and he said, "Let's just stay here."

She held his head. She said, "If I were a jewel lying out on thin ice would you skate out to rescue me?"

Mason felt her fingers against his ear, the pressure of her elbow on his back. His eyes were closed and the rhythm of her breathing lifted and lowered his head. She smelled faintly of soap, of Mr. Ferry's house. He said, "Yes, I'd rescue you."

"Even if you might die?"

"I'd risk it. I wouldn't even think about it."

"That's important," she said. "That you don't think about it. That you just go. That's what I love about you." She sat up. Folded her legs under her. She was wearing the red turtleneck she'd worn on the day she stopped outside the Bagel Shop on her way to voice lessons. It made her neck longer and it was as if her head was disconnected from her body.

She said, "The thing I liked best at Mr. Ferry's was all the books. I think sometimes if I could surround myself with books, maybe live in a library or a bookstore, then I'd be happy." She paused and took Mason's hand and said, "He doesn't need them all."

"What do you mean?"

"He can't even read. They're like trophies he can't see. Some time soon take a book for me."

"I can't do that, Lena."

"Why not? He wouldn't even notice."

"I just can't. Besides, I'm not sure he wouldn't notice."

"Okay." She let go of his hand. "I figured why not borrow a book or two. But fine." She bounced off the bed and went to the bathroom. Mason heard the toilet flush and then it was quiet. Outside, the wind was snapping at a loose shingle. The branches of a tree scraped the gutter.

Lena called, "Come here."

She was in Mason's parents' room, looking through his mother's closet. "Look at this," she said, holding up an orange leather miniskirt. She threw it on the bed and her arm created an arc and then fell back. She turned again to the closet and said, her voice distant, "Let's get dressed and then we'll go out. Your mom wouldn't mind, would she? She's got everything."

"We're not going out, but you can try them on."

Lena turned to face him and asked, "You sure?" but she was already stripping down to her underwear. She put on red pantyhose. The orange skirt. A black top and tall boots with big heels. She bent over to zip the boots and her rear appeared as a pumpkin.

Mason pulled Lena onto the bed. The boots hit his shin. She pushed him away and stood. Mason loved the line of her haunch. He followed her into the kitchen where they sat and drank Mason's father's beer. Lena said that in the skirt and tights and the top she felt like someone else, someone who couldn't be Lena Schellendal. "I love that," she said. "If you closed your eyes we could be somewhere else. Another city. Like Paris. You wanna call me Claire or Sophie or what?"

"Bernadette," Mason said.

"Yeah, and you're Gustave or Philippe and we're drinking aperitifs and later we'll have a late dinner and then we'll go home and you'll bend me over and nail me like the good French boy you are. I'm so dirty."

"I don't think so," Mason said. He saw her front teeth, the small gap there.

She watched him for a bit, then said, "I like you."

Mason shrugged. Touched the hand that she had wrapped around her beer.

"Lots of girls do," she said. "They talk. Your name comes up. One time Annie Oliver was standing beside me putting on lipstick, this was in the girls' bathroom at school, and she said, 'Mason Crowe, he's so *laconic*, I'd get pervy for him.'"

"She said that?"

"Yeah. So I had another look."

"And?"

"She was right."

"Annie's weird. We read some poetry once at a coffee house. I went, then she went. She laughs really high and fast and her breasts are too big."

Lena uncrossed her legs, passed a hand over her knees, and said, "Don't you ever wonder what'll happen? To us? To the world?"

Mason said that he didn't know. He said that growing old didn't excite him and that the prospect of living like his father and mother was depressing. "The other day they were talking about sex," he said.

"In front of you? My parents never would. They don't even fuck."[8] She held her beer in the air and said, "I don't want to go there."

When they had finished their beer they went back into Mason's parents' bedroom, where Lena removed her clothes. Mason took the skirt and hung it up. He put the pantyhose away, pushing them deep into his mother's lingerie drawer, feeling there the texture of silk and nylon, the eroticism of empty panties.

Lena showered and dressed while Mason made tuna melts and then they sat in the kitchen and ate and at one point Lena

---

[8] They do. The night before, actually. At one in the morning Mrs. Schellendal straddled her husband and put him inside her and he held her breasts and she reached behind and cupped his balls and cried out and then ducked her head forward and bit his hand and later he said, "I love your cunt."

said, "Look at us, Bernadette and Gustave," and she simpered and Mason was keenly aware of the possibility that he could lose her.

⁓

Lena called Mason and said that her father wanted to meet him. He was invited for supper a week from Saturday. "Okay?" she said.

"Do I have a choice?" Mason asked.

"Not really." Lena's voice dropped on the last syllable, her tone aimless, as if much of life was inevitable and simply to be borne. Then she said, much too brightly, "Wanna hang out?" She said she was going to the mall. She wanted to do some shopping and see a movie. "My Dad gave me his Visa. We had a fight and he's trying to appease me."

They met in the food court of Polo Park. Lena was red-cheeked from the cold. She wore a Russian-looking hat with fur flaps. She said she wanted to see Ethan Hawke in *Hamlet*. She loved Ethan Hawke. Mason wasn't sure if he wanted to but he just nodded and said, "Okay."

Lena started talking about Ms. Abendschade and how Ms. Abendschade was so strict about interpretation and how she probably wouldn't like the play being set in modern times with video cameras and computers and skyscrapers.

"A travesty," Lena said. "She loved that word."

"Rigorous," Mason said. "That was her favourite. 'Class, what is required of you is rigorous thought, rigorous examination, rigorous reflection.'"

"Come," Lena said, "Let's go shopping." She flashed a white hand and stood. She pulled Mason up and they trolled the mall. Lena tried on a dark blue dress. Mason told her it was too short. "Bend over and all you get is panty."

She bent over and looked at herself in the mirror. "It's fine," she said.

She bought it. Carried it out in a black bag with a hemp handle. It dangled from her fingers like something both despicable and delicate. She bought a pair of shoes and a T-shirt that was tiny and accented her belly. Some panties and a bra, a jean jacket, a pair of leather gloves, a bracelet of leather and beads, a tube of lipstick, eye shadow, Body Shop lotion. She offered to buy Mason a jacket. He refused. She stood holding her bags beneath the glassed ceiling of the mall and said, "All this stuff."

They went to the movie and sat in the back row and ate licorice, and at one point, when Hamlet was angry with his mother, Lena turned to Mason and said, "Put your hand between my legs."

He reached for her and they fooled around and the bags rustled at their feet and Lena said, "Buying things always makes me horny."

The movie wasn't like the play. It was too brief, too chopped up, and Mason kept thinking how Lena was right, Ms. Abendschade wouldn't have liked it. She would have called it doltish or said it wasn't rigorous enough. Ethan Hawke didn't love his mother. According to Ms. Abendschade, Hamlet wanted to sleep with his mother, was terribly jealous of Claudius, but even so, "the reechy kisses" and the "incestuous sheets" couldn't goad him to action.

Lena pushed her mouth against Mason's neck and sucked. Took his hand and put it near her crotch where he fumbled with her zipper. Licorice on her breath.

And finally, Hamlet called out, "I'm dead, Horatio." Much had been made of that in class as well. Ms. Abendschade had been using a broomstick as a sword and she had brandished it and said, her face red with excitement, "Hamlet stands there, slain, and utters the words, 'I'm dead.' Not 'I'm dying,' but 'I'm dead.'"

They wandered through the mall after, Lena clutching her bags and Mason glowing in the memories of Lena's body and slaughtered Danes. He smelled his fingers as they stood by the upper railing, near the clock and the fountain, and looked down. It was then that they saw Mason's mother. She was standing by a display of watches and jewellery. She was leaning against a man and for a moment Mason believed that his father had suddenly returned home. She touched the back of the man's head and he turned and Mason saw his face. It wasn't his father. Mason didn't know him. He was a stranger.

"Look," Mason said. He nodded in the direction of his mother.

Lena studied the scene below them. Her hand took Mason's elbow. "That's your mom, then," she said. She didn't seem surprised.

His mother turned and looked up at the clock and said something and Mason stepped back from the railing and pulled Lena with him. Then Mason leaned forward and looked down and he saw his mother talking and holding the man's arm and the man began to laugh. He was handsome and looked younger than his mother, and then his mother laughed again and the man's hands, covered with leather gloves, lifted and held Mason's mother's face and he said something to her and she took his arm and they walked on and disappeared.

"Jesus Christ," Mason said.

Lena looked at him. She seemed small and inconsequential.

"Come on," Lena said. She took his arm and led him past the closed shops and down the escalators to the outside doors and across the street where they waited for the bus. Mason kept looking around as if expecting his mother to reappear.

They took the bus up to the Liquor Commission and Mason walked Lena home. She asked him to come in to meet her awful sisters and her awful parents but Mason stopped at the steps and looked at the house and said, "No, no, I'll come on Saturday. Should I dress up?"

Lena laughed. "How? As Zorro? Sure, that would be fine. Don't forget to memorize something. Anything simple from the Old Testament is good."

He said that he had a passage picked out. It was easy and he even liked it but he didn't know whether it was from the Old Testament.

"Doesn't matter," she said. "You're so lovely." She pushed her tongue deep into his startled mouth and only later did he realize that that was how it would always be, she would decide what was good and fair and dirty and raw and ugly and lovely and he, he would nod and say, Yes.

"I was just asking," he said, "Because if I show up all formal it might not look good. You see?"

"Wear that silky shirt. That blue slippery one. I love it." She squeezed his hand. "Don't worry about your mother. She's cool." And then she turned and went inside and Mason walked down the stairs and stood on the sidewalk looking in. He could see one of Lena's sisters doing handstands. She was wearing a skirt and the legs went up and the skirt tumbled and the legs were white and long and the underwear was blue and then the legs disappeared and Mason wished with a dull ache that he had a sister. All the secrets he could have learned. A sister was flagrant and easy and obvious. A sister was a teacher. No competition, no threat. And a sister would know what to do with his mother.

He walked home over the bridge. It was colder. Snow had been promised. The river was high and wild and fast, and as happened each time he crossed the bridge, Mason wondered if a car would run up on the sidewalk and hit the backs of his knees and throw him over the balustrade and he would somersault and hit the water and die.

When he got home the house was empty. A single light was on in the hall. He called for his mother. There was no answer. He took off his boots and walked around the house to check for burglars and perverts. He was alone. He ate a bowl of cereal and listened to the wind. He thought of putting on some music but didn't really feel like it. He rinsed his bowl and left it in the sink. He went up to his mother's room and lay down on her bed. After a bit he stood and rummaged through his mother's drawers. Thongs both white and black, lacy underwear that could serve no other purpose than to excite, hose, socks, dried flowers, a spent bottle of Chanel No. 5, a pack of old cigarettes, a Ziploc bag with letters, ribbons from her athletic high school days, loose change, and in the back, tucked into a box, a vibrator and body lubricant. Mason took out the vibrator. Turned it on. It was innocuous, the scent of metal and plastic, perhaps strawberry. He put the vibrator away and rummaged some more, thinking he might find a diary in which his mother would reveal the name of the man at the mall. There was no diary. He lay down on the bed and fell asleep and he dreamed that Lena was sitting on Mr. Ferry's lap reading to him and Mason's mother entered the room and called out, "Mason?"

He woke. His mother was sitting beside him holding his hand. Her own hands were cold. She released him and removed her shoes. Stood and hiked her skirt and rolled her pantyhose down. She sat and pulled them off. Her back was to him and he could see the straps of her bra through her top. She smelled of something different; leather perhaps, someone else, cologne.

"Where were you?" Mason asked.

"I was out with Rhonda. Drank too much. Listened to music. Talked." She paused. "Close your eyes," she said and she stood and pulled down her skirt and stooped to pick it up and Mason watched and saw her tiny black panties and the smack of her thigh. She tossed the skirt onto the bed and put on loose pants. Tied the drawstring. Said, "What did you do?"

Mason looked at her. She hadn't faced him yet. He said, "Read. Waited for you." He was studying his mother's profile. She went into the bathroom and Mason followed her.

He said, "I saw you."

She picked up a brush and brushed her hair. She was cold and efficient as she looked at him in the mirror. She said, "Oh, where?"

"At the mall."

"Really? When?"

"Tonight."

She considered this. Turned and looked at Mason. Asked, "Why didn't you say hi?"

Mason shrugged.

"You and Lena?" she asked.

Mason said, Yes, him and Lena. Then he asked, "What's his name?"

She sighed and said, "His name's Aldous and he's just a friend. He's a friend of a friend."

"When's Dad coming back?" Mason asked.

"Next week. He called yesterday and said he could either come back and drive taxi or work as a carpenter out of town. He was offered a job framing houses in Kenora. He didn't take it. Not yet."

"What'll happen?" Mason asked. "You'll move there?"

"No. No. I couldn't leave my job. Who'd buy you food and clothes?"

"He'd live there?"

"He would." The prospect seemed to please her. Her mouth lifted and though it might have been a grimace Mason saw it as a smile. She said, "He likes to live away from home. Haven't you noticed?" She turned again and looked at him. "Don't blame me for all of it, Mason."

Mason went to the kitchen and looked out the window. It had begun to rain and there was ice forming on the windowpane. He heard his mother behind him and saw her image reflected in the darkness of the pane. She said, "Marriage is like a car, Mason, it needs repair sometimes and your father doesn't like to repair things. He'd rather run."

Mason didn't think this was true. Adultery was worse than running. There was nothing creative or good or pleasant about having your mother sleep with a man who was not your father.

His mother said, "You think I'm selfish. Is that it?"

"Aren't you?"

"Don't blame anyone," she said, and then she said that sex and heartbreak could tumble down around the heads of anyone, young or old, and he shouldn't think that was his domain. It wasn't. Love wasn't just a privilege of youth. "Do you love Lena?" she asked. She had reached up into the cupboard and was pouring herself a glass of Scotch. She dipped her finger in and licked it. Eyed Mason. Took a sip.

He said, "I'm not married to Lena. I didn't promise her anything." Then he said what he'd been thinking. He told his mother that she had had her chance and now it was his chance and she was stealing away the best years of his life. And what kind of name was that? Did he think he was Huxley or some Aryan stud? Mason finished and began to cry and his mother looked shocked. She put her glass down and said, "Mason," and walked over and pulled his head against her breasts and said, "Mason, Mason, Mason." When he was finished crying she took his chin in her hands and looked at him and said, "These aren't your best years. It gets better, believe me," and she poured him a small amount of Scotch and handed it to him. "Here," she said, as if this were the comfort he needed. He took it and drank and shuddered. She poured him more and they sat at the table. She crossed her legs and said this wasn't a contest between Mason's father and Aldous. "It's possible to love more than one person. This may not be a good thing but it's a fact." She lifted her glass and looked at it.

Mason said, "So Danny gets it from you." Her face was younger in the soft yellow light of the dining-room lamp. "You know. The sex. The fucking-around thing."

"I don't do the *fucking-around thing*." Her speech was slow, as if her tongue had been lashed to the roof of her mouth. She dipped her finger in her drink again, licked it, and studied Mason as if considering her next words. Then she said, "Two times, that's all. Two times I had sex with Aldous."[9]

"Why are you telling me this? I don't care," he said.

His mother, ignoring him, dragged him in further. She said, "He makes me feel alive. Well? You might as well know."

---

[9] She is not being entirely honest. It depends on how you define sex. She sucked him off once in Assiniboine Park, bending across the stick shift of his Boxster, and they had actual penetration twice, once in his apartment in the middle of the afternoon, a day she called in sick, and the other time in the corner of a dark crowded bar, when he took her by surprise from behind. She had allowed this. That surprised him – that she had allowed this – and it surprised her as well. And so, three times.

"Go away," Mason said.

His mother looked surprised. She said, "You hate me. Is that it?"

"I don't like you. Not right now. Maybe tomorrow again or next week, but right now I think you're pretty lousy."

His mother said that he was right. She was lousy. She sighed and stood and went to rinse her glass and Mason saw the curve of her waist and the dip of her head and her arm reaching up to replace the glass in the cupboard and he wondered if Aldous had a bigger penis than his father.[10]

He figured that his father didn't know. On Sunday morning, Mason found his parents in the kitchen reading the paper and drinking coffee. His father was happy. He was telling Mason's mother a story and his voice went up and down and when he was finished he laughed. His mother was wearing white pants and a black sleeveless top. She'd been eating toast. She lowered the newspaper and asked Mason to pour her more coffee. Mason did this and then got a glass of orange juice and went into the next room to watch TV. He wondered what his father would do when he found out.

Over the next week Mason tried to avoid his parents but he kept bumping into his mother. Once, she came into his room and stood in his doorway and waited until he turned down his stereo and then she asked, "Have you told your

---

[10] He did. It was thicker and longer.

father?" She paused and then continued, "Because if you're planning on it could you let me know? Before you do that?"

"I'm not going to say anything," Mason said. "I'll leave that to you."

His mother looked around at the walls of his room and then back at him and said, "Are you okay?" Her arms were crossed as if she were hugging herself. He could tell she was nervous and that she wanted him to say something. He was quiet. She said, just before turning to leave, "I shouldn't have told you what I told you, about Aldous and me. That was unfair. To everybody. I guess I was angry. Anyway." She sighed and stepped out of the room and shut the door and Mason sat there wondering if she might come back, but she didn't. Later in the day, after Mason's father had gone to work, she left the house dressed in a black dress and a red coat. She didn't say goodbye or tell Mason where she was going. The coat looked brand new.

That following Saturday evening Mason went to the Schellendal house for supper. Lena and her sisters surrounded him. They dropped in age by twos so that the youngest, Emily, was eleven. She was also the most mysterious; silent, circumspect, and left-handed. Lena's grandmother was there: stooped and blue-haired, she commanded attention at the far side of the table. Nana – that's what the girls called her. Mr. Schellendal had fried pickerel in butter and flour and now served everyone straight from the pan. He wore a tea towel at his waist and took it off just before seating himself. The family prayed. They held hands and Mr. Schellendal thanked God for the fish and the salad and the fresh frozen beans and good health and for Mason, Lena's friend. Emily did not close her eyes. Neither did Mason, who sat between Lena and her mother, and whose hand was slightly damp.

They ate and the girls talked and Mrs. Schellendal paid attention to Mason, replenishing his plate. The thirteen-year-old, Margot, got the giggles and excused herself and returned with her hair combed back and pulled into a tight ponytail. Over dessert Mrs. Schellendal asked Mason what his father did.

Mason said that he was a salesman. And then, perhaps because he wanted to make his own family life sound more interesting, he said that his father also wrote plays. He did this late at night when most people were sleeping. His father didn't like to talk about his writing.

"You never told me that," Lena said.

"That's wonderful," Mrs. Schellendal said. "Years ago, in a community play, I acted."

"She was Cordelia," Lena's father said. He lifted a hand, leaned forward, and focused on his wife. "'Nothing?'" he cried out.

"'Nothing,'" she answered.

"'Nothing will come of nothing. Speak again.'"

"'Unhappy that I am I cannot heave my heart into my mouth. I love your Majesty according to my bond, no more nor less.'"

Mrs. Schellendal paused, her gaze seeking out the grandmother and then Mason and finally her daughters. Lena began a slow mocking clap. Mason glanced at the girls and then at Lena's father. He seemed oblivious to Lena, who had stopped clapping. Emily smirked and held her fork like a shovel.

Margot said, "Dad, you do that every time we have guests. It's old. Boring."

"It's all we know, isn't it, Beth?"

Mrs. Schellendal agreed. When Mason turned towards her he was very close to her ear, a perfect whorl and the attached lobe. Across the table, Lena's sister Rosemary, whom Mason recognized from school, twirled her fork and studied him. He noticed this.

Lena's father said, "It runs in the family, this need for attention." He pointed an index finger at himself. "Not me, of course. Just the girls. This is why they all take singing lessons. They want to be famous. Though I fear they do not take criticism well."

"What's to criticize?" Lena asked.

Her father raised his head and said, "Willst du ein Knopf am Kirchturm sein, werden dich die Krahen hacken."[11]

Lena's grandmother said, "Oh, now, must we?"

Lena pressed against Mason's shoulder and whispered, "You okay?"

Mason nodded. Mystified, he looked at the two youngest girls who seemed happily unaware, and then over at Mr. Schellendal, who asked, "Do you want to be a writer like your father, Mason?"

---

[11] "If you want to be a bright button in the church tower, expect the crows to peck at you." The Schellendal family has heard this before. It reflects Mr. Schellendal's distrust of ego, his affection for hard work and self-effacement. Later, Mason will ask Lena what her father meant and she will translate: "Who do you think you are?"

"He is," Lena said. "He writes poetry."

"Love poems?" Emily asked. She raised her left hand and moved her fork in a slow circle. She was, Mason thought, the most like Lena.

"Not really," Mason said.

"They're not that obvious," Lena said.

Her father asked Mason if he had a particular poet he liked to read. Robert Frost, perhaps.

Mason answered, breathlessly, that Frost was a great poet. Though his poetry seemed simple, it wasn't. He turned to Lena, who was staring at her father. Suddenly anchorless, Mason said that poetry could come in all shapes and sizes and that even the Bible had its poetry. Perhaps it was nervousness or perhaps he believed that this was expected of him but he began to recite what he had learned from the Bible, pausing briefly after the first line. But then he continued and he was aware of the girls watching him with amused looks and when he reached the line, "So, there is nothing new under the sun," Lena's father held up a hand and said, "You don't have to prove anything, Mason." Then, as if to dispute his own advice, he asked, "Who wrote that?"

"Solomon," Lena said.

Mr. Schellendal ignored her and asked Mason, "Why do you think Solomon had such a bleak view? What was he saying?"

Rosemary looked up suddenly; her smallness surprised Mason. She was stubbornly silent. Lena, across from him, shrugged. He felt Mrs. Schellendal's presence, the sweet acquiescent sorrow she carried. "I don't know," he said, and as he said this he caught Mr. Schellendal's gaze and he thought, I have put your daughter's breasts in my mouth.

Lena's grandmother said that there was too much arguing in the family. "Ask a question like that of six people, Silas, and you'll get six different answers. Maybe the boy doesn't care what Solomon meant. Do you, Mason?"

Mason looked around the table. Lena said, "Nana hates arguments."

"This wasn't an argument," Mr. Schellendal said.

"My own parents always fought," Nana said. "Every meal they'd argue. About the food, the weather, politics. It's pointless."

"Of course it's pointless," Mrs. Schellendal said.

"Don't humour me," Nana cried. Her hand lifted. "I'm not dead yet."

Emily stood and began to clear the table. She took her nana's plate first and bent down and hugged her.

"Thank you," Nana said, "dear, dear child," and she looked directly at Lena's father, who was settling back into his chair and folding his napkin.

After supper they all went into the family room and watched videos of the girls growing up. Mason sat beside Lena. Emily curled up against his other shoulder. There were shots of the girls as infants, the girls skating, the girls at their cousin's wedding, the girls celebrating birthdays. Throughout, Emily and Lena and Margot squealed and called out comments. Rosemary said nothing. Not even when the film cut to a church and showed her baptism the year before.

Mr. Schellendal said, "Rosemary's our only daughter who has chosen to be baptized."

It was a lesson for Mason. Rosemary walked down into a tank of water. She stood beside an older man who put his arm around her.

"That's Pastor Gary," Mrs. Schellendal called out. She was sitting on a small stool, her back very straight. Her feet were crossed and were tucked to one side of the stool.

Rosemary looked nervous; her face was small and white. Then she fell back into the water and reappeared, a wet rag, in the arms of the pastor.

"Whooosh," Lena whispered in Mason's ear. She put her hand on his thigh. He felt Emily's warmth against his arm.

Then there were images of the girls on the beach in Florida. "Disney World," screeched Emily. Lena was wearing a bright blue two-piece. She looked chubby but seemed unaware of it as she pranced before the camera.

"Show-off," Margot said.

"I'm fat," Lena said.

Emily giggled. "Big tummy."

"Naww," Mason said.

"My favourite boy," Lena said, and she lifted her face and kissed him on the cheek. Mr. Schellendal was watching. Lena kissed him again. Mr. Schellendal said that they'd seen enough and he turned off the video. He stood in the middle of the room and said, "Well, Mason, it was wonderful that you could come. We always like to meet our daughters' friends. Don't we, Beth?"

"Yes, Mason," Mrs. Schellendal said. Then she turned to Lena, "Do you want to drive Mason home?"

"Ahh," Mr. Schellendal said, "He can go on his own. He looks in shape. Do you play any sports, Mason?"

"Tennis," Mason said. "Not now, though. In summer."

Mr. Schellendal seemed surprised. He swung his big head and said, "Tennis, huh."

Lena said she would walk Mason home halfway, up to the bridge. "Okay?" She took Mason's hand and squeezed.

Outside, Lena shivered in the late October air and said, "My sisters were jealous, my mother was jealous. Even my father was jealous. Nana liked you."

"She was very nice, defending me. I felt like an idiot. Why did Solomon have such a bleak view of life? Do you know that one? I couldn't think. I mean I could come up with an answer now, just like that, but whoaa, when I was sitting there it was like an exam. He asked that question and I was looking at your sisters and thinking how they were all really pretty and how maybe they could help me with the answer but nobody said anything. Everybody just stared and I panicked. So I thought about your mother's ring and how big the diamond was. She's got hands like you." When they reached the bridge they stood facing each other. Across the street the hospital sign glowed red and white. Lena's breath rose into the air.

"I should have warned you not to just dive into the Bible verses. My father likes to plan these things and you threw him off – which was nice to watch." She said that no one ever passed the tests. She said that the most devout missionaries could not pass. "My father hates all the boys I date. Don't worry, there haven't been many, three, max. It's just, my father likes to meddle." She sighed then and banged Mason's shoulder and said that overall she was happy with the evening. "My mother seemed to like you. And Rosemary."

"Your silent sister. She sat there and listened. Even when we were watching the video of her baptism she just sat there, like it was someone else up there."

"Rosemary's so secretive. She slips in and out of the house and sees boys my father would hate. She floats through a dark world and my parents only see the light. Rosemary's good at hiding."

"Maybe you should do the same thing," Mason said. "It would keep your father happy."

"I don't give a shit about my father's happiness."

"Sure you do," Mason said. He put his arm around Lena's neck and pulled.

⁓

"He doesn't want me to see you any more," Lena said. She was sitting beside Mason in a back corner at Cousins, which was located across from The Nook. Lena had just gotten off work and they had arranged to meet. It was cold, mid-November, and Lena was wearing an old hip-length coat that she took off and hung on the back of a chair. She still had her uniform on, a pale yellow dress, the hem of which she'd altered; this made the dress a lot shorter and she kept tugging at it and shifting her hips. Her lips were dry and cracked. Her face had an odd pallor; the whiteness of her skin had darkened in the several weeks since the dinner at her house and Mason had an urge to scrub at it.

"So what are we going to do?" Mason said.

Lena lit a cigarette and looked away.

"What's wrong with me?"

"It's not *you*. He just gets worried and of course I can't be going out with some pagan. Who you are is way out there somewhere not even close to who I am and there's nothing he'd like better than to find a perfect Christian boy for me who speaks both German and in tongues. The other day he saw you standing on our sidewalk and he said, "Who's that?" knowing very well who it was and he asked *me* this. Got me from my room and pointed out at the sidewalk at you and said, 'Who's that?' I said, 'My goodness, it looks like my boyfriend, Mason,' and he said, 'I don't want you seeing him any more.' I figure you gotta stop mooning outside my house."

"Okay, I won't. Jesus Christ. Your house is a fortress. No room for Mason Crowe."

"Do something then. Get a ladder and scale the wall. God, I've missed your little heathen body."

Mason took Lena's free hand and pulled it across the table towards him and held it between his palms. He studied her face. "You're kind of pale, like you were sick."

"I *am* sick."

He asked her if she was going to obey her father. "Are you going to stop seeing me?"

"'Course not."

"What are you going to do?"

"Run away. Or, we could get married." She smiled. It was a mocking smile and it made Mason wary.

He imagined Lena in a white dress and himself in a tux. Flowers. A garden. Photos. His parents off to the side. I do.

"Say our vows and there we are," Lena said. "I would be Mrs. Crowe. Huh." She touched her nose and studied the scene around her. She said that the restaurant had an odd odour, that her sense of smell was very acute these days. It was the medication. "Did you know that every Tuesday I go talk to my psychiatrist. A fat woman who gets excited when I talk about sex."

"You talk about sex with her?" Mason asked. "Not about us, I hope."

"Sure I do. She thinks you're quite a guy. Don't worry, I call you Gustave." She gave him a smug look and lit a cigarette and exhaled upwards. "You haven't gotten me any books yet, have you? That'd be a reason to drop by. 'Hi, Mr. Schellendal, I just happened to have this book, could you give it to your daughter?' It'd make you look intelligent, rich, caring. Mason, my intellectual. He's impressed by serious boys." She put out her cigarette. Lifted his hand and bit his finger.

Her hair was dirty and he took a few strands and pulled at them and said that he'd rather talk to her mother, who was much more approachable. Then he said she shouldn't worry because he had nothing to hide and besides, her father couldn't chain her to the bed in her room.

They parted on the sidewalk by Sherbrook and Westminster. Lena looked up at Mason and touched his mouth with a mitten. "Bye," she said and put her arms around his neck and held him, and he thought for a moment he might end up hating her. He wrapped his arms around her and said, "Lena."

ڡ

The book was on top of one of the shorter bookcases by the window. Mason picked it up and looked at it. *The Collected Poems of Robert Browning.* The cover was green. A picture of Robert himself, a low beard and waxy face, bushy eyebrows, man long dead. Mason slipped it into his bag. Mr. Ferry came back from the kitchen and settled himself and asked, "How's Lena?"

Mason said he didn't want to talk about Lena.

Mr. Ferry said that that was no problem. He said that the way of the world was a mystery. He swung his hand at his wineglass. It tipped and spilled and broke on the floor. His head swivelled towards Mason and then back to the spot where the glass had been. "Did you move it?" he asked.

"No, I didn't."

"Could you clean it up, please?"

Mason stood and went into the kitchen and searched for a rag and a dustpan and broom. "In the closet by the fridge," Mr. Ferry called from the other room. Mason found what he needed and came back and pushed the broken glass onto the dustpan. He wiped up the wine and returned the rag and dustpan to the kitchen. He returned with a new glass and poured more wine for Mr. Ferry and set the glass in his hand.

"Thank you," Mr. Ferry said. "Did I spill on the books?"

"No, they're fine." There was a stack of three paperbacks. A corner of the Browning peeked out from his bag.

Mason read then, from a translated book of Russian poetry, but his tongue was thick and he stumbled over the words and the poems made little sense except for one about how speech is divided up into parts but by then he was tired and Mr. Ferry let him go early. He walked home, the stolen book tucked into his backpack.

He put the book in his room where it sat until one night he picked it up and read several poems. The following week he took another book. The writings of Jakob Boehme. He felt no guilt, in fact he took pleasure in placing the book on his own shelf, reasoning that Mr. Ferry would not miss it. Over the next weeks he took twelve more books. He didn't read them, he wasn't sure if he even planned to read them in the future. He just took them, as if by possessing them he was making his way in the world. Once, when Mr. Ferry left the room, he pushed *The Riverside Shakespeare* into his backpack and later, walking home, its heft weighed on his shoulders and he thought, "All those words."

One Tuesday Mason arrived and Mr. Ferry had been drinking and seemed uneasy. He lifted his glass when he heard Mason and he said, "Here's to all the necessary things." He drank while Mason took off his boots and hat and jacket.

"Is it cold?" he asked, tilting his head.

"Yes," Mason said.

There had been a heavy snowfall, snowdrifts had built against the sides of houses, and the temperature had dropped. Car exhaust made objects disappear.

"A drink?" Mr. Ferry asked. He motioned at the wine bottle.

"No. Thank you."

Mason sat down and Mr. Ferry said, "I was thinking about Lena just this morning and her visit, what was it, several months ago? In any case, I was thinking she should come again, only stay a little longer. She ran off so quickly. How is she?"

Mason said she was fine. She was busy working and he didn't know if she'd have time to come back. He said she was shy.

"Really. I thought she was more haughty than shy, but those two can be confused, can't they? She's got a beautiful name. All kinds of possibilities. Lean against the fence. Scarcity. Inclination. Fall. It's perfect." He paused, held up a hand, and let it drop. "You know, of course, that there will be others. They will accumulate like debts. And you will love each consecutive girl a little less. But there will always be Lena. You don't want to hear this, do you?"

Mason didn't answer. He looked at the old man's bare feet sticking out of his open slippers, his toenails, the bluish hue of his ankles.

Mr. Ferry wasn't finished. He said he wanted to talk about stories. He said that the goal of telling a story was not to amuse. The writer was not a magician sent forth to beguile, neither was the goal to teach as if a story were a map rolled out and held flat with weights and the reader a lost traveller bent over that map trying to find the way. The purpose of a story was to enchant, and the reason we like stories, he said, is because they are truer than our own lives.

He said, "The story I will tell you is something you might have heard before. But that doesn't make it any less important. In fact, in this whole world there are only a few stories to tell. It is how we tell them that is important."

Mason was watching Mr. Ferry, who was focused and intent on telling this story. He was hunched forward and his hands were folded in his lap. He appeared to be looking at a particular spot on the floor.

"I once knew a woman called A.," Mr. Ferry said, "who one October found herself at a hotel in Gimli which looked out onto the lake. She was married but she had come alone to take some time to gather her thoughts. She was unhappy and had told her husband this and her husband had sent her off to rediscover herself. These were his foolish words.

"While there she met G., a man on holiday. The two of them spent time together strolling the boardwalk and looking out over the masts of the sailboats to the brown water of the lake which stretched eastward like a shallow ocean. They both had time to idle away and they did this indolently, as if the things of the world did not concern them. A week passed and one evening on the pier G. turned and kissed A. on the mouth and said with a quiet voice, 'Let's go to your room.'

"After, G. sat at the table eating an apple and he studied his new lover who lounged at the edge of the bed, distraught, it seemed, because she had deceived herself. G. did not understand, in fact the scene bored him, but still he held and comforted her and later they went out along the pier. There was not a soul around. They sat on a bench. White clouds above the lake. The evening, the sky, the beautiful woman beside him, all of this enthralled G. and he thought that everything in the world was really beautiful, everything but our own thoughts and actions when we lose sight of our dignity.

"In all this A. took obvious pleasure but she saw herself as a vulgar woman and when she left Gimli to return to her husband she told G. that it was a good thing. 'It's fate,' she said.

"But of course the affair did not end, and one day A.'s husband learned of the betrayal and found A. in her bedroom. She was sitting in blue panties before the mirror holding a powder puff. He loved her. He really did love her. He realized that he was jealous and he stepped close to his wife and clasped her shoulders. He saw his brown hairy hands on her white shoulders. He asked her to be honest and she half-turned, her upper body twisting at the hips and she sat, a lifeless being, a mannequin made of wax and silk lingerie and she said very slowly, 'I never miss you.'

"'So you don't love me,' the husband said, and A. said, 'No.'

"'Aha, I see,' said the husband, and then he said, 'I'm going to kill you.' And A. said, 'Kill me.'

"The husband was filled with hatred, for his wife and for himself, and he thought he should do something, should bring some order back into his life, and the thought that he could make order gave him strength and he left his wife and went out into the city to look for the man who was the lover of his wife but he did not find the man nor did he want to find the man.

The husband was pathetic and weak and if he had lived in a time when duels were acceptable he would have suffered shame rather than be shot. He loved his wife."

At this point Mr. Ferry stopped talking. His eyes were closed.

Mason asked, "And so?"

Mr. Ferry turned his head as if surprised by the question or as if he were only now aware that he had an audience.

"Ah, yes," he said, "what happened." He lifted his hand and splayed his fingers. He said, "What would you have liked to have happened? For the wife to come back to the pathetic husband? For the husband to shoot the lover? Nothing happened. The couple grew old together. A. saw G. several times after that and then never again. That's what happened. Then one day A. left her husband and he continued to live in his house by himself only he no longer saw what was around him. He cut himself off." Mr. Ferry stopped talking.

Mason waited. Then he asked a question to which he already knew the answer. "Were you in that story?"

Mr. Ferry lifted his head. "Which?"

"The story you just told."

"Did you recognize me?"

"I don't know. I'm not sure why you told me it."

"That's good," Mr. Ferry said. "To not be sure is good." Then he turned his head to Mason and said, "I might be recognized. I was once foolish and sent my wife Anabel off on her own to be cured of something I didn't understand. She fell in love and I was jealous and hated her. Did I threaten to kill her? Once perhaps. Though I didn't do anything. Eventually she left me but not for the man she briefly loved. And now I am blind and I sit and live in the perfect world of other people's stories." He paused. Drank some wine, and then continued. "There you go, those are some of the facts. But it isn't exactly my story. I didn't put my brown hairy hands on Anabel's white shoulders and she wasn't sitting before a mirror in blue panties holding a powder puff. That image comes from a novel about the Hapsburg Empire. The Trotta family. Or G. thinking the world is really beautiful, everything but our own thoughts and actions when we lose sight of our dignity. That line I took from a Chekhov story. So, I stole from two stories. What do you think?" He folded his hands in his lap.

"What do you mean?"

"About stealing." He turned his head like a bird about to strike.

"What do you mean, stealing a story?"

"For example, a story."

"I don't care," Mason said.

"You should. It's important to discern. The question is, is it okay to steal a story, or parts of it, if you let someone know it's stolen? Is that better than just outright theft?"

"Probably," Mason said.

Mr. Ferry wasn't finished. He said, "Kierkegaard wanted to be a novelist. It was as if he recognized that a story was different from a book of philosophy. It has more possibilities. One of his ideas was about a man who wishes to write a novel in which one of the characters goes mad; while working on it he himself goes mad by degrees, and finishes it in the first person. He never did write a novel. But what if I did this?

Decided to write a novel about a sixteen-year-old boy who reads Kierkegaard to a blind man and show the boy in all his innocence and guises and put a microscope on his love life and burrow into the mind of his girlfriend and, throughout the story about the boy and girl, I would scatter Kierkegaard's words like seeds, only I wouldn't acknowledge that these were his words, they would just appear, like signposts to the attentive reader. Every writer steals in some way from other writers, be it ideas, or specific lines, or inspiration. And indeed, my own theft is perhaps less harmful since it is more readily discovered, since I am confessing to the theft in advance. What do you think of that?"

Mason didn't know where Mr. Ferry was going with this. He supposed it had something to do with the stolen books but this didn't frighten him. He recognized himself as the sixteen-year-old boy, at least he thought he did, and this piqued his curiosity and he wondered how Mr. Ferry could put a microscope on a teenager's love life, what did he know, and he realized, as he had listened to Mr. Ferry, that he did not understand the man and in some ways he was alarmed by him.

Outside it was dark. Mason turned on the lamp at Mr. Ferry's elbow and asked Mr. Ferry if he wanted something to drink besides wine. Water? Tea? He said he didn't. Mason looked around the dim room. He was depressed. Mr. Ferry took things much too seriously. The story, the room, the lack of light, the books on the shelves, all this depressed Mason. He found it hard to breathe.

"I'm sorry," Mr. Ferry said, "I've talked too much. I do that. I'm full of nonsense sometimes. Here." He reached for

Mason's hand and held it. Patted it. "You want to read? What would you like?"

"I'm not sure, Mr. Ferry. The books we've been reading lately haven't been much fun. I'm sorry."

"Oh, no, don't be sorry. We'll read something else. More upbeat. A happy author. We'll think of a happy author. You choose." He motioned at the shelves.

Mason sat and waited. Mr. Ferry still held his hand. He wanted to pull it away but he didn't know how. Mr. Ferry squeezed and held on.

"The thing is," Mr. Ferry said, "Happy books aren't as interesting. They want us to believe that everybody lives forever." He turned his blind eyes onto Mason's forehead.

"I have to go," Mason said.

He got up and went into the foyer and put on his jacket, boots, and hat, said goodbye, and went out the front door. He stood in the wind and then instead of going home he walked over the Maryland Bridge and turned down towards Lena's house and when he got there he stood on the sidewalk and looked at the bright windows. The curtains weren't drawn yet and he could see Margot playing the piano. Emily passed before the front window. He didn't see Lena. It was snowing and his face was cold and the wind hurt his ears. He walked up to a corner store and looked at the chocolate bars. A man came in the store. It was Lena's father and he was with Emily. Mason watched them buy a loaf of bread and argue about gum that Emily wanted. In the end Emily got the gum and she pushed her small face against the sleeve of her father's coat as he bent towards the cashier and counted out the change. His head was large and he seemed very content with who he was. He said, "No, no, not at all," and then he said, "Every Tuesday," and he touched the top of his daughter's head. As they turned to leave, Emily saw Mason and she pulled on her father's sleeve and nodded across the aisle. Mr. Schellendal stopped and looked over his shoulder and when Mason responded by lifting his hand, Mr. Schellendal turned and, pulling his young daughter, left the store.

The following day Mr. Schellendal phoned Mason and asked him to come by the bank. Mason didn't want to but Mr. Schellendal was forceful and convincing. He sensed Mason's hesitation and said that there was nothing to worry about. He wasn't dangerous. He said, "There are some things we need to talk about and I'd like you to meet me here at the bank some time soon." They arranged a time and Mason hung up and stood by the window. Two garbage trucks idled on the street outside and three men stood beside the trucks and talked and looked around and then talked some more. They smoked and laughed and Mason thought about the men. They either had wives and babies or they lived alone and went out drinking in the evening looking for women. They would not be bad men. They were collectors of garbage and that didn't make them good or bad. Mason thought they might be nothing, really. They weren't important in any large sense. Perhaps they were important to their children or to the women they met or even to themselves but they weren't important to him or Lena or the president of some company or the prime minister of

Canada, who was, when the cameras weren't trained on him, also of no consequence. A nobody.

When Mason arrived at the bank the following day he sat in the lobby and drank coffee and watched a dark-haired woman in a skirt and jacket answer the phone. Lena's father swung out into the waiting area and called to Mason and brought him into his office. Then he said he'd be right back and he left Mason by himself. Mason looked around. There was a photograph of the Schellendal family on the wall. They were standing in front of a silver camper trailer and there were mountains in the background. Lena was younger, maybe fourteen, and she was holding her father's arm and looking up past his chin at something outside of the picture. Her sisters were smiling and her mother was wearing a baseball cap and a halter top and shorts. Mrs. Schellendal was beautiful. He could see that. On the desk were a sheaf of business cards and a pen and an empty cup of coffee from Tim Hortons and a basket of golf tees. Lena's father returned and he sat down on the same side of the desk as Mason. He leaned forward and said, "You know why you're here so let's get to it. I am not an ogre. I am simply a father who is concerned about a daughter who is complex and difficult and who is searching. That's what she's doing and I'm not sure how to deal with it. Do you understand?"

Mason looked at his own hands and said, "I think so."

"With Lena you have to be very sure. She can't abide uncertainty." Mr. Schellendal leaned back in his chair, crossed his legs, and laid an index finger across his cheek. "Did she tell you that I don't want her seeing you any more?"

Mason nodded. "Yes."

"Did she say why?"

"Because I'm not a Christian?"

Mr. Schellendal shook his head. "That's not true. That's a convenient reason. She's done that to other boys. Made them memorize and then quote Scripture as if I were a Bible-thumping gatekeeper full of revenge. I'm not." He paused and waved a hand and said, "How old are you, Mason?"

"Sixteen."

"You should be playing football, running around with other boys. You're young."

"I don't like football."

"Well, tennis then. Lena told me that you're an excellent tennis player. That's what she said, Excellent. Usually she tells me nothing. In any case, all this to say that you're too young to be worried about girls."

"I love her."

Mr. Schellendal raised his eyebrows. "No, you don't, Mason. You have no idea what love is."

"I think I do."

Mr. Schellendal sighed. He said, "Lena's not well, Mason. Physically she looks capable but the body has a soul and a mind and that's the problem here. You are not the first boy who has loved her nor will you be the last. She is very lovable. I love her. She is unpredictable and out of control and I imagine she makes your life exciting but she is not well. For several years now she has been seeing doctors. She takes medication and sometimes the medication makes her impetuous and irrational. Do you see?"

Mason didn't, but he said he did.

"Has she asked you to marry her?"

Mason looked away.

"Again, you are not the first. She actually tried to marry a boy named Kevin. This when she was only fifteen. That's right. Is that normal?"

"I don't believe you," Mason said.

"Of course you don't. And you shouldn't. You're young. Love is wonderful and exclusive and why should Lena betray you? Good for you."

"May I go now?" Mason asked.

Mr. Schellendal rose and said, "The thing is, we don't want her hurt or pregnant or dead in a car crash or doing drugs or anything else that would ruin her chances. Do you see?"

Mason nodded and let Mr. Schellendal guide him from the office. They walked through the lobby and Mason saw Mr. Schellendal's dark square shoulders and he wondered what his own father would look like in a suit. They parted near the cash machine, Mr. Schellendal ducking his head slightly and saying goodbye as Mason turned and stepped outside. Snow fell. Large flakes scudded sideways. He thought he should write a poem called "The Death of Lena Schellendal." Send it to Lena's father and have him understand some things.

Mason didn't go to school the next day. His mother left early in the morning and his father went out at midday to run some errands. Just the week before, Danny had moved his boxes and stuff back home, quit his job at the restaurant, and left for Montreal. During that week Danny had commanded a lot of attention and Mason was glad now to be alone in the house. He woke late and sat in the kitchen and ate Shreddies and thought about Lena and he thought about Mr. Schellendal's warnings, and the fact that Lena could not abide uncertainty. And so in the afternoon he phoned Lena and left a message for her to call. She came by and found him watching TV. She sat down beside him and looped an arm around his neck.

"Hey," she said. "You okay?"

Mason shrugged.

Lena tried to touch him but he pulled away.

"Okay then," she said. She stood.

"I saw your Dad yesterday," he said.

"Oh, poor Mason. That's why. He said nasty things about me and you believed him."

Mason shook his head. Lena kneeled on the couch and kissed his forehead and eyes and cheeks and his mouth. Her own mouth was wet and soft and Mason saw that nothing mattered.

"It doesn't matter," he said. "I said I didn't believe him."

"Of course you didn't. He makes things up."

"He told me about Kevin."

"Oh, man." Lena laughed, a guilty hiccup.

"That you tried to marry him."

"That was a lark. I was sixteen."

"Fifteen."

"Okay, fifteen."

"Am I a lark?"

"God, no." She paused. "What else?"

"He said he doesn't want you dropping acid or smoking crack."

Lena smiled. "Yeah, right."

"Okay, okay, at least not pregnant and smoking crack," Mason said. She was still on her knees as if she were praying or begging. Mason touched her forearms. Ran his hands down to her elbows. "You're amazing," he said. "You won't get pregnant, will you? Or die?"

"Never. Never." She looked up at him, expectant. "And?"

"That's all," he said. "Hold me."

They lay on the couch and Mason crushed Lena to him. He put his face against her neck and breathed in and out and after a while he felt himself slipping into a space where he and Lena were one and all fears of madness and escape disappeared and he could feel her hip against his crotch and the buckle of her belt and an elbow in his ribs. She smelled of cooked food and cigarette smoke and the van and Mr. Koop's. Her arms, her face, had the smoothness of eggs. Her blood beat through a vein in her neck and Mason marvelled at the intricacy of Lena's body, what she was made of.

In the week that followed, Mason phoned her house, went by, called The Nook, but always he either had just missed her or was put off by a cautionary tone or the words, "She's gone." A wall had been put up around her. He went, on a Wednesday afternoon, to the Bagel Shop on Academy and he bought coffee and watched for Lena as she passed by on her way to music lessons but she neither came nor went and he wondered if her lessons were a thing of the past. He did not know and this surprised him that he did not know. He met Rosemary, the second-oldest sister, in the street one day. He said, "Lena," and she looked away and then back at him again. She had a silver nose ring and Mason saw that she was softer than Lena, not as pretty. She was plain and short and her feet were small.

"Is she okay?" Mason asked. "I haven't been able to find her. She doesn't call me back. She's not working."

Rosemary wrinkled her nose. "She said you were sweet."

"Did she?"

"She does stupid things," Rosemary said. "She's all happy and hey-ho and then she locks herself away. She's in a lock-up phase. What are you doing?"

"Nothing, I suppose."

"Want to walk with me up to voice lessons?"

He said he could do that. Rosemary was different from the night of the dinner, more talkative and confident, and this surprised Mason. As they walked he imagined the Schellendal girls as interchangeable, a throaty chorus line, a quartet that traipsed this familiar path to Mrs. Malcolm's house and stood, backs straight, and practised scales. Did they all sing? Was Lena like Rosemary like Margot like Emily?

They walked over the bridge and past the Lutheran Church with its "Little Lambs Nursery" sign and on down past the Bagel Shop and left on Elm and while they walked Rosemary said, "The thing is, with my parents, they can't stand Lena's boyfriends. It's not you, believe me, they hate them all. Nothing is good enough. Especially my father, who gets so sad. I had a boyfriend once and nobody knew. Nobody cared. Jimmy Mutch and he had this tattoo on his shoulder. The jack of spades. He was really smart. He took Calculus and Theory of Knowledge and quoted Descartes, I think, therefore I am, only with Jimmy it was, I drink, therefore I am. And nobody cared. See?" She lifted her shoulders and tossed her hair. She moved her music books to her other arm and pushed her free hand into the crook of his elbow. She was wearing a long scarf of many colours and one end floated behind her like a tail and because she was so short Mason had to look down at the top of her head and he thought that anybody passing them by might see them as brother and sister.

"Could you tell Lena to call me?" Mason said.

"Sure," Rosemary said. "I'll shove a note under her door. *Call Mason.*"

"If I write a note would you give it to her?"

"Yeah. Sure, I could." Rosemary lifted her face and looked at Mason and he saw that she had eyebrows like Lena and he had a thought that maybe Lena wasn't the right Schellendal girl for him and when Rosemary said, turning her head to talk to the air, as if this were an afterthought and not a serious thing to be considered, "If you wanna hang out some time, you know, call me," Mason saw that the future was shaped by forces greater than himself and he said, "Sure. Whatever."

He didn't have a pen and so Rosemary had to search her pockets and backpack. She came up with a scrap piece of paper and a red pen and he held the paper against his knee and didn't know what to say. He thought about Mr. Ferry's words about how a story wasn't a map to point the way and he thought how, no matter what he said, he'd sound desperate. So he wrote, *Hey, you in your fortress, let me in.* He folded the paper and gave it to Rosemary. The tips of his fingers were cold. He blew on his hands. Rosemary pushed the note into her pocket and said goodbye and then she walked on and Mason turned and went back the way he had come.

When he got home his mother was in the living room with the man she'd been holding on to at the mall. She stood and said, "Mason, this is Aldous," and she turned her left foot out at an angle. Aldous stood and shook Mason's hand and said his name as if it were a foreign word. Perhaps it was. He was German. His speech was thick and truncated, though he spoke English well. His last name was Schmidt. He told Mason this as they shook hands. He was a carefully dressed man and only a little taller than his mother, whom he called Penny. He said, "Penny has talked about you. She's very proud of you."

Mason looked at his mother who said, "Don't look at me like that. I won't have my evening ruined." She turned to Aldous and said, "Another?" and then she wagged a wrist and said, "Mason, can you get Mr. Schmidt another Coke? Just Coke, with some ice."

Mason took Aldous's glass and went to the kitchen and poured Coke into the glass and dropped two ice cubes in and he returned to the living room and handed the glass back to Aldous, who said, "Thank you." He had a long face and long hair. He said, "How old are you, Mason?"

"Sixteen."

Aldous said, "At sixteen I quit school and worked on the oil fields in Alberta. I never finished high school. I don't have a university degree." He looked at Mason's mother. "Did you know that, Penny?"

"No, I didn't." She was standing in the middle of the room, wearing a dark suede skirt, and she kept running one hand down the side of her thigh. She had her boots on; they were shiny black with low heels and they came up to just below her knees, so there was a slash of her legs between the skirt and the boots, but it was a striking slash because she was wearing dark purple tights. Mason wondered what would happen if his father came home. His mother was looking at Aldous with big eyes. She said, "Aldous is a millionaire. Many times over. He has no education but he's successful. How does that happen?" She was looking at Mason now.

"It's not that amazing," Aldous said. "It's a combination of luck and vision. I saw that mud was the answer, and, bingo, I was right."

"Aldous sells mud to drilling companies," Mrs. Crowe said. "Isn't that strange? Making millions off of mud?" She was very excited by the word millions.

Mason asked Aldous, "So, you drive a Porsche, or what?"

"Don't get snippy," Mrs. Crowe said.

"Oh, that's fine," Aldous said. "The whole point of being young is to rebel. To protest. Isn't it?"

It wasn't clear to whom he had addressed this question and Mason refused to respond. His mother was moving around the room like she was the only woman in the world. He said, "I'm going to my room, okay?"

"Good," his mother said. Then she said to Aldous, "Mason's a big reader. He'll go to his room now and read and he'll be fine."

"What do you read?" Aldous asked.

"*Mein Kampf.* Pornography."

Aldous looked at Mrs. Crowe, who gave Mason a withering look. Then she said, "Let's go out. You want to come, Mason? We were thinking Chinese food, weren't we, Aldous?"

Mason said he wasn't hungry. He said he was expecting Lena to call and he didn't want to miss her.

"Lena," Mrs. Crowe sighed. Mason thought he might cry so he turned his face away. His mother and Aldous left quickly, and in their wake Mason experienced the vacuum of the house, a silence that swirled around him and darkened the rooms. He watched TV and opened a Caramilk bar and sucked at it slowly as evening came. He fell asleep on the couch and woke to the phone ringing. It was Lena. She said that her heels and fingertips were cracking. The dry weather attacked her feet and hands and they bled and at night she applied Vaseline and then put on socks and mitts. Mason imagined her as a mummy. He said, "Did Rosemary give you the note?"

She said, "My father's a bully. I'm not interested in sex these days. That worries me. My doctor says it's the pills." Her voice was weak, she seemed wary.

"You don't have to worry about me," Mason said.

"I'm not. I never think of you."

Mason didn't answer. He could hear Lena breathing.

"Does that surprise you?" she asked. "Because it shouldn't."

Mason said it didn't surprise him. He saw his mother's empty wine glass on the end table by the couch. There was a trace of her lipstick on the rim and he thought of Aldous and he said, "I have no idea what's going on. You've locked yourself away and then you say you never think of me."

"Do you like my sister?"

"Which one?"

"Rosemary. She said you walked to music lessons together and you were really sweet and all I could think of was when you used to spy on me. Are you following her now?"

"No, I'm not *following* her and I don't like her. Not in that way."

"She's sweet. Not as sexy as me but she's more stable. You know?" She paused and Mason waited and then she said, "These days the world, people, things, they all disappoint me. I don't think people are generally very smart. I had a dream the other night and it was way into the future and people then were looking back at us now and laughing. We're so important. We think we know everything. We don't. We're worse than a bunch of baboons. With baboons, at least, the fucking has some order. I could live the life of an ape. Did you know that one male baboon runs the horde?"[12]

---

[12] Lena is subconsciously borrowing from her doctor, who just the other day told her that some people fear relationships with real live people and can relate only to phantoms of their own fantasies, or to things, or animals. "Are you saying that's me?" Lena had asked, and the doctor said, "No, not yet. You're still very much Lena."

Mason said he didn't know that. He said, "You wanna come over here? We could be a horde of two. My mother's out eating egg foo yong with some guy called Aldous. A thick German."

"Where's your Dad?"

"Driving taxi tonight."

"Really? That's wild. He's driving taxi and she's fucking another man."

"I didn't say they were fucking."

"Well, aren't they?

Mason paused. "Maybe they are."

"Didn't you ask her?"

"She told me they had sex twice."

"She *said* that? My mother would never talk about that. Or even do it."

"She was mad at me. She said it when she was mad at me." Mason paused, then asked. "Lena? You wanna come over? I want to be with you."

"Aww, Mason. I'll come. Don't move, okay?" And she hung up.

She arrived with cold cheeks and snow on her coat and icy fingers. She threw her hat and scarf and coat across a chair and bent towards Mason and he saw the width of her hips and the band of flesh at her waist and he held her wrists.

"I've escaped," she said. Her eyes were bright. She'd coloured her hair red.

"Amazing."

"I can't stay long."

He said, "Let's get undressed."

She shook her head but he held her wrists with one hand and put the other hand on her shirt and felt her bra and breast. She allowed this. He unbuttoned her shirt and removed it. She was wearing a cream-coloured bra. He removed her white pants. She didn't stop him or help him. Her panties were black. She looked older.

"It's been so long," Mason said. He pushed her down on the couch and undid his pants and took them off. He was standing above her and she was looking past him at the ceiling, her hands at her sides. He tugged her panties down past her knees to her ankles and lay down on top of her. She said, "I don't have a condom."

"I'll pull out," he said.

He put himself inside her. She was dry and she winced and went, "Oh." This excited Mason and he closed his eyes and moved inside her and felt her right breast with his right hand. His arm was like a brace across her chest. He lifted his torso just before he came and he pulled out and squirted on her hip and the couch cushion. He took his T-shirt and wiped her. The couch. He was breathing quickly. Lena was watching him and her stomach moved as she breathed. He lay down on her again, his head against her chest, and they stayed like that without speaking. Lena's arms were at her sides. Her bare knees, his own bare buttocks, the back of his legs, his mismatched socks. The sound of her heart, her head turned to the side, her panties like manacles at her ankles.

2

Mason Crowe – she saw him first in Ms. Abendschade's class and even then she had decided upon him. That whole spring and summer she let his being penetrate hers. She observed him sitting there when she walked to voice lessons. He was so obvious. Sometimes she wanted to enter the Bagel Shop and face him but she never did. The waiting, the anticipation was a painful pleasure.

In early September she confronted him outside her house. She said that there was no one home and did he want to come in. She was happy when he said yes. She played piano for him and she was aware of him watching her and she felt naked and wished that both of them were naked. Her hands were trembling but she hid this with jokes and small talk. She explained that she had quit school and she said, "I'm throwing my life away," but really she was thinking that she would like to touch him. She said she knew everything about him and she listed off his activities and the facts of his life and his surprise pleased her. He didn't eat the pear she had given him. She said, "You should stay away from me. I am mad." She took his hand when she said this. He could have told her to do anything and she would have done it. He said, "What do you mean?" She said, "I can tell a hawk from a handsaw, not that kind of mad. More a melancholy sort of mad."

One time, when they drove up to get eggs from Koops', she stopped the van and pulled him into the back and undressed herself and him and she told him that they could have sex. His body was thin and light. She discovered the down on his lower back and said, "Look at you." She straddled his bum and squeezed blackheads from his shoulders and held them out like trophies for him to see. She liked his smell, the way he walked, his bare feet against the floor of the van, the way he looked at her as if she were a mysterious object, something worth considering. She wanted to fit inside him. She wrote his name everywhere: on bathroom walls, with a pen on the inside of her thighs, in the grease of the grill at The Nook, on cards she never sent.

She had long legs that were too thin and her left breast was smaller than her right. Her nipples were copper aureoles, slightly bumpy and large. She looked at herself naked in the mirror. Her hips and the slight roundness at her belly that held yards of entrails that carried her shit. Her body was made of water and enzymes and blood. She was not ashamed of her nakedness.[13]

---

[13] In her journal she sketches pictures of herself naked and draws arrows and then labels her body parts. When she looks at herself in the mirror she cannot tell the difference between ugly and beautiful. She writes, "Ein Affe hinein guckt" (An ape looks in).

Or his. In those early days, when they were first discovering each other, she studied his dark sac with the mercurial balls that moved, it seemed, on their own, two slippery mouthfuls that carried all those seeds. She knew by heart the texture of his nipples, the hairless chest, the smell of his armpits, the frame of his ribs as he lay down, arms raised and thrown back. Between his anus and his scrotum ran a raised furrow like a perfect line dissecting the fundament, as if a man were an assembly-line product, two halves glued together.

There were times as they lay together on his bed in the late afternoon when Lena felt the weight of something on her head and during those moments she imagined she was a shell and Mason was a shell and what they had seen and touched, their skin and hair and orifices, all of that was the covering of the empty shell. When this thought arrived she panicked and opened her eyes and sought out Mason and, finding him, was relieved.

One night she sat in her bedroom with her three sisters and showed them the tattoo she had gotten the day before. It was on the inside of her thigh, just below the crotch, a tiny black anchor, and Margot asked, wide-eyed, "You let a man do that to you?"

"He was very practical," Lena said. "I had to forge Mom's signature for this."

"You have so much hair," Margot said.

Rosemary went, "Gaawd."

"Isn't it pretty?" Lena asked.

Margot said that she didn't think it was pretty. "Looks like Devon Ashcombe's head," she said.

"No," Lena said, "I mean the tattoo."

"Mom'll kill you if she sees that," Rosemary said.

"How's she gonna see it?" Lena asked. She stood by the mirror and inspected her back. There was a pimple near her shoulder blade. In the mirror she saw Rosemary's head and neck, her small nose.

"Do you love Mason?" Emily asked.

"Absolutely," Lena said.

"Have you seen him naked?"

Margot and Rosemary giggled, though they waited for the answer.

"Hmmm hmmm."

"Really?"

"Really."

"Do you like him better with clothes on or with clothes off?" This was still Emily, quite serious.

"It depends."

"On what?"

"On what we're doing."

Margot asked, "Have you had sex?"

"It's obvious," Rosemary said.

Margot asked, "Does it hurt?"

Lena said no, though there were times when it was slightly uncomfortable, like opening your mouth too wide for the dentist.

"Is he circumcised?" Margot asked.

"What's *that*?" Emily asked.

Rosemary explained. She was clinical and moved her hands about.

Margot said she'd watched a porno at Willow Poole's house and all of them were circumcised. She pronounced "them" with a certain horror.

"You shouldn't be watching stuff like that," Lena said. "You're barely thirteen and what they show you is warped." She studied her face in the mirror. Her sisters watched her. She could see all three of them reversed in the mirror. She said, "I shouldn't have told you about Mason. He wouldn't like it."

"Daddy'll kill you," Emily said.

"He can't do anything. That's important to understand. Mom and Dad are helpless. Just look in their eyes when you say you aren't going to obey. They're scared." She took a pair of jeans from her drawer and sat on the edge of the bed. Pushed a foot through one leg and paused to examine her toes.

Rosemary said, "Look who's brave. You wouldn't be talking so big if you knew that Mom and Dad were talking about sending you away somewhere."

Lena turned towards Rosemary, her one leg still bare. "What are you talking about, send me away. I'm not a pet. They can't." She stood and faced all three sisters. Saw them, at that moment, as Russian dolls, with her as the biggest doll. She was pleased by the poetry in the image but the responsibility frightened her. She said, "Oh," and then she finished putting on her jeans and asked, "When did they say that?"

Rosemary hugged her knees and said, "They were just talking. I overheard them. I'm sorry, Lena."

Lena thought about where she could be sent. She wanted to see Mason. To hold him. She sighed and said, "Anyways, why would Mom and Dad send me away? They like to keep track of me. You three are lucky, you know. I'm doing all the work here. Emily, you're especially lucky." Emily looked up with anticipation. "By the time you're my age, Mom and Dad'll be completely broken. That's what happens. What else did Dad say?"

Rosemary lifted her small shoulders. She lay down on the bed and reached up a hand and played with Margot's hair. "He said you're depressed."

"Oh, he's so smart. Isn't he? Isn't he smart? Depressed. What does he know? Because I dropped out of school? Because I think? I don't want to talk about him. Mason's Dad? He just leaves everybody alone. That we could be so lucky."

At the dinner table that evening Lena told her father she was thinking of quitting her job at The Nook. When she said this she looked at him and waited for his answer. He put his fork and knife down and looked over at Lena's mother and then back at Lena and said, "Do we want to talk about this now?"

"I don't think so," Lena's mother said. "It's not fair to the girls and it certainly isn't fair to me. I worked hard at this meal and I don't want it ruined by an argument."

"Fine, get out your Palm Pilot, Dad. Let's make an appointment."

"Don't, Lena." This was her mother.

Her father nodded slowly. He said, "You could go back to school."

"I'm doing correspondence, Dad. Remember? Right now I'm writing an essay on Robert Herrick. Do you know who Robert Herrick is?"

"Don't be rude, Lena," her mother said.

Lena ignored her. She said, "School is a factory. The world likes factories. I'm not in favour of them."

"We worry about your health," her father said. "And spending time with Mason. You don't need uncertainty in your life. You know what happened last time with that Kevin boy. For whatever reason you obsess and the obsession makes you sad and we hate to see you sad."

"Not sad. Not sad. Insane, you mean. I embarrass you, don't I?"

"You aren't insane, Lena. That's some kind of romantic notion you like to promote. You were depressed. I won't say more. Not now."

Margot said she was tired.

Lena looked at her family and said they should take a vote. "Who thinks I'm insane?"

"Stop it, Lena." Rosemary was staring at the table as she said this.

Lena paused. She stood. "Thanks," she said, and she went up to her room and looked out the window down onto the street. She bit her hand, hard, and studied the marks her teeth had left. Emily began to practise piano. Someone was putting dishes in the dishwasher. Outside it had begun to snow, lightly, and the streetlights offered up the swirling flakes. Her mother knocked on the door and called out but Lena didn't answer. Her mother said her name once more and then moved back down the hall and Lena imagined her perfect legs, the thighs pushing against the dark skirt she'd been wearing, the white blouse and her hair pulled back and the hard lines of her jaw. She was good-looking. Once, at a neighbourhood party, Lena had seen her mother play a role in a skit with a neighbour, Mr. Shelton. They had held hands and whimpered and at that moment, with an overwhelming sorrow, Lena had pictured Mr. Shelton unbuttoning her mother's blouse.

She wished, sometimes, that she was as beautiful as her mother. She put her finger against the cold glass of the window. Wrote her name in the frost. She sat on her bed and looked at her sketchbook, the self-portrait she'd done months ago, back when she'd been full of hope and brilliance. All the parts of her body chopped up and laid out and labelled. It didn't seem so brilliant now. It was too obvious. She placed the book back under her bed and went downstairs and put on her jacket and stood in the darkness of the foyer. Her mother was in the family room and called out but Lena ignored her. She went outside and walked down to the park bench by the river and she sat down and smoked a cigarette. She could see into the uncovered windows of the house beside the park and there was a man standing at the sink talking to someone she couldn't see. Once, a hand appeared and touched his shoulder, but then it disappeared, and finally the man drew the blind on the window and he disappeared as well. The falling snow had covered her shoulders, her head, and her thighs. She stood and walked over the bridge and went to Mason's house. When he answered the door she held his hands and said, "I wanted to surprise you." He took her in to the living room where they sat and watched TV. Lena put her head against Mason's shoulder.

Mason's mother entered the room and offered Lena something to drink and eat but Lena said thanks, she'd just eaten. She said, "I like your bracelet, Mrs. Crowe."

"Oh," Mason's mother looked at her wrist and then at Lena and said, "Thank you."

When they were alone again, Lena said, "I don't know what's happening to me."

She took his hand and put it on her breast. She said, "What do you like about me? My body, I mean."

"Everything," Mason said. "I like everything."

"Be specific," Lena said. "Me, I like your hands. I like your bum. I like the hair under your arms." She paused. "So, what do you like?"

Mason looked at his hand. "I like this. Your breasts."

"Ya? What else?"

"And I like feeling your head with my hands when we have sex. Sometimes it's like your head is everything, even though I'm inside you. You know? I wonder what you're thinking about when we're doing it. Or if you're even thinking. That's why I like holding your head."

"That's nice," Lena whispered. "Tell me more."

"It's all so thin," Mason said. "I mean the wall between the outside and the inside." He touched Lena's arm. "What we're made of. Sometimes I can't believe it. I can't believe that you would allow me to put myself inside you. To me it's unbelievable. I love you though. That's not what I'm saying. I'm talking about the act. And then it's over and we separate and hard as I try I can't get you back in the same way. Not until the next time."

Lena kissed Mason on the mouth. "Shut up," she said. "I want to do everything with you. Whatever you want. If we do everything there'll be no reason to go elsewhere."

"I won't go anywhere else."

"And I don't want you to. Aren't there things you'd like to try? You said you liked to be inside me." She put her nose against Mason's cheek and breathed in. "Hmmm," she said. "Do you want to try other places, like my bum? Does that interest you? You must have thought about it. Haven't you?"

"Maybe. A little. But not with you. It's like there are girls out there who do that kind of thing but not the girl I'm with. You know? It just seems weird and kind of embarrassing."

"Doesn't have to be. Only we will know about it." Lena was curious. She told Mason that and then she said that there was nothing wrong with anal sex and if she was ever going to do it she wanted it to be with him. She unbuttoned his jeans and put her hand down his shorts. "Look how hard you are. Come on." She zipped him up and took his hand and pulled him out into the kitchen. Mrs. Crowe was eating cheese and crackers and reading. She looked up at them and Mason said, "We're going down to my room. Just for a bit. Lena has to go soon." Mrs. Crowe smiled and waved a knife at them.

Mason told Lena to go ahead, he'd be right there. She went downstairs and lay down on the bed and looked at the ceiling. Her feet were still cold from the walk over. She went to the basement washroom and washed herself. Saw her hipbones in the mirror. She put a bit of toothpaste on her tongue and sucked on it. She went back to Mason's bedroom and took off her jeans and panties. Left her top on. Her head rested at an angle on the pillow and she could see the door and her legs and the hair at her crotch. She thought she should be scared but she wasn't. She heard Mason and his mother talking upstairs, then Mason's steps on the landing. Mason came in and looked at her and looked away. "Don't have to use a condom," Lena said. Mason still would not look at her and this made her feel stronger. He had a tube of lubricant in his hand and she took it from him. His hand was shaking. She opened the lubricant and spread it on herself and put some on Mason's cock. She could hear him breathing. She kneeled on the bed, bent forward and rested her forehead against a pillow, and said, "Fuck me, Mason."

Even with the lubricant it hurt. Mason asked, "Does it hurt?" but Lena said, "No." Her face was pressed against the blanket now and she could smell laundry detergent and the sweet fruity scent of the lubricant and she thought of the air outside and Mrs. Crowe eating crackers upstairs and her own father back home preparing a punishment for her. When Mason came Lena turned her head to look at his face and his eyes were closed and his chin pushed up and sideways and he seemed disgusted.[14]

ᔐ

---

[14] Mason is, in fact, more surprised than disgusted. Whereas Lena desperately wants to lay claim to Mason, he has anal sex with her because she suggests it and because other boys and girls are doing it and he wonders what it would feel like. His face is registering both pleasure and dread.

In mid-December, Lena went Christmas shopping and bought Mason a CD, a Hank Williams III. She hated the holiday season; the songs, the cheer, and the panic she felt. Over the past week Lena had wanted to phone Mason but she forced herself to wait, and when they did finally meet again, outside of The Nook on a cold day, Mason said, "I haven't seen you. Where have you been?"

Lena looked away. Across the street an old woman walked a small dog. A car honked. Lena said, "On Monday I slept, on Tuesday I bought a new coat, on Wednesday I thought I saw you on the street but it was someone else, someone with a goatee and long feet, and on Thursday I thought about you for a few minutes. Today is Friday. Here I am. I'm aware of you now because you're in front of me. It's funny. I think, Oh, I'd like to see you, but then I see you and I wonder why I wanted to see you." She said, "We have all kinds of problems. Even if I love you I have to push you away. There is my world and then there is yours. You know nothing about me."

To all of this Mason made no reply.

The holidays came and on Christmas Eve Lena's family went carolling, the six of them walking over to Lions Manor. They gathered in the lobby around the grand piano and sang to old men and women. Lena envied their lack of restlessness, their simple needs. She hadn't wanted to go but her father said, "You must." She wore an oversized army coat with a high collar, her father's boots, and the Russian hat with the fur flaps. Her sisters, Rosemary especially, were giddy and silly. They linked arms and, three abreast, sang sharply, as if to please their father. Later, the girls circled the room, shaking hands with the extended claws, calling out "Merry Christmas" and "Happy holidays." What joy.

On Christmas Day they had a turkey dinner. Nana came. Mr. and Mrs. Schellendal had also invited a poor single mother and her two children, a girl of three and a boy of eight. The boy smelled like someone who had diarrhea. Lena sat beside him at the table and had to excuse herself. She went up to her room and lay down and looked at the poster of Jim Morrison.

Rosemary knocked on her door. Said, "Lena?"

Lena didn't answer. Rosemary came in and said, "Mom wants you downstairs."

"Sure, she does."

"We're having carrot pudding."

Lena shrugged and said, "Junior there smells like shit."

"Poor little kid," Rosemary said.

"I hate being the missionary family," Lena said.

Rosemary lay down on her stomach beside Lena. "Mason called again."

"Yeah? I figured he would."

"He sounds so lost."

"He is."

"Why don't you see him?"

"I don't know. He just wants to have sex? I'm a bitch?"

"Dad answered the phone yesterday. He was mean."

"What did he say?"

"He said you were indisposed."

"Do *you* want him?" Lena asked. She turned on her side and took Rosemary's hand. "He likes you. He said you were the best of the Schellendal sisters. The most honest."

"You don't own him, Lena. He's not a present to give away."

"I do though," Lena said. "He listens to me. I could do anything to him and he would forgive me."

"He said I was the best?"

Lena nodded. Put her hand on Rosemary's neck. "He's a great kisser," she said. She pushed her nose against Rosemary's chin. They were lying against the pillows and facing each other. Lena kissed Rosemary lightly on the mouth. "Remember when we were younger and used to practise. Boys are harder than girls, you ever noticed that?" She kissed Rosemary again, pushed her tongue into her mouth and Rosemary let her. She closed her eyes and then opened them again and held her hand on Lena's hip. Lena pulled away and saw her sister's wet mouth. "He likes to do that until it hurts."

Rosemary rolled off the bed. "Don't want a hand-me-down," she said.

They went back downstairs together and Rosemary sat beside the fecal-smelling boy while Lena slid in beside her mother. They ate carrot pudding with a nutmeg sauce while the woman who was visiting told the family about her nose infection. Lena slowly ate her pudding and looked at the hairs on her father's fingers. When the woman was done speaking Lena laughed. Her mother pushed the back of a hand against Lena's thigh. "Don't," she whispered.

Lena was facing the woman. She said, "My parents think I'm mad. Do you think I'm mad?" The woman was thin and weak and Lena thought that there was nothing sexual about her. She couldn't imagine any man wanting her.

"Lena." Her father, across the table, raised his head quickly.

The woman looked at Lena, at Mr. Schellendal and then at her own children.

Lena continued, ignoring her father's glare, "I'm going to go away to some place and in that place I will be healed and then I'll come home again. Right, Dad?"

Margot giggled. She'd placed her chin on the edge of the table and watched the scene.

"What are you talking about?" Mr. Schellendal asked.

"Yes, what *are* you talking about?" her mother said.

Lena snorted. Laid her spoon down beside her bowl. She addressed the woman. "If your son was troubled would you send him away? Would you call up some doctors in white coats and say, 'Come pick up my son. I don't want him any more'?"

Lena could see that the woman was flustered and this pleased her. Her father said, "Stop this, Lena," and her mother was pinching the flesh on her upper arm.

"Ouch," she said, and she pulled away. She faced the visitor. "Would you like more carrot pudding? It's everybody's favourite here. Especially my father's." She looked at her father who had pushed away from the table and was suggesting a move to the living room. He was demanding it, Lena could see that. And so the group moved away from the table, but Lena remained seated, refusing her mother's entreaties to join the others, hearing the squeals of Margot and Emily and, once, the stinky boy came back into the dining room and stared at Lena and she stared back. "Boo," she went, but he didn't budge and then she whispered, "Piece

of shit," and his face twisted and he backed away and returned
to the living room.

Then, without calling ahead, Mason came over that evening.
Lena came down and stood outside with him in socks and a
sweater. Together they exhaled plumes of fog that mingled and
rose upwards. "You've got a lot of guts, coming here," Lena
said. "What if my father sees you?"

Mason shrugged. "What's he going to do? Flog me?" He
handed her a package. "Here," he said. "I got this for you.
Merry Christmas."

Lena took it. "It's a book."

"Maybe. Or it could be a box of chocolates disguised as
a book."

"You can't come in," Lena said.

"I know." Mason pushed his hands into his pockets.

"I don't have a present for you," Lena said. She looked
behind her, thinking about the CD. She turned back.

"It doesn't matter. That's not why I gave you that."

She wanted to put her arms around him. Say his name.
"Bye," she said.

"Bye." She stood there and watched him step down the
stairs and she wanted to call out to him but she didn't and this
pleased her; that she would have the strength to deny herself
something that she actually wanted.

The book was *A Portrait of the Artist As a Young Man*. It was
black and old and smelled of Mr. Ferry's house. Inside, on the

cover, was the name Hyam Ferry. "You stole it," Lena whispered.[15] She was in bed. She was wearing long underwear and a cotton nightgown with Pooh characters on it. She was alone. There was no inscription to her in the book, in fact, Mason had not left a card or said anything in a note. For several weeks after that she carried the book around with her. At breakfast, she laid it beside her plate and when she watched TV she held it on her lap. Her father asked her at dinner one night what that black book was. Lena said it was a gift from a friend. It was rare, she said, and worth a lot of money. Her father looked at her mother, who shook her head and asked the girls if they were ready for dessert.

She still refused to see Mason, who called twice a day. Once, he showed up at the door and said he was taking her to a movie. She said, "You can't. Besides, these days I'm ugly and fat."

"What are you talking about?" Mason asked.

"Take Rosemary," Lena said, and she went upstairs and got her sister and sent the two of them on their way. Mason's lack of

---

[15] This book was not one of the ones he'd stolen. Mr. Ferry actually gave it to Mason. He told him to fetch it from the upstairs library and then he advised Mason to read all of Joyce. Read this and pass it on, he said. So, Mason read it and is now passing it on to Lena. He thinks she might like the religious sections, the dark guilt, the plunging into the depths, the soul as a basketful of water – lamp and basket, lamp and basket. He does not expect anything from Lena. In fact, he is surprised when she comes to the door. He has been talking to Rosemary at school and she has been giving him bits of information about Lena.

protest and Rosemary's visible giddiness produced a brief bout of jealousy in Lena, who spent the evening in her room, waiting and looking out at the street. At one point she sat on her bed and took her journal, her art book, *Portrait*, a photo of Mason and her sitting on Mason's front steps, a bowl of shells collected on Vancouver Island, and she studied and fingered all these objects. When Rosemary came home Lena went to her room and watched her undress and she was surprised at how beautiful Rosemary's body was, the tautness of her stomach, the padded bra, the tiny panties, and she said, "Did he kiss you?"

"No. He talked about you the whole time."

"Did he?" Lena was pleased.

"You're stupid," Rosemary said.

"There are more important things than love," Lena said.

"See? Stupid." Rosemary turned away.

"He didn't touch you? Hold your hand? Even suggest it?"

"What do you want?"

Lena didn't answer. That night she came to Rosemary's bed and crawled in and asked, "Is this okay?"

"Sure," Rosemary said.

Lena curled into her sister. Put one arm over her waist and the other under her own head. Played with Rosemary's hair and pressed her face against her neck. They didn't say anything, just fell asleep like that, and in the morning when Lena woke, it seemed that she was outside of herself, looking down on the scene of two sisters lying in bed together; there was a door and if Lena were to open the door she would find herself on the other side, only she did not know how to open the door.

Death. The idea of it was there. One afternoon when she

was alone in the house she went out into the garage and found the box her father had built for killing small animals. It was the size of a small TV and it had a door with a rubber seal and a hole and a clamp where the hose snapped in. The box had a small window. Once she had watched her father asphyxiate a squirrel. "You must be careful," he had explained as he attached the hose to the tailpipe, "That no exhaust leaks into the garage." Then he had turned on the car's ignition and they had watched together. "See," her father said, "It just falls asleep." And this was true; there was nothing ugly or violent about the squirrel's death. Her father had killed Pontoon, their cat, in the same way. Lena had watched and when it was over she looked down at Pontoon who was laid out on the cement floor like a small rug. She saw her father's large hands and the black pipe and she saw her own feet, her grey runners. "We should put him on a blanket," she said.

Her parents had argued that night. Lena heard them beyond the dining room door.

"He wasn't sick," her mother said.

Mr. Schellendal muttered something.

Mrs. Schellendal said, "You got tired of him. You got tired of his shit, of cleaning up after him. You couldn't train him so you killed him."

"He was suffering."

There was silence for a while and then her mother's soft voice, impossible to understand, and then a low groan and her mother said, "I hope I never get sick," and her father chuckled and her mother said "Here," and then Margot came running into the room.

At that moment, that age, she had loved her father. His scent, the hairs on his fingers, the pull of his suit jacket across his shoulders, the clip of money in his pocket, the dark shadow of bristle on his jaw at 7 p.m. She liked to sit on her father's lap and plant kisses on his forehead and mouth, especially when her mother was watching. She protected her father. Made certain he had nothing to worry about. She made him a little card every night and placed it on his plate and when he got home from work, he'd bend to kiss her and ask, "How's my big girl," and maybe, if he was happy, he'd nuzzle her neck.

From the first days when Lena began to work at The Nook, she and Julianne had tried to guess customer's occupations. Julianne would slide into the kitchen and call out the order for the real estate lady, the one with the copper hair and the stiletto heels. "Money," Julianne said.

Lena was better with the men. There were the hospital workers but there were also insurance salesmen and computer guys and carpenters and plumbers and salesmen and bar owners and teachers and accountants and dads with kids. Musicians were easy, especially the young ones who dreamed of glory. They rarely tipped. One time an older man in a black overcoat and a hat and black gloves had come in and stamped his feet and removed his gloves and took off his hat and sat himself in the back booth. "Limo driver," Julianne said.

"Banker," Raymond, the cook, said.

"No, no," Lena said, "Believe me, I know about bankers. He's a CEO of some company."

Lena served him. He had nice hands. His hair was grey but his face was younger. Lena figured he was about fifty. He ordered poached eggs on rye, no butter, and tea. He spoke softly and when he was done he folded the menu, handed it to Lena, and said, "Thank you."

Lena brought him his tea. He said, "Thank you." She placed his eggs and toast before him and he said, "Thank you."

She went to the back and said, "He's very polite."

Julianne wondered if he had money and if he did, was he married.

"He's wearing a wedding band," Lena said.

Later, Lena brought him the bill. She laid it on the table and said, "This might seem impolite but Julianne Jefford, the other waitress who works here, and I, Lena Schellendal, were curious about your occupation. Julianne thought you were an actor and I said you were a banker because my Dad's a banker and he dresses like you, very nicely, but we were wondering, you know? Is this rude?"

The man looked at the bill. He raised his eyebrows. He reached into his coat pocket and pulled out his wallet. He stood and put on his coat and then his gloves and he removed a ten-dollar bill from his wallet and handed it to Lena and said, "Thank you, Lena," and then he took a business card from his wallet, laid it on the table, and he left.

"He drives a fucking hearse," Julianne said when Lena showed her the card. "So cool."

"A funeral director," Lena said, "That's what it says. He doesn't drive, he prepares the bodies. You should have seen his hands, they were beautiful."

"Creepy," Julianne said.

Lena didn't think so. She waited for him to come back, but he never did. She imagined him slipping out of his black coat and putting on a lab jacket and touching the naked body of some girl who had died too young. Did he look at the girl sexually? Was that impossible? He had seemed so polite and for a few weeks, waiting for his return, Lena had wondered how one became a mortician. Lena told Julianne that the whole concept of jobs and careers and work was depressing. The everyday flow of humanity to offices and work sites and then the flow back home. And for what? Julianne said that people needed to work. There was nothing else. Take away a person's job and they were lost. She said that for every job there was a need. People needed to crap and read and drive and eat and watch TV and run and sleep and borrow money. The problem, Lena responded, was the stupidity of the jobs, the mindlessness.

Then, one afternoon in early January, Lena's father came into The Nook. He was wearing a dark overcoat and black gloves and he stood inside the door and removed his gloves and then he went to the back booth and sat down. Julianne served him. She came into the back and said, "Another mortician."

Lena looked, said, "Oh, man," and stepped back into the kitchen. She looked at Julianne and said, "He's a banker. My dad."

Julianne pushed Lena out into the restaurant and said, "Well, go serve him then."

Lena walked up to the table and said, "Hi."

Mr. Schellendal picked up his gloves and laid them neatly by the napkin holder. "Hi, Lena," he said. "I thought I might as well see where you work."

"Not much," Lena said. "Good food though."

"Well, sure it is. What would you recommend?"

"You want lunch, there's minestrone and garlic bread. Or a salad. We serve breakfast all day. If you want that then have poached eggs on rye. It's the safest. The bacon's okay, just not top-quality. Ham's too salty, try the sausages."

"Okay, that's good. I'll have the sausages and eggs. Will you have a chance to sit down? Just for a bit?"

Lena shrugged, said she'd see. She went to the back and Julianne said, "Go, talk to him."

So Lena sat and she drank coffee and Julianne brought the food and Lena said, "Dad, this is Julianne," and her father reached out a hand and shook and Julianne said, "Hiya." Lena watched her father eat. He seemed ill at ease: he dropped his fork and Lena fetched him a clean one; he offered her a slice of toast, which she refused; he dabbed at his mouth with a napkin and then studied it, as if expecting to find some surprise there; he told her an uninteresting story about one of the cashiers at the bank. When he was finished eating, Lena lit a cigarette and blew the smoke at the ceiling. He looked at her but didn't say anything.

He asked, "Do you like it here?"

"Yeah, I like it."

He said, "Your mom and I were talking the other day and we both agreed that we were happy you haven't quit."

"I don't want to work here the rest of my life. I figured out that I serve at least 100 eggs a day. At five days a week over the next thirty years that would be about 800,000 eggs."

Mr. Schellendal seemed at a loss. He said, "Julianne's a friend."

"Yeah. We work together and sometimes hang out. She lives on her own." She made a slight O with her mouth and exhaled smoke and looked up at the ceiling. She asked, "Shouldn't you be at work?"

Her father said that he'd been at a meeting in this area and he was passing by and he'd seen Lena in the window and decided on a whim to stop.

"On a whim?" Lena said. "Wow. That must be a first."

Her father's mouth went hard and he looked at her and said, "You're so angry." He pulled a pamphlet from his pocket and slid it across the table at her. "Here. I found this. It's not like I think you're going to do something foolish. It's just I read it and I thought you should read it, so there it is." He moved his hands nervously across the tabletop and he picked up his gloves. Lena asked if he wanted more coffee. He said he didn't. He said that Nana wanted to take Lena to a movie some time, would that be okay? She shrugged and said Fine, and then she said she had to work. She stood and took his plate and his cutlery and his dirty napkin and carried them to the kitchen. He watched her go and she knew that he was watching and she imagined that he saw the shape of her calves below the hemline of her dress, and the Band-Aid peeking above the heel of her shoe, and her hair pinned up, and her exposed neck.

Later, after closing time, she looked at the pamphlet her father had given her. It was called "Youth and Depression" and there was a cartoon figure of a teenager looking glum and there was a definition of depression – a very deep and prolonged feeling of hopelessness – and there were the symptoms – withdrawal, anxiety, and turning to alcohol, drugs, promiscuity, and suicide – and finally there was the suggestion that God might be able to help. Lena threw out the pamphlet and that night, in her room, she made a pencil sketch of a girl on her back with her legs spread, knees bent, and beside the drawing she wrote the dictionary definition for "promiscuous": "casual, as in casual shoes, casual labour, casual sex. Or: indiscriminate, as in promiscuous massacre, promiscuous hospitality." The word massacre attached to promiscuous interested Lena.

෨

Lena's grandma called her the following Saturday morning and asked if she wanted to go to a matinee. "I'll pay, dear," she said. Her grandmother went to the movies almost every day. Her choices were arbitrary, until she stumbled upon a movie she loved and then she saw that movie six or seven times, memorizing the lines, telling everybody what a wonderful film it was. "You must see it," she would say. She was seventy-four years old. Sex and violence did not bother her. She liked a good story, she liked romance, adventure, action. She admired certain actors; she loved Sean Connery and Anthony Hopkins. Her husband had died fifteen years earlier. He hadn't liked the movies and she liked to say she was making up for all those lost years. Movies, she said, were magic.

She picked Lena up at the house. Lena wore a short skirt and pale pink tights and black boots and a leather jacket and as she settled into the car her grandma looked her over and said, "You look lovely."

"Really, Nana? Thank you."

They went to Grant Park, and waiting in line to buy tickets, Lena's grandmother said, "I don't know this movie, though I've heard about it. The girls in it are young so I thought you might like it."

They found seats and Lena's grandmother gave Lena money to buy treats. She returned to the foyer, bought popcorn and drinks, and then ferried them back, sat down, and asked, "Are you okay, Nana? Do you have to go to the washroom?"

"Perfectly fine. I peed before I left. Your father thinks you're sad these days. Are you?"

Lena shrugged.

"Don't worry. Your father sees darkness everywhere. He needs to relax." She sighed. Said, "I don't know what happened to him. Your poor mother. Thank you for the popcorn, sweetie."

"You're welcome, Nana."

Lena thought the movie was too out-there. The main character was a terrible dresser and she liked to make a point of wearing clothes that clashed and at times it appeared she might be depressed but it was never quite clear and then she had a fling with an older man and ran away. It was all too easy. After, when her grandma asked what she thought, Lena said, "I loved it."

"See. I knew it. Let's go eat something."

They went to the Pizza Place in the mall and sat in the smoking section and Lena drank Coke and ate garlic bread while her grandma nibbled like an ancient rabbit at Caesar salad; torn bits of lettuce fell around her plate. She wiped at her mouth with a paper napkin. Lena noticed some girls from school. When they looked at her, she turned away.

"Do you know those girls?" her grandma asked. She was putting on lipstick, angling her compact, and brushing away the trace of Parmesan at the corner of her mouth.

Lena said they were from school but she didn't know them. They were very popular girls who knew they were popular.

"I was never popular," her grandma said. "Didn't matter though. Certainly doesn't matter today, does it? I was in love with a boy called Ralph who wasn't popular either but very handsome indeed. He died parachuting. He was seventeen and loved to fly. But you've heard this story before."

"That's okay, Nana."

"He was going to land on my yard for my birthday. I don't know, but I had the feeling he was going to propose after he landed. You know how instinct works, well I had that instinct. And I would have said yes. As it turned out, he landed in a sheep farmer's field a mile away. I didn't go to look at the body."

"Oh, Nana, that's terrible."

"It's okay. I survived." She snapped her compact and stuffed it back in her purse. "Smoke," she said. "Go ahead. You're going to anyway so you might as well have my permission."

Lena lit a cigarette and asked, "Remember Mason, from our house?"

"Of course I remember. A sweet handsome boy."

"Did you like him?"

"Sure I did. Though he was scared of your father."

"Of course he was. Dad doesn't want me to see him."

Her grandma sighed. Waved a hand at the wafting smoke, said, "No, no," when Lena said, "Sorry," and then said that her son was too strict, too enamoured with building a fence around his family. "Where will that get you?" she asked. "Everybody just wants to climb the fence and escape." She rummaged through her purse and pulled out a Kleenex and blew her nose and put the tissue back. "Do you like this Mason?"

"Very. Though I think I will send him away."

"Why? Because of your father?"

"No. Because I have to stand alone. That way I will become a better person."

"Oh, Lena, sweetheart, you already are a better person."

"No, I'm not, Nana. I'm not."

After, they walked out into the din of the mall and wandered past the shops and Lena took her grandma's arm and guided her into a card shop where they bought cards with flowers and spring scenes and bright colours. One was a watercolour of a Winnipeg scene, so Lena bought it and sent it to Mason. Inside she wrote, "To my local boy."

One night, after work, Julianne suggested that she and Lena go check out a new club on Bannatyne. Lena had her mother's car so they drove over to Julianne's apartment where they drank some wine and showered and put on fresh clothes. Lena wore a leather skirt of Julianne's, and a tight black top and a belt with studs and high boots. They sat on wooden chairs in the living room and smoked a joint and at one point Julianne lifted her hand, announced that tonight she wanted to get laid. Lena felt a brief dizziness that turned quickly into resignation. She said, "I feel so peaceful."

The club was full; people seemed to know each other and Lena sat with Julianne and watched couples dance and talk and drink. A man sat down beside her and said that his name was Steve. Lena looked at him. He was holding beer. Julianne patted Lena's arm and stood and walked over to the bar.

Steve watched her go and then he turned to Lena. "Are you talking to strangers?"

Lena shrugged. "If they're interesting," she said. He had big hands.

"I'm interesting," he said.

"How's that?"

"What do you mean?"

"What *makes* you interesting?" Lena was already tired of this man.

"I scuba dive."

"Wow." Lena looked around the bar as if there might be someone to help her. Julianne was talking to a short man with glasses. They were leaning into each other and laughing.

Steve said, "Every time I dive it's like I'm reborn."

Lena looked at his face. It was square and soft. He had perfect teeth. He was at least thirty.

"How old are you?" she asked.

"Twenty-three," he said. He touched her arm.

"I doubt it," Lena said.

"I saw you here and I saw you drinking Caesars and I wondered why you'd sit here drinking by yourself. How old are you?"

"Thirty-seven. I'm not by myself. Besides the girl who was just sitting here, there's my family too. They're just in the washroom."

Steve looked around. Lena studied his mouth and wondered what it would be like to touch him. This was probably what he wanted. His head, his neck, his shoulders, they were all bigger than Mason's. Mason was a string.

"Let's dance," Steve said.

"I don't know you."

"Just friendly, nothing to it."

Lena shrugged. She said she would drink one more and then she might be ready to dance. She lit a cigarette. Steve seemed pleased with her answer. He turned his stool so his knee touched her leg. She didn't pull away. The band played a loud number and Steve leaned in close and talked in her ear. About nothing. At one point Lena excused herself and went to the bathroom. She walked as if she knew that Steve was watching her and assessing her. She saw Julianne and pointed at the washroom. Julianne nodded. In the washroom two women were talking.

"She doesn't shave."

"Maybe Carl likes that."

"Would he?"

"Brush me off here."

"There?"

"Yeah."

"She must give off a smell or something that men like. It can't be her looks."

The women left. Lena wiped and flushed. She adjusted her skirt and stepped out and saw herself in the mirror. She said, "Practise your beauty." Her face was pale. She looked plain. "Hi, Steve," she said. When she spoke her mouth went slightly crooked. Mason liked that. She rinsed her fingers and dried them. Went back into the bar and saw the two women from the washroom. They were dancing together. She couldn't see Julianne. Steve looked up from his beer and watched her come. She sat down and said, "You were watching me. When I left. Did you like my ass?"

Steve looked around the bar. He said, "What's wrong?"

"Nothing. What do you think we're going to do?"

"I don't know. Maybe we won't do anything," Steve said. He looked disappointed. Ready for flight.

"You're hopeful, though."

"I guess. Aren't you?"

"No, I don't think so." Lena paused. Ordered another drink and said, "You don't know me."

"What's your name, then?"

"Lena." She lifted her glass and drank and watched Steve watching her. She put her drink down. Steve was pushing against her thigh again. She looked him down and up. She said, "You think you know me, don't you. You think that life is simple, but what else do you know about me, other than the colour of my hair or the size of my tits."

"You're quite vulgar."

"What else?"

"I don't know."

"I have a boyfriend. Mason Crowe. He's sixteen."

"Sixteen?"

"That's right. My father, if he knew I was here talking to you, would kill you. I have three sisters. My voice range is three octaves. I don't shave my armpits. I see a doctor every second Tuesday. Lena Schellendal is my name, Canada is my nation, Winnipeg is my dwelling place, and heaven my expectation. I like to memorize things. Do you know James Joyce?"

Steve said he didn't.

"Why should you? He was my boyfriend for a while. Before Mason came along. A perverted Irish boy who liked to have sex standing up. He went blind."

"How old was he?"

"A hundred and three."

"Jesus, you're full of shit."

"Am I? Well. Come." She took Steve by the elbow and pulled him out onto the dance floor. His pants were too tight and he was clumsy. His nose was big. He tried to take her hands but she pulled away and danced alone across from him while he watched and shuffled his feet. Once, he leaned forward and pushed his mouth against her ear and called out, "You can dance." The feel of him, his chin on her cheek and his hand against her hip. Later, at the bar, he kissed her hand and then took her face and turned it towards him and looked into her eyes and kissed her on the mouth. She let him. She didn't open her mouth, though he wanted this, and she kept her eyes open and she saw the ring in his ear, his shirt collar, and his neck. Soon after that she pulled him out onto the dance floor again and they kissed then too, except Steve kept moving his hands around on her back and she tried to let him know, through sharp movements of her shoulders, that she didn't want that. She didn't like him, but she liked kissing him.

When they were sitting and drinking again he told her that both his parents were dead.

"I don't believe you," she said. "You want pity."

"No, I don't. But they are dead. They were killed in a car accident. I live with my little brother. I should be home right now taking care of him but sometimes I just want to go out and be bad."

"Oh, so this is being bad. Naughty boy."

He took her hand. His shirtsleeves were rolled up and his forearms were large. With her free hand she touched his arm. She thought, in a giddy moment of drunkenness, that he was good-looking. They sat like that and drank while Lena studied Steve's neck and his arms. She pushed her finger against his forearm and then lifted her hand and drank again. At some point their hands came together and stayed put and that's how Julianne found her. She pushed her body against Lena's back and said she was tired and wanted to go. She said that the little man with the glasses was a loser. "Too perverted for my tastes," she said. "Whatcha gonna do?"

Lena said that she was going to hang on to Steve for a while.

Julianne looked at Steve. She whispered in Lena's ear, "His head's too big."

Lena giggled.

"Don't do anything stupid," Julianne said. "Like drive him home when you're drunk. You don't know him."

"It's okay."

Julianne said she'd take a taxi home. She squeezed Lena's elbow and passed a hand through the air at Steve. Then she slipped away.

At 2:00 a.m. Lena and Steve left the club and stood on the sidewalk. Two prostitutes in fur coats across the street, a neon sign advertising a restaurant. Steve said, "I took a taxi here. How about you?"

"My mom's car, you want a ride?" She didn't want him to, but asked anyway.

"Sure." He was happy. He said, "You want me to drive? You drank a lot."

She waved him away. "No, no, I'll go slow."

In the car he talked. He said he loved Winnipeg. The rivers, the smallness, the chance to meet a girl like her. "Lena," he said.

"Be quiet," she said.

He directed her. Up Kenaston and onto Grant. Down through Charleswood and then left towards the Perimeter.

"You sure this is the right way?" Lena asked. She wouldn't find her way home. She was shivering. Her head ached.

"I'm sure. It's my place."

"A house?"

"Yeah."

They crossed the tracks and stopped at the Perimeter. "Straight through," Steve said.

"There's no house," Lena said. "I don't see a house." She was breathless. The alcohol had made her breathless. She was scared now, aware of Steve's size. The way he'd pushed against her earlier in the bar.

"Down that road," he said.

A tractor-trailer passed. A car. A pickup. Lena was holding the wheel with both hands and the darkness surrounded them and she began to cry. Not loud or hard but there were tears. "This is nowhere," she said. "You brought me out here to fuck me. Didn't you? You don't have a house out here. Please don't fuck me. This is my mother's car."

"Aww, man," Steve reached out to touch her arm.

Lena screamed, "Don't."

"Okay. Okay, listen. I won't touch you. We're almost there. Watch the traffic. It's divided. Then go straight. My house is orange. It's 49."

"You're not lying? You won't hurt me?"

"Lena. Lena."

"My father'll kill me." She drove again. Crossed the divided highway and followed the thin road up past a few unlit houses and when Steve pointed out his orange house with the single lit window she slowed and aimed for the driveway and drove into the ditch. The car settled, leaning slightly on the driver's side.

"I missed," Lena said.

"You're drunk," Steve said.

"My dad'll kill me," Lena said. She looked around, as if suddenly aware of the mess of the evening. "Oh, fuck." This was her voice and she was surprised at the sound of its despair.

"Not the end of the world," Steve said. "Come in and we'll call a tow truck."

"This isn't good. Nobody's going to come out here at this time of night. Aww, man."

"Well, come in anyway, you can't sit out here."

She climbed out into the ditch and pushed her way around the nose of the car and called out to Steve who was walking to the house. "Could we push, do you think?"

He ignored her and kept walking. She followed him and entered the house. There was a boy sleeping on the sofa in the living room. Steve had disappeared. He came back and motioned at the boy and said, "My brother Mick."

Lena looked at the boy, who was young, not more than thirteen.

Steve took her coat and hung it up. He said she could use the phone and call for a ride. Or she could sleep in the chair. He said that her age surprised him, now that he could see her in a normal room under normal light, and if he'd known she was so young he'd have left her alone.

"So, I ruined your evening?" she asked.

"You should be at home. What are you thinking?" Then he said he was working in the morning, the early shift, and he was going to bed. "Call someone. Your parents, or that sixteen-year-old boyfriend. Okay? Good night," he said and he left her standing in the middle of the room.

She sat down and waited. She heard Steve in the bathroom, the flushed toilet, the brushing of teeth, a tap running. A door opened, another closed. All was quiet. She was more clear-headed now and she realized that she had failed in some way and that the failure was poignant and memorable. The room she sat in had the one sofa and two chairs and a painting of black-and-white squares diminishing into the distance. There was a phone. She stood by the window and looked out at her car. A wind was blowing and new drifts were forming against the passenger door. The house, the yard, the land out there, was desolate. She considered calling someone but wasn't sure who. Julianne had no car and she couldn't phone her parents. Mason would do something. She knew that. She picked up the phone and punched in Mason's number. It rang a long time. Then Mason answered. Lena said, "Mason, I'm stranded and I need your help. I went out for drinks and then I was driving home and I hit the ditch. Can you come get me?"

Mason's voice was still caught in sleep. "Where are you?" he asked. Lena imagined him in his shorts, his limbs bare. She was sorry. She wanted to be with him.

"I don't know," she said. "Out in the country. Somewhere. South of the Perimeter."

"What are you doing out there? Are you okay?"

"I was driving someone home. And then I hit the ditch. I was on the road and then *swoosh*, I was off the road. It was simple. Can you come?"

"Who?" Mason asked. "Who were you driving home?"

Lena sighed. "A guy. Steve. From the bar. It was no big deal. Nothing happened. He's old, about twenty-five, and he's got a little brother called Mick."

Mason didn't say anything.

"I'm sorry, Mason. I am. Can you come?"

"I can't," he said. He sounded pleased. "My mom's car's not here."

Mick was awake and watching Lena. He lifted his hand and made a visor. "What do you expect me to do?" Lena asked. "I can't phone my father." Then she said, all business. "What about your father?"

"He's at work. How would I get him? The night dispatcher's a bitch."

"Tell her it's an emergency. Your sister's in trouble or something. Okay? Mason, okay?"

Mason was thinking. Lena watched Mick, who was rubbing his eyes. Mason said, "I need your address."

Lena put the receiver against her chest. She called out to Mick, "What's the house number here? This street."

Mick rolled his head towards her. His face was chubby, his eyebrows dark. He gave the address and Lena passed it on to Mason who said, "I don't believe you. That nothing happened."

Lena was watching Mick who was watching her. She was tired. She said, "It's true, Mason. All of it is true."

"I'm upset," he said, "You know?"

"Sure. I know. I'm sorry."

"Are you? How do I know that? You're in trouble and so you call me. But you never called me earlier. You say we have all kinds of problems and then you tell me to go away when I show up at your house and now, when you get yourself into some stupid mess, you call."

"I think about you all the time, Mason. I was planning on calling you earlier tonight but then Julianne suggested checking out that new nightclub and we headed downtown and all this other stuff happened. Look, can I give you my phone number, or what?" She read it off the phone in front of her and asked Mason if he got it.

"You fuck things up, Lena. I don't know what to do."

"Call your Dad." Lena hung up and looked at Mick. "I'm Lena," she said.

Mick shrugged. Kept watching her.

"You're Mick," Lena said, pointing a finger at him. "Steve told me that. Your brother." She looked around the room. "How old are you, Mick?"

"Twelve."

"You go to school?"

Mick nodded.

"I remember when I was twelve. Grade 7, I think. I went to this little school with really high ceilings, and I had a teacher called Mr. Hatfield. He read *The Call of the Wild* to us. It was about Buck, a dog. Buck gets sold up north where he's a sled dog and he gets tossed from owner to owner and some beat him and some don't and all the time he tries his best. I remember that. I remember that it was a sad book but it ends happy." She stopped, then said, "So, your brother takes care of you?"

Mick nodded again.

"You're probably wondering what I'm doing here, eh?"

"You're Steve's friend."

"I guess. I gave him a ride home and my car got stuck. If you look out the window you'll see. It's in the ditch."

"Are you Jessica's friend?"

"I don't know. Who's she?"

"My brother's girlfriend."

"Oh. No, actually, I don't know Jessica. I have a boyfriend, his name's Mason. I just talked to him on the phone." Lena paused and leaned forward, elbows on her knees, and looked at Mick, who looked at her. Neither of them spoke. Mick yawned. Lena said, "You're tired. Go back to sleep."

Mick closed his eyes. After a bit his arm jumped and his fingers moved. Lena watched him and thought of Emily, her sister. Then she must have slept too because Mr. Crowe shook her awake. He was standing over her. He had his boots and jacket on and he was bent forward and when she opened her eyes she said, "Mason," and she smiled.

Then she sat up and said, "Oh, hi, Mr. Crowe," and she stood. Mick was still sleeping.

"I walked in," Mr. Crowe said. "I knocked but nobody answered. I saw your car out there so I knew you were here. Who's that?"

"Mick."

Mr. Crowe said okay and looked around the room. Then he said, "You'll want a ride. Mason called the dispatcher. I was out by the airport and she radioed and said my daughter, Lena, needed a ride. She gave me the address, so I came. Are you okay? I called Mason but he didn't really tell me what was going on other than there was some guy called Steve and you were stuck at his house."

"I'm sorry, Mr. Crowe. I didn't know what to do. My dad'll kill me."

"Oh, I don't think so. Though he's probably worried about you right now. Did you call him?"

"I can't. He'll just rant and I won't be able to say anything. I'll talk to him at home."

They left the house together and walked towards the taxi that was standing on the road, engine running. They passed by Lena's car and Mr. Crowe looked at it but Lena kept walking and got into the taxi. The car was warm and the dashboard lights glowed. Lena felt safe. Mr. Crowe got in and blew on his hands and said, "Miserable." He started to drive and he didn't say anything for a long time. Lena wanted to explain herself but she wasn't sure how to start and so, finally, she said, "I'm sorry, Mr. Crowe."

"It's okay."

Lena said, "I guess you think I'm pretty awful."

"I don't think that."

"Well I am. I was really stupid to drive Steve home. I didn't even know him and there we were in the middle of nowhere and he could have done anything."

"He didn't though, did he?" Mr. Crowe said.

"No, he didn't." She said, "That boy on the couch. Mick. He was living with his brother because his mom and dad were dead. He was so sweet. I told him to go to sleep and he did. Just like that."

Mr. Crowe didn't say anything though he seemed to have been listening. The taxi was warm and Lena liked the bigness of it, the legroom. It was like a cave. Mr. Crowe drove with one finger. He had a jaw like Mason's, kind of wide and obvious. Lena thought that Mason would be like his father some day, maybe even drive a taxi, and she would be married to him and he would come home to Kraft Dinner that she'd made and they'd eat it in front of the TV and talk about the day. She'd be in school, medicine maybe; that'd make her father happy.

She said to Mr. Crowe, "It's weird, if you were my father you'd be lecturing me right now. Blah, blah, blah about responsibility and danger and the evils of the world."

Mr. Crowe looked at her. Said, "I'm not your father."

"So right."

"Mason was pretty upset," Mr. Crowe said. "He's sixteen and I guess he can't quite figure out why you'd be driving home a strange guy. I figure he's got a point. Unless you know something he doesn't."

"I don't know any more than he does," Lena said. She saw that things were not simple. She wondered if Mr. Crowe knew about his wife seeing another man. And if he was doing anything about it. She said, "Sometimes adults think they know everything. But they don't. There are lots of things taking place. Apocalyptic things. When you were a kid you probably didn't have to worry about the polar ice cap melting and Ebola and cloning sheep."

Mr. Crowe nodded at this. He said, "I don't think any of that will touch your life, Lena. At least I don't think you should let it worry you. I think if we all took care of the little world around us then the larger world would be fine."

"Do you think it's possible to love more than one person?" Lena asked.

Mr. Crowe pushed a hand through his hair. He said, "Perhaps, though I think there are things more important than love. Not greater, I wouldn't say that, just more important."

"My mother told me once that she could have loved another man. She said she didn't love my dad when they married. She *grew* to love him. That's weird."

"The word is overused," Mr. Crowe said. "It's thrown about like so much nonsense. People sometimes don't know what they mean."

They were in Lena's neighbourhood now. The dimly lit streets, the bare trees, the dark houses. Mr. Crowe pulled up in front of Lena's house. The living-room light was on. Lena could see her father sitting on the couch. His head, the lamp-light pouring down over his crown. He shifted, looked out at the street.

"That's my Dad," Lena said. She waited and then turned to Mr. Crowe and said, "Thanks, Mr. Crowe. Tell Mason I'll call him, okay."

Mr. Crowe nodded and said, "Good luck." Lena stepped out onto the street, closed the taxi door, and Mr. Crowe drove off. She watched the car disappear and then she turned to look at her house. Her father was still looking out the window but he could not see her and she stood for a long time and watched him as he waited for her to come home.

Nothing happened. Or at least nothing obvious or tangible. There had been no screaming, no lecture, no consequences. Lena's father had the car picked up by a local tow-truck driver and it was delivered the following day when Lena was in her room. She had just woken and she stood in her nightgown by the window and watched her mother's car being backed into the garage. Over the next ten days, since the night out with Steve, she did not leave the house. She slept and ate packages of dried apples and drank water and several times her mother came into her room and attempted conversations but Lena only answered with elliptical comments and the occasional yes or no. Her sisters circled her. They allowed her control of the bathroom and they whispered down the hallway. Mason did not call her, neither did she call him. One night Rosemary crept into Lena's room and sat on her bed and said, "Mom and Dad are talking about you. They really do want to send you somewhere."

Lena had been lying on top of her blanket, staring up at the ceiling. She was dressed. She had her shoes on. Her coat. As if she had imagined the possibility of leaving, even though she knew it wouldn't happen. She lay there and didn't speak for the longest time. Then she whispered, "Where?"

"To a hospital. Dad said."

"Huh," Lena went. She held up a hand. It was shaking.

"That's crazy. Why don't you just do something? Get up. Go back to school."

Lena took Rosemary's hand and said, "Don't worry. I will. I promise."

"Do you?"

"Yes." Then she asked, "How's Mason?"

Rosemary shrugged. "Why ask me?"

"Has he kissed you yet?"

"Why do you keep asking me that?"

"I can't remember what he looks like. I try to picture him, thinking that'll make me happy, and I can't find him. He's a zero."

"He looks the same. You saw him a couple of weeks ago."

"I know he looks the same. It's just I can't picture him."

"Are you okay, Lena? Should I call Mom?"

"She can't do anything. Anyways, it's all so sad."

"It doesn't have to be sad, Lena."

"You can say that again and again but it still is, you see."

"You want me to sleep with you?"

"You don't want to. I smell."

"That's okay."

"So, I *do* smell. I thought it was something in the garbage and then I realized it was me. This morning Mom said I should shower and I planned on it but I kept waiting for the right moment."

"You want me to help you? Here, come." And Rosemary took Lena and pulled her up so she was sitting at the edge of the bed. She held her arm and walked her down to the bathroom and Lena stood with her arms at her side as Rosemary undressed her. When she was naked Rosemary told her to pee. She sat down and watched as Rosemary turned on the shower. Rosemary asked, "Can you do it yourself?"

Lena didn't answer. She was looking at the caulking on the shower wall. Mould like a blue flower. Rosemary undressed, helped Lena into the shower, then climbed in behind her. "Get your hair wet," Rosemary said. She pushed Lena's head under the nozzle and then pulled her away and lathered shampoo in.

She scrubbed Lena's head for a long time and then rinsed her off. Then she soaped Lena's body and scrubbed her armpits and crotch. Lena looked down at Rosemary's hand between her legs. "Thank you," she said. Rosemary said, "I'm going to shave you," and she switched the shower off and ran water into the tub. Sat Lena down at the edge of the tub and Rosemary knelt in the water and spread their father's shaving lotion over Lena's calves. She used their mother's razor. "You'll be all perfect," Rosemary said and planted a kiss on Lena's knee.

"Am I beautiful?" Lena asked.

"Very beautiful," Rosemary said. "Here, raise your arm." She shaved her right armpit and then her left and as she worked Lena watched her arm move back and forth.

"Your elbow is amazing," Lena said.

Rosemary helped Lena out of the tub and dried her off. Lena felt the towel and looked at Rosemary's arms and head and legs and said, "Oh, you're naked." Then she said, "Do you want to know something funny? Mason and I had anal sex." Rosemary took her own housecoat from the back of the bathroom door and put it on Lena.

"I wanted to try it," Lena said. "I don't think he did. He did it for me. I wanted to eat him up. Haven't you ever liked a guy so badly you wanted to devour him?"

Rosemary didn't answer. She guided Lena back to her bed and tucked her in and placed a hand on her forehead and then climbed in beside her and wrapped an arm around her stomach and said, "There now, go to sleep."

On a cold clear day, Lena left the house when no one was home. She walked up to Cousins and ordered a coffee and date cake and sat at a back table. Jeff, an older man she knew from working at The Nook, said hi to her and looked at her face, her breasts, and then her hands. He asked her if she was still working. Lena shook her head and put her hands under the table.

Jeff said that was too bad and went to sit at a corner table. Two girls came in who Lena knew from high school. She looked away but one of the girls saw her and came over and said, "Hey, Lena, got any cigarettes?"

Lena pushed her pack across the table and looked at the girl's coat, the pale lines against dark wool. Megan, that was the girl's name. An upturned piggy nose. Two cigarettes in the fat fingers of her right hand. "Thanks," she said, and went back to her friend and sat down and they blew smoke at the ceiling and once Megan said something and looked over at Lena and then she turned back to the other girl and shrugged. Little nose pointing upwards. She had no idea what the world was about, Lena thought.

She left her uneaten cake and she put on her coat. On her way out she stopped beside the girls and handed Megan the pack of cigarettes and said, "Here, I won't need these," and then she stepped out onto the street. It was nearing four o'clock and rush-hour traffic was starting. She walked over to Maryland and up past Bridge Motors. The attendant, wearing a dark green parka and thick mitts, was pumping gas. Lena bent her bare head against the wind. She walked to the centre of the bridge and leaned over the balustrade and looked down. Back in the fall, crossing this bridge to Mason's house, she had liked to stop and look down at the muddy river. Once, two rowers slid by, their boats thin and white and silent. An older man had passed her and asked, "Are you okay," and Lena said that she was fine. She was working on a science project. Mass and speed and distance. She took a penny from her pocket, threw it over the railing, and watched it fall. The man walked away, but he turned several times to look at Lena, and the last time he looked she waved and he disappeared around the corner.

Now, in the middle of winter, she walked across the bridge and descended the embankment towards the river. She stood on the bank for a long time and looked at the snow and ice. A small sign warned people to stay off the ice. She walked back up towards the street and onto the bridge and went back to the middle and climbed up onto the wide concrete railing and she sat looking upriver, her feet dangling. A car honked behind her. Another slowed. On the bank of the river, to her left, a man was shingling the roof of a house. The traffic behind her; above her, the sky, and below, the ice of the river. She was wearing her mother's fur coat. It was old and had a hole under the arm but it was warm. Seen from a distance she thought she might look like a large stuffed animal. A woman walking across the bridge looked at her and then continued on. Two young girls wearing the blue skirts of St. Mary's Academy passed her and giggled. Below her, on the ice, Lena saw a man. He opened his mouth but she could not hear. She leaned forward; the coat pulled at her shoulders. The man picked up a megaphone and called out, "Shoot a bullet in his head, snip, snap,

snout and my tale is out; tip, tap, tin and another can begin."
The man laughed. He was wearing a top hat and shorts and he
was barefoot and danced a jig. He was beautiful. There was the
sky. She looked up. Saw the dim light of an afternoon moon,
the pale ceiling, the meagre sun. She looked down. The man
was gone. She panicked and called out. Her voice was a low
moan and she looked around to see who was crying. Another
car honked. She saw a red-haired teenage boy lean out of the
window of a passing car. He shouted, "Jump." The car was
silver, a silver Rabbit full of boys. The single word "jump" startled her. In the distance, on the sidewalk, there was a man in a
brown knee-length coat. He was walking towards her. He had
a briefcase with a strap and the strap went over his shoulder
and he was holding his hand out to her. She turned away and
looked down and saw her boots and the ice below. The man in
the brown coat was close to her now. He was talking but she
couldn't understand him. A muffled gurgle. He reached for her
and she tried to slide away, but his arms came around tight
across the front of her coat, and someone grunted and called
out, "Ohhh." She was lying on her back, the man's face above
her. The pale sky beyond. She was convinced that she had
fallen and was floating near the bowl of heaven.

The room she was in had a desk and a lamp and there was a
clock radio and on the wall there were posters of famous
paintings and she recognized one as Géricault's *Raft of the*

Medusa. Her Art teacher at school had shown them slides of nineteenth-century works and Géricault's painting had been talked about and admired and much had been made of the bodies of the men and one girl had said, "Do you think they were saved?" Her father had wondered, during his last visit, what merit could be found in putting that kind of painting in a place like this.

Mrs. Schellendal had said, "It's not that bad. What do you want, unicorns?"

Lena was sitting on her bed. The three of them were drinking Sprite from plastic cups and nibbling at Liquorice Allsorts that Lena's mother had brought. The sound of her father chewing made Lena sad. Her mother was wearing wool pants and she sat with her legs crossed, one ankle moving back and forth. She took Lena's hand and wouldn't let it go. Finally, Lena freed herself and went to the bathroom. She sat and listened to the rise and fall of her parents' voices. She couldn't hear what they were saying. She put her elbows on her knees. Her skin was dry. When her mother knocked at the bathroom door and called out for her Lena flushed and looked at herself in the mirror. She said her own name, Lena Schellendal, and then she turned and opened the door.

She liked where she was. She felt safe. Her bed was small but the sheets were clean and there was a tiny window that looked out onto a green space. She was not allowed to leave the ward without supervision. She could phone out but rarely did. The only visitors were her parents and during the visits they sat in her room. One time, they talked about Lena's sisters. Rosemary was playing basketball, Margot had had a birthday, Emily had chipped a tooth. She missed Lena.

"Did you tell her where I was?" Lena asked.

Mrs. Schellendal waved a hand. She said, too brightly, "Have you made any friends here?"

"Hordes, Mom. We have a great time."

"These aren't the kind of people you want her to get close to," Mr. Schellendal said.

"How's banking, Dad?" Lena asked. She had a headache. Her father's hands were huge.

"Let's not start," Mrs. Schellendal said. "Your father and I have been thinking about a family vacation. Maybe go to Cuba or Mexico. The girls are very excited."

Lena stood and went to look out the window. She said, "I can't go. Dr. Deane said it would be healthier if I didn't get too excited."

"It's just a plan," Mrs. Schellendal said. "First we want you better." She went to Lena and hugged her. "We're so sorry, Lena. We're trying to figure all of this out and we need your help." She placed a hand on her head.

Lena didn't say anything. There was her mother's body, her thinness, the scent that came from a silver tin and was rubbed onto her wrists and neck. Her father breathing and smothering her hands with his and then as they were leaving, stooping towards her as if to pick her up but only touching her. "Goodbye, Lena," he said and slipped an envelope into her hand.

She opened it in her room. It contained five twenty-dollar bills and a handwritten note that said, "Lena, I want you to forgive me. I love you." Then, in a more swooping style, he had copied out some lines:

> So we'll live,
> And pray, and sing, and tell old tales, and laugh
> At gilded butterflies, and hear poor rogues
> Talk of court news: and we'll talk with them too
> Who loses and who wins; who's in, who's out;
> And take upon 's the mystery of things,
> As if we were God's spies: and we'll wear out
> In a walled prison, packs and sects of great ones,
> That ebb and flow by the moon.

At night Lena couldn't sleep. She sat on her bed and fingered the card and reread it and wondered why her father hadn't chosen a Bible verse instead. She walked down the hall to the lounge and sat with Carol, the ward worker, and Billy, a fifteen-year-old who had burned down the family house. Billy said that he wanted to smoke.

Carol said, "You can't. You're not allowed to have matches."

"I could just slip out and stand in the snow. Five minutes."

"Go to bed, Billy."

"Lena, you got smokes?" Billy asked.

Lena shook her head.

"Sure you do. I can see you're a smoker. Get me one, will you?"

"Shut up, Billy," Carol said. "Watch TV and shut up."

Billy looked at Carol. He said, "Okay. Okay."

After a bit Carol said, "You kids hungry? I could eat some toast."

She stood and Lena saw her big rear and the flab on her elbows. She walked to the kitchen. Billy said to Lena, "You got a boyfriend?"

"Fuck off," Lena said.

Billy nodded. "My girlfriend's name is April. She's sixteen." He looked at Lena. "Next time she comes to visit I'll introduce you. Then you'll believe me."

"I believe you."

Carol came back with three plates of toast and jam. Billy ate his fast, Lena looked at hers, and Carol chewed daintily, tiny bites for such a large mouth. Later, when Lena went back to bed, she wept until she fell asleep.

The following evening Rosemary came to visit and brought with her a bag of macaroons from Mordens. They sat on the bed and ate them and Lena said, "Weird people here, Rose. Little Billy's a pyro who'd like to get in my panties and Alice throws knives, and the other day we went swimming, can you believe it, swimming, and I'm surrounded by freaks, only I look in the mirror and I see I'm a freak too. Mom brought me cigarettes."

They went down to the front door in their parkas and huddled against the wind and smoked. Hector, a ward worker, went down with them.

"Emily thinks you're at music camp," Rosemary said. "She was pushing Mom and Dad, asking about you. They have you studying flute."

"Good. And Margot?"

"She knows. She writes in her journal and shows me. Poems about bell jars and sex and boys and suicide by gassing. Very passionate."

"Oh, man, Rosemary. Tell her to stop."

"She thinks you're perfect."

Lena huddled against the wind. "Look at me. Bring her with you next time. I'll talk to her."

"Mason called and asked me if I wanted to go to this poetry reading with him. Mason read a poem about watching a girl. I figure that was you."

"Really?" Lena was pleased. Then she asked, "He knew where I was?"

"He'd already heard. He asked lots of questions, general things like, Is she okay? and I answered him the best I could."

Lena beat her cold hands together and exhaled into the air.

They went back upstairs and sat on the bed and finished the macaroons. Rosemary pulled a Coke from her backpack and they shared it. When she left she hugged Lena and then Lena watched her walk down the hallway of the ward and out through the green swinging doors and she was glad she didn't have to go along.

One day, in her third week at the hospital, Mason came to visit. It was eight o'clock on a Thursday evening and he walked into the common room and said, "Hi, Lena." In the room there was a TV and several couches and board games and a card table and a CD player and, over in the corner, folded into a large red chair, there was one other girl. She was reading *Anna Karenina*. Lena was sitting on a long couch. Her feet were propped on a coffee table in front of her and there were wads of Kleenex stuck between her toes and when she saw Mason she looked around and then she looked back at Mason and lifted a foot slightly and said, "Isn't this pretty?"

Mason nodded. He said it was pretty. "Orange," he said. He sat down across from Lena.

"Meredith did it," Lena said. "Meredith just left on an evening pass with her mother. Too bad you couldn't meet her. She's very beautiful."

Lena was wearing baggy jeans with frayed bottoms and a T-shirt that said *Angel*. Her lips were chapped. He said, "Your hair is really long."

Lena pulled at it with one hand. "Yeah. Yeah. It is." Then she said, "Were you scared to come here?"

Mason looked over at the girl who was reading Tolstoy. Her head was bent forward.

"Don't worry about Ann," Lena said quietly. "She doesn't listen. And don't be too impressed. She just pretends to read. She's been on page 639 for the last week." She paused and asked, "Did Rosemary tell you I was here?"

"Julianne did. I see her sometimes in the cafeteria and one time when we were alone she asked if I knew. I didn't. Which surprised me, because you'd think *I* of all people should know. But then again I haven't seen you since you called from some guy's house. Right? But we don't have to talk about that and anyways that's way back there and gone. I know that. You don't have to tell me. My father filled me in, you know. He told me you were repentant. That's the word he used, repentant, and then he said that there was nothing new under the sun and remember that time when I was over at your house and I quoted the Bible like an idiot and used that same line? Well, it was like the strangest thing, hearing him say that line and remembering that day at your dinner table with your father all dressed up and your mother in her black dress and your grandma and sisters, the whole family. It's amazing, when you think about it, how lucky you are to have your sisters."

"Mason." Lena had placed her feet on the floor and she was sitting forward and looking at him, her chest pressed against her forearms. "It's okay," she said. "You don't have to entertain me." She looked down at her knees and waited and then she said, "I don't remember what happened. Only the man grabbing me from behind and this other man with a top hat calling out to me from down below on the river ice. Things like that." She opened her hands and looked up. Mason was wearing a black sweater. He was biting at a fingernail, leaning back against the couch and pretending to be nonchalant. He was nervous, she could tell. She wished that they were alone. She touched his hand, the one resting on his thigh, and she held it.

"So, what's up? Are you working? Still reading to that blind man?" she asked. She could feel him slipping away. He kept glancing at the girl with the open book and then over at the clock.

"Yeah, Tuesdays and Thursdays still. Mr. Ferry asked about you. I didn't know what to say, so I said you were in the hospital."

"Everybody knows, I guess."

"Not everybody. Anyways, it doesn't matter. Mr. Ferry said you were unhappy."

Lena snorted. "How'd he get to be so smart. And he's *not* unhappy?"

"I don't know," Mason said. "Just last week I saw a woman at his house. She was maybe thirty or thirty-five, and she was sitting on the couch and Mr. Ferry was sitting beside her and though they weren't holding hands or anything it was like I'd walked into something private. She was a big woman, and there was this fur coat lying on the arm of the couch and Mr. Ferry didn't introduce us. He just told me to wait in the library and I heard him say goodbye to the woman. I didn't hear what they said, just a lot of whispering, and then she left. I don't know who she was."

"He was probably paying her."

"You think so? She might have been his niece, or someone."

Lena said that she wasn't the person to ask. There was a glass of water beside her and she picked it up and drank from it. "Want some?" she asked, lifting the glass. Mason said no.

Lena pulled her feet up against her thighs and began to remove the wadded Kleenex from between her toes. She said that she didn't expect anything from Mason. She was glad he'd come to visit and she didn't know what his motives were and he didn't have to tell her. Maybe *he* didn't even know.

"I do know, though," Mason said. "I wanted to see you. It might surprise you but that's the truth."

Lena put her chin on her knees. She said, "Rosemary told me you wrote a poem about watching a girl."

"I did. She came to hear me. It was at The Blue Note and there were other kids doing things. Singing. One girl belly danced." He paused. "I guess you're wondering why I'm hanging around with Rosemary."

"I've thought about it. No big deal. You fucked her yet?"

"Jesus, Lena." He looked at her. Then he said, "Don't talk like that."

She closed her eyes as if considering this advice. She said, "Lots of material here for your brilliant poems," she said. "Crazy people. If you want to be a goddam poet you've got to see things." She touched her forehead. She was looking at his hands and she said, "I feel like I tricked you. I never meant to."

"What do you mean? You didn't make me do anything. I chose," Mason said.

"See," she said, "You don't understand. This isn't about what you like or what you choose. This is about *me* choosing. Does this sound mad? It is. But I think that if I say no to something, something really important, the most important thing in my life, that then I will save myself." There was the sound of Mason breathing and the muted voices of patients out in the hall. She looked at his eyes.

He said, "That's crazy, Lena. You're not making any sense."

"It's over," she said.

He didn't answer. He stood and put on his jacket and she watched him walk out into the hall and then he disappeared. She sat and waited for him to come back but he didn't. The girl in the corner glanced at her and Lena said, "What are *you* looking at?"

A while later Billy came into the common room and sat down across from her and grinned. She studied him and waited for him to speak but he said nothing. She reached into her jeans pocket and pulled out one of the twenties her father had given her. She pushed it across the table at Billy and said, "Here, buy yourself some cigarettes."

Billy looked at the money and he picked it up and put it in his shirt pocket. He said, "That was your boyfriend, then."

Lena was aware of Billy's long hair, the way he pushed it behind his ears and how it curled and touched his neck. He was tall and thin and his face was long and dark. She said, "What do you want from me, Billy?"

He grinned. Said, "I like you, Lena. You're *in*teresting."

She stood and walked to her room. After a few minutes there was a knock and then the door opened and Billy entered. Lena didn't look up, just said, "Close the door." They sat on the bed and looked at each other and Lena told him to suck on her fingers and he did as he was told. He tried to touch her breasts but she said, "No." She took his head and pushed his face against her chest. Her hands felt his ribs. She pushed him away and unbuckled his jeans, pulled them down to his knees. Then his underwear. A dark little boner that she touched and studied. His breathing was quicker. She worked at him until he came into her hand.

She didn't eat her dinner that night. Green beans, a pork cutlet, and applesauce stared up at her from the tray. She stuck a spoon in the pudding and left it there. Billy passed by her room and stopped and then kept walking. That evening he strutted around the ward.

"Little rooster," Carol said.

Billy grinned and eyed Lena, who turned away.

The following morning Lena's mother appeared on the ward. Billy had bragged and the doctor had been informed and Lena's parents had been called. Her mother entered with a hard stride and she berated the nurses and threw Lena's clothes into her suitcase and then sat on her bed and said, "Why?" Lena didn't answer. Dr. Deane was called and she arrived breathless and harried and she closed the door to the room and sat across from Mrs. Schellendal and said, "Pull yourself together."

"You," Lena's mother said, "are supposed to be taking care of my daughter, and this is what happens? Unbelievable."

Dr. Deane looked at Lena and then at Mrs. Schellendal. She said, "Forget about yourself. For just a moment. And take your daughter for a while and love her."

Lena was standing by the closed door. She saw her mother's black boots and her navy skirt and her freshly manicured nails and she imagined her mother sitting on a chair in a salon, yesterday or the day before, while Lena was in the hospital.

"You got your nails done," Lena said.

Mrs. Schellendal looked at her hands. Seemed surprised. Nodded and sighed and said, "Come, Lena."

In the car, which was located in a three-storey parkade opposite the hospital, Mrs. Schellendal placed her gloved hands on the steering wheel and said, "I want to take you out of town for a few days, just the two of us."

Lena panicked, looked around the car, and considered for a moment stepping back outside and running through the gloomy parkade, back to the ward where Billy waited for her.

"Where?" she whispered. Her knees were cold. She placed her red woollen mittens on them.

"Oh," said her mother, too brightly – Lena would realize later, when it became clear that this was not her mother's idea of fun – "to that nice little hotel in Gimli which looks out on the lake."

"Why are we going *there*? What about everybody else?"

"Your father suggested it. I agreed. Your sisters would be jealous if they knew."

"Take them, then. I don't want to go," Lena said. Her mother was severe, acting in a manner Lena did not recognize. The weight of everything on her neck, right there, where her head bent slightly as she leaned out the window to receive the receipt for parking. She closed the window, looked over at Lena, and sighed.

"Oh, Lena," she said and then she said no more. When they reached the outskirts of the city she pulled into a doughnut shop and slipped from the car and returned with juice for Lena and coffee for herself.

Back on the highway, Lena huddled against the passenger door and looked out the window. A clump of trees, a farm-yard, a dog in the ditch, its tail in the air. The snow on the fields was like a desert, with the drifts and waves shaped by the wind and the emptiness.

Lena's mother spilled some coffee on her skirt. She scrubbed at it with a dry Kleenex and said, "I just dry-cleaned this. My goodness." She put the ball of Kleenex on the dash, placed both hands back on the wheel, and looked straight ahead. After a lengthy silence she said, "I have to tell you something but I'm afraid to. I'm afraid because it's something sad and God knows I don't want you upset. You have to promise me, Lena, that when I say what I have to say, you won't do anything rash. Okay?"

Lena had turned towards her mother. The leather of the seats creaked and she saw her mother's profile and the width of the sky beyond the driver's window. "You're leaving Dad," she said.

"Oh. Oh, Lena. No. No, no. Not at all. I love your father." She laughed, though it seemed to Lena that it wasn't really a laugh but more a moan. Her mother continued, almost breathlessly. "It's Nana. You know that she was old and she had problems with her heart." She paused, swung her head towards Lena and then back at the road.

Lena was aware of her mother's hands and the tremor in her voice. "What happened?"

"It was in her sleep."

"What do you mean?"

"Nana died." She reached out and took Lena's hand.

Lena was quiet for a bit and then she said, "Nana's dead?"

Her mother nodded. "She had a heart attack ten days ago, in her home, at night. Your father called her the following day and when he got no response he went over and found her. I'm sorry, Lena." She was wiping at her eyes and, seeing this, Lena turned her head away and forced herself not to cry at the same time as her mother.

"You didn't tell me," Lena said, "It happened ten days ago and you never told me."

Her mother had stopped crying. "Believe me, Lena, I wanted to. But Dr. Deane thought that the timing was bad.

She was worried about your response, how you'd handle it. I thought you should know; however, I was in the minority."

"The funeral."

"We had it last week, Lena."

"Poor Nana."

Her chest felt like it was being crushed.

Their room was on the third floor and it looked out over the ice of the lake. Twin beds, twin desks, a bathroom for two with twin towel racks. Lena took a shower and after, she stood in the sunlight that arrived in stripes through the half-opened venetian blinds. Her body was pale. Her knuckles and knees and elbows were dry. She studied her breasts. Touched the anchor on her thigh. Thought of Mason and wondered if he'd known, when he came to visit, that her Nana was dead. She walked out into the room wearing the white bathrobe her mother had bought her. Sat at the foot of her bed and watched TV while her mother read in the bed beside her. That night, as her mother slept, Lena listened to her snore and hearing this, she began to weep. When she finally fell asleep she dreamed briefly and bizarrely of a woman who spoke only German and wanted to cut off all of Lena's hair. In the morning, at breakfast, she asked her mother what *Ewigkeit* meant.

"Eternal. Eternity." Her mother was eating a soft-boiled egg in a cup. There was butter and pepper and salt and her mother's wrist and a band of gold where her watch hung like a bracelet. "That's interesting. Your father and I were talking just the other day about you studying German."

"I don't want to study German. That's Dad's language. Full of *Ich*s."

Mrs. Schellendal waved her spoon. "You're too hard on him. He loves you. In many ways he has always protected you."

Lena lifted her eyebrows and blew out her cheeks. "That card he gave me, with that quote. Was that your idea?"

"No, he wanted to send you something."

"But the words. You gave them to him. At least guided him toward them."

"Is that so bad?" her mother asked. "We don't know what to do, Lena. If there were something magical we could say, we'd say it. But we don't know."

Lena said, "Talking isn't everything. You think if I told you things then all would be fine. It wouldn't."

The waiter appeared and took away Lena's plate and cutlery. He had big forearms and Lena was aware of his bulk and the way he walked, lightly, as if tiptoeing across soft ground. She watched him till he had disappeared through the kitchen door and then she said, "Did Nana know? About me being in the hospital? And everything?"

Her mother shook her head. "No. She didn't. We never told her."

Lena thought about this. She said, "That's good." Then she looked away and back at her mother. "Your nails are nice," she said. "Absolutely perfect."

She spent the day in her room, looking out at the lake and watching TV. Later in the evening she went down to the pool and swam and then sat in the hot tub and watched a boy of about sixteen swim with his younger sister. She closed her eyes.

The next day she and her mother walked around the town. They stopped at an antique shop where her mother bought a piano lamp, bronze with a green base. Outside, the wind was cold, and loose snow swirled through the streets. There was a dog in the shop, a setter with mournful eyes. Lena sat on a stool and held the dog's ear and said, "Hey, how are ya?"

They ate dinner that evening in the hotel dining room. There was music playing and Lena recognized some of the pieces from her piano lessons and from her sisters practising after school. She was wearing a tight skirt and she shifted now and pulled at its hem. Her feet were bare in her fat-soled shoes. She looked around the restaurant and wished that it were more full.

"Empty restaurants are depressing," she said.

"Should we go?" her mother asked. "We could go out to that pizza place across the street. Though we'd have to get our coats."

Lena said, "No, I was just saying." Then she said, "Remember the time we came here as a family? I was ten and one afternoon we walked down to the beach and you and Dad were arguing. I remember what Dad said. 'Can you keep just *one* thought in your head? Is that possible?' That's what he said. You were arguing about how often you had sex. Even at that age I was aware of what you and Dad talked about. You stomped off and left us alone on the beach for the afternoon. Dad was super nice to all of us girls. It was like we were you for the afternoon. I remember loving it."

"I don't think we stayed here," her mother said.

"We *did*," Lena said. "On the second floor. I remember shooting pool with Dad. It was our special time together after all the other girls were sleeping."

Then her mother asked what had happened in the hospital.

"What do you mean?"

"With that boy. What happened with that boy?"

"Nothing important, Mom. We were together for five minutes."

Her mother wanted to know if it was true. "Did you have sex with him?"

"Huh. Is that what the doctor said?"

"Not exactly."

"What did she say? She never asked me for the facts."

"Dr. Deane said that the boy said you had had sex."

"Well, we didn't."

Her mother was pleased and relieved. "I thought so," she said. "The idea was preposterous. That's what I told your dad."

"I beat him off," Lena said.

"Oh, Lena." Her mother looked away. Then she frowned and asked, "Did he force you?"

"Actually, no, Mom. He didn't."

"Lena. Why?"

Lena shrugged. She said, "I was curious. It didn't have anything to do with sex. I didn't take off my clothes. He didn't touch me. There's nothing wrong with me and nothing happened to me." She lifted the glass of wine her mother had poured her and drank from it. She put the glass down. A little wine had spilled and it spread across the white tablecloth. The music was playing. One of the songs was Borowski's

"Adoration" and Lena lifted her head and said, "I played this for Mason. When we first met."

Her mother's mouth moved into what appeared to be a smile. Lena's throat was not working properly. She swallowed and closed her eyes; opened them and said, as if this were an answer to a question she had been asked, "That day on the bridge, when I tried to jump, I was scared."

"Of course you were," her mother said.

"No, no, you don't understand. The thing is, I was afraid that I wouldn't be able to die, that I would live. That was the awful thing." She stopped.

"Oh, Lena." Her mother reached out and took her hand. She said, "I want us to be happy. I want you to be happy."

Now they were all alone, the couple that had been sitting in the corner had left. The music played.

The following afternoon, walking by herself along the pier that gave out onto the frozen lake, she saw herself as others must have seen her: a girl in a dark-green coat stepping carefully along an icy walk. She felt a sudden lightness that was unfamiliar, and for a brief moment it was as if a window had opened, let in the light, and then shut again.

3

I n the spring, when the river-ice melted and the water rose and flooded the banks and the trees grew leaves and the grass offered up its musty scent, Mason's brother Danny came back from Montreal. He had left with great hopes and he was returning empty-handed: he had no job and he had no money. His failure – and this is what he called it, "my perfect failure" – had left him subdued and drifting.

A few weeks earlier, Mrs. Crowe had moved out of the house, and was now living with Aldous in his condominium by the river. One evening when Mr. Crowe was at work, Danny sat down across from Mason at the kitchen table, pulled the wrapper off a beer bottle, and said, "I talked to Dad yesterday. He's pretty devastated by Mom and this Schmidt." He said Schmidt as if it were an unfortunate or foul name. "If I were Dad I'd slash the tires on his car."

"A Boxster," Mason said. "A beautiful red Boxster."

"All the better. The thing is, it's like Dad just sat there. Didn't he know what was going on? She must have come home smelling of some other guy?"

"'I'm going dancing with Rhonda.' 'Rhonda and I are going out for drinks.' That's what she'd say. Anyways, Mom had all kinds of time to herself. She wasn't very happy."

"Oh, you know that?" Danny asked. "She confessed this? Sat you down one day and said, You know, Mason, I'm not a very happy woman so I think I'll fuck this man Schmidt who drives a red Boxster."

"She didn't look happy. That's all. Now she does."

Danny grinned. "She likes things and Schmidt gives her things. Bingo. Happiness. I told Dad he had to do something beyond work. Like a hobby. Or go out with friends."

"He doesn't have a lot of friends," Mason said. "There was Mom. That's what he had."

Danny waved his hand, as if announcing the termination of that topic. He drank from his beer and then reached into his pocket and pulled out a plastic bag and rolled a joint. He lit up and said, "Wanna?" and Mason took it and they passed it back and forth without talking. The lamp above the table was yellow and it cast a sombre hue over Mason's books. His pen lay on his notebook and pointed at the last word he'd written, *heinous*. He was writing an essay on *Crime and Punishment* for Ms. Abendschade, who had, in the last few months, become shrill and impatient. Beth Ly figured she was perpetually PMS, Sally Hayes said it was early menopause – "Look at her fiery cheeks," and Jane Fenske, who seemed to know, said it was way too early, Abendschade was only thirty-six. "She's pregnant," Fenske announced, and blinked her wide eyes.

"The crime was heinous." Or, "A heinous crime." Definite, or indefinite? Ms. Abendschade liked clarity. She liked short, quick sentences because, as she said, most high school students didn't know how to write long sentences that looped back on themselves and inevitably the sentences, like snakes, ended up meeting their own tails and the arguments became circular and dangerous, if not downright poisonous. She seemed pleased with her extended wit. The fact remained that the crime *was* heinous: a young man kills two women by splitting their heads open with an axe.

The best part of the novel was the murder. The axe falling, the second killing, the escape, the blood. Ms. Abendschade did not seem particularly pleased with the novel. It was a chore. She was, she said, not a big fan of Dostoevsky and would have rather taught Tolstoy or Pushkin but neither of those writers was available in the book room and so it was the epileptic Russian (her words) that the class would read.

"In the scope of Russian literature," Ms. Abendschade said, "if you use the metaphor of light, Dostoevsky would appear as a distant star to Tolstoy's sun." She had said this on a Monday morning, a few days after Mason had visited Lena in the hospital. Because of his troubled state Mason had challenged Ms. Abendschade and said, "Who cares. Both Tolstoy and Dostoevsky are dead. It doesn't matter."

"Oh, Mason. Oh. But it does matter." Ms. Abendschade's cheeks burned. She was wearing a grey cardigan with tiny sheep stitched along the hem. The sheep were white with large cloven feet and their ears were erect and too small. They looked like pigs. Her cardigan was zipped up past her stomach and so it was impossible to see any slight swelling where the fetus would have been pushing at her abdomen. Abendschade pregnant. It made her soft and pliable and sleepy and round. Her impatience might have been fatigue. Jane Fenske had said all pregnant women get extremely tired in the first trimester. And it was with this fatigue that Ms. Abendschade had looked at Mason as he challenged her. She shook her head quizzically, impatiently, paused as if to reveal something profound, and then said, "The point is not the author's life but the book's life."

This type of comment from Ms. Abendschade normally would have pleased Mason, but he was thinking of Lena. Of Lena deciding. Sitting in her room she writes a list and it is either long or not and she closes her eyes and points with her pen and hits "bridge," or she is seduced by the word itself, a movement from here to there, crossing over, better than razors and pills and gas and guns. In his selfishness Mason wanted to believe that she is thinking of him, that she sits on the bridge, her legs dangling out over the river, her head twisting round, checking the passing traffic, "Look, you fine happy commuters, I'm going to kill myself," and somewhere in the chaos she considers Mason Crowe, boyfriend, minor poet, Mr. Ferry's reader, the lover she pushes onto the floor of the van and says, all grace and beauty, "We can have sex, but we have to watch the eggs."

Perhaps, Mason thought, the idea had always been incubating in her head, a smooth oval shape in the shadows of her brain that one day cracked open and offered oblivion. Sex and death lie in the dark. Lena in his mother's orange skirt, Lena turning her head back to guide his cock into her, Lena swivelling on the bridge. It is Mason and Lena lying together naked on his bed and Lena saying, "No one knows who I am. I can smile at you but really I am thinking I would like to die."[16]

Danny, who was hungry, had found some peanuts and chips. He also had a bowl of ice cream before him and he was spinning his spoon and watching Mason. He confessed, without any prompting, that he missed Maryann. His voice was low and despondent. He said, "You still seeing that girl? Lena, right?"

Mason nodded. He said, "Right," but he didn't commit either way. He didn't want to share Lena with Danny, even if at this point Lena was out there somewhere, unconnected. Since she had gotten out of the hospital he had seen her several times, once, briefly at a party on the weekend and they had talked and Lena had seemed interested in being near him. They had danced and Lena had looped her arms around his neck and asked, "Do you miss me?" and he had said, "Yes," though he wasn't sure what the right answer was. She had said,

---

[16] That night had been tempestuous and full of disagreement. Earlier, Lena had filmed her and Mason having sex. "You can erase the tape," she told Mason when he protested. "This is very important to me. I want to see what we look like." She had acted. Fought for position and looked at the camera and called out more shrilly than necessary. It was comical, only she thought it was serious. When she watched it later she said, "Look at me, I'm fat. I should join a gym." Still, she watched it twice and was surprised at how beautiful she appeared from the back. The slope of her buttocks and the curve of her back, Mason's hand holding the back of her head. She looked like a monk. She convinced Mason to make love as they watched themselves on video. "Look at us," she cried out.

"I'm better now. Almost. Whole. For a while I was just parts. A hand. A leg. A face. Now I'm one piece." And she hugged him and he'd wondered if she remembered her last words to him in the hospital.

Just yesterday he had seen her as he walked to school and this was odd because his path to school did not lead by Lena's house, but there she had been, like a stalker, and they had stopped and exchanged some words and Lena had said, as she walked away, "It was nice to see you again, Mason." She said his name clearly and slowly, as if, he thought, by holding it in her mouth she could maybe possess him again.

Danny was talking, going on about his drawing and his art and how he figured that might be his future. "Being a chef is lousy," he said. "You create something that gets devoured in half an hour. Just like that." He snapped his fingers. "And then the next day it gets shit out. With art, at least, it lasts. You can look at it one day and a year later it's still there."

Mason didn't think his brother was a very good artist. He'd seen some nudes of Maryann, pencil sketches and a few in charcoal, and though they were precise and vaguely erotic, they certainly wouldn't make Danny famous. Perhaps it was a fact, Mason thought, that everyone in the Crowe family was doomed to fail and only by getting out, like his mother had done, would they save themselves.

His mother had moved out on a Friday night. The week, unusual for late March, had been humid and hot and the air was closed in and heavy. Mason was home alone with his mother, sitting on her bed watching her pack suitcases and boxes. She was barefoot and wore shorts and an old T-shirt. Her hair was tucked under a blue bandana.

"I know this girl, Jane Fenske," Mason said, "who became narcoleptic after her parents broke up." This was true. Wide-eyed Fenske was not really so wide-eyed. Several times in class she'd fallen asleep and it was common knowledge, confessed by Jane herself, that her sleeping disorder had been brought on by her parents' divorce.

Mason's mother said, "Oh, Mason." Then she sat beside him and hugged him and whispered, "This isn't about you. You have to understand that." His face pressed against her shoulder. The smoothness of her neck. She stood and held him at arm's length. "You can come visit any time. Stay the night, keep some clothes at the apartment. Will you do that, Mason?"

He said he wasn't sure. He would think about it.

There had been many pairs of shoes and underwear and there were garters and skirts and dresses and jeans and more shoes and sandals and silky things and bottles of body wash and perfume and all the paraphernalia of hygiene. Mason had kept his eye open for the vibrator but it didn't appear, perhaps already ferried to Schmidt's grand palace where it could be used willy-nilly with no fear of a son marching in on the perversions.

Mason carried bags and boxes out to his mother's car. It was around 7 p.m. and the sun had just disappeared but it was still warm and the sky was still more light than dark. At Aldous's place, in the parking lot, two boys were shooting baskets, their voices calling out to each other in tones of camaraderie. Up in the condo it was cool and there were fresh-cut flowers in a crystal vase on the dining-room table and Christmas lights flickered on the railing of the balcony. Mason's mother had explained that Aldous was gone for the weekend. She surveyed the room, released her hair from her bandana, and sighed. Earlier, she had offered Mason her car, and now she dangled the keys in her left hand. "Are you okay, sweetie?" she asked.

He looked around at the clean brightness of his mother's new place. He looked right at her, thinking that he should sound convincing, and he said, "Yes. I'm okay." He took the keys and she moved towards him and he saw over her shoulder the almost-dark sky and the tiny lights.

"Come here," she said. She held him, and her voice, muffled in his collar, came to him from some other place: "This is my chance. I want this to work." At the door, she said, "You can stay, we'll watch a movie," but he was past the threshold aiming for the elevator and she sang out, "I'll pick up the car tomorrow morning, all right?"

Downstairs he climbed into his mother's Nissan and stared out through the windshield. A couple, both dressed in black, crossed in front of him and passed on. He drove around by himself for an hour, criss-crossing the centre of the city, stopping to buy cigarettes at one point and catching sight of a group of Squeegee kids from school who hung out by the Gas Station Theatre. He saw Crystal, the lover of Baudelaire, holding hands with one of the boys. She was tossing her heavy mane sideways as she talked. Mason drove on, down Corydon and past Bar Italia where Turbine liked to go, pretending that he was both an artist and good at pool, a yellow Gitane dangling from his mouth. He eventually wound his way back to

Wellington and parked close to the Rehabilitation Centre for Children. He walked down to the back of the hospital and climbed the metal ladder to the roof. Found himself sitting with his feet dangling over the edge, looking out towards the river. He smoked a cigarette and when he was done he spun it out into the darkness; a flaring arc and then nothing. He thought about his mother, sitting in her new place, away from his father and him and Danny. She might be bathing right now, or folding her clothes, or sitting out on the balcony looking out over the river. Maybe she would think about him. He lit another cigarette and thought that if he had been brave he would have stopped by Lena's. Or called her and said, "Hi, Lena. I have a car and I'd like to take you out for a while." He considered this and then put the idea away. He lay back against the tarred roof and looked up at the inkiness of the sky.

Over the following weeks, Mason got into the habit of borrowing his mother's car. Sometimes he just drove aimlessly, once he parked on the street across from the Schellendal house and he watched for Lena or her sisters but saw nothing. He hadn't seen Turbine at school in the last week so one night, on a Friday, he phoned him. Turbine's mother answered and when Mason asked to speak to Turbine there was a long silence. Finally, he heard her speaking to someone else and then she came back to the phone and asked, "Who is it?"

"Mason Crowe. I'm a friend from school."

A shorter silence this time and finally Turbine answered.

"What's going on?" Mason asked.

Turbine's voice was quiet and his speech was less quick. He said that his parents were taking him out of school and sending him to a boarding school in Ottawa.

Mason waited for an explanation and when it didn't come, he asked, "What for?"

"Huh, well. My parents were out of town last weekend and I had that party, remember, and the condo got trashed? Where were you?"

"I couldn't make it. I had stuff. You know. Sorry."

"No, hey, that's fine. The party was amazing but really you didn't miss much. Anyway, my parents want some reformation in my life and it's not happening here, so Ottawa is supposed to cure me."

"Jesus."

"I'm leaving tomorrow." Turbine laughed and then he stopped laughing and said, "My parents have clout. They got me into this fucking boarding school. I have to wear a uniform. All-boys."

"No way. You poor shit." Mason was trying to be nonchalant, but he was also thinking about how hard it would be for Turbine, and he was feeling sorry for him. "I guess I'll miss you," he said.

"You want to come over and give me a hug?" Turbine snorted through his nose to indicate that he wasn't being serious.

"We could meet at the rehab hospital," Mason said. "Have a last ritual something. Or we could go to a party. There's one at Cindy Duong's."

"My parents won't let me out." Turbine paused and then said, "Hey, how are things with that Schellendal girl? Lena, right?"

"Yeah. Yeah. Lena."

"Very nice, Mason. You have taste."

"I guess. I just never had much luck."

"And now?" Turbine laughed.

Mason considered the question and then he said, "I feel lucky."

Turbine said that he felt lucky, too. Then he said, "I figure good things will happen to me." They talked a bit more and then Turbine said he had to go. He said that he would phone Mason in a few weeks. Let him know what was up. They could e-mail maybe. Then they said goodbye.

After Mason hung up he thought about Turbine and then he thought about Lena and what he'd said about Lena, about feeling lucky. He left the house and got into his mother's car. Finally, he went to Cindy Duong's house. He drove by the house and saw the lights on, kids standing and drinking and smoking on the front lawn. It was a big house. From the upstairs balcony a boy leaned over the parapet and called out. Mason drove around the block, parked, and walked back towards the house. He moved past the gauntlet of football players and drama queens and entered a large house that was well on the road to being destroyed. A young boy with long hair hung on to a massive chandelier from which dangled a bra, a sock, a pink shirt, boxer shorts, and an orange skirt that reminded Mason of Lena. He left the apelike creature who, on the verge of letting go, was calling for help, and he entered the inner room, where he found Gary Kessle, a boy from one of his classes, drinking tequila with a girl half his size. The girl was chattering in Spanish and Gary was nodding and taking deep breaths and exhaling slowly.

"María," Gary said, and grinned stupidly. He moved his hand in tiny circles as if feeling for something.

"*Hola*," María said. She looked at Mason. She licked at the salt on her wrist, drank quickly from a small glass, and then sucked at a lime.

"María's from Santiago," Gary said. "She's very good."

Mason looked down at the dark part in María's hair and backed out of the kitchen. As he left, he poured himself a glass of Smirnoff and soda. He stood in the large front room. A boy in a Maple Leafs jersey stood at the top of the stairs and silently fell backwards. His large body knocked out part of the banister and he came to rest in the foyer, his head lying on the tile floor. Kids stepped over and around him.

Mason danced, briefly and for no particular reason, with a girl who looked barely thirteen. She was chubby and wore a very short skirt. Amy. She pretended to be drunk and held onto Mason's neck and rubbed her nose against his jaw and ground her hips against his. He held his half-full glass behind her back and tried not to spill.

"I know you," Amy said. She pressed her breasts against his rib cage. "You're Rosemary Schellendal's sister's boyfriend. Rosemary's in my class."

Mason reached his glass over Amy's head and drank. She looked up at him. "Sorry," Mason said, and he freed himself and wandered back into the kitchen. In the art studio – a beautiful glassed-in area off the kitchen which held an easel and a firing oven and a long table with pastel drawings and half-finished oil canvases – a girl was standing on top of one of the paintings and she was dancing and taking off her clothes as boys and girls gathered below her and chanted. The girl stumbled and a tall boy caught her and pushed her back up onto the table. A wide-faced blond-haired girl near Mason stamped her feet and hollered and tossed an arm over her boyfriend's shoulder and kissed him on the mouth. The girl on the table took off her shirt. She reached behind her back and unclipped her bra and let it drop. Mason stepped back and looked away. He caught sight of Sadia Chahal's face at the entrance to the studio. Sadia saw him and turned to go. Mason slipped back through the kitchen and caught up to Sadia beneath the chandelier, now without the hanging boy.

"That was stupid," Mason said. He was walking beside Sadia, brushing up against her shoulder. She exited the house and he kept up with her as she cut across the lawn out towards the road. Mason asked her if she was alone and she said she was. "I came with some friends from school, but they left. You've got a car?"

He said he did. He gestured down the street.

"You have plans?" she asked, and the way she asked it indicated that she had none, and Mason said he could drive her somewhere if she liked.

"I'd like," she said.

When they were in the car Mason became more aware of Sadia: her sharp nose, the outline of her jaw, and her small shoulders. She was wearing jeans and a short tight top. As he drove the air came in through the open window and she held her long hair back from her face with her right hand. He saw the angle of her bent arm and he said, understanding the callousness of the question, but wanting to ask it, "Your sister. Seeta. How is she?"

Sadia looked at Mason. "Of course," she said. And then she looked out the window and turned back to him and said, "She's changed. Does whatever Ajit says. He's selling RVs and he wears a suit and polishes his shoes every night. He's not a philosopher. My parents don't like him."

Mason nodded, as if this were a kind of justice. "They didn't like me either. There was a time, and you're gonna think this is weird, but there was a time when I believed that I would marry your sister. I pictured us in a little apartment downtown and she'd work or go to university and I'd have graduated from high school and be going to university too."

"That's not weird. Impossible, but not weird. I used to imagine living with Mr. Anthony, the woods teacher. Whenever I was in class and working at this little wooden urn I was building, he'd come over to the band saw or the lathe and show me something and try to look down my top and stupid me, I thought it'd be fun to get pervy with him."

Mason tried to picture Sadia with Mr. Anthony. It wasn't easy.

Sadia said, "Seeta's happy, though. She's coming to visit next week. You could see her if you want."

Mason said that he wasn't sure. "What would we talk about? Tennis? Danny? Your father's rake?"

"Hah, Seeta told me about that." She gave a quick snort and pushed a fist lightly against Mason's shoulder. Mason drove on. He sensed the evening closing in on him: the few minutes dancing with chubby Amy; the girl on the table unclasping her bra; even this moment here, sitting beside Sadia Chahal, pretending it meant something but wishing for more than this. He was suddenly and fiercely aware of Lena's presence out there somewhere and he wondered if he should get rid of Sadia, drop her off at home, and go find Lena.

And then Sadia, who had been looking out the window, sat up and said, as if she understood Mason's thoughts, that she didn't want to go home. She wanted to be dropped off at Brenda Darby's house. She directed Mason and they ended up in a large gated area. The stone house, the grounds, the coach house, the metal sculptures. Sadia got out and poked her head back into the open door and asked Mason to wait. She disappeared and Mason waited. It was one in the morning. He was sitting in his mother's car, alone. Sadia reappeared. She ran down the sloping driveway, her heels slipping out sideways, and she called out in a fluted, whispery voice, "It's okay. Brenda's awake. Her parents are out. I called my mom and said I was spending the night here. Brenda says if you want, you can come in. We can go for a swim. They just got the pool going this weekend."

Mason was tired. He said he didn't have anything to wear. Sadia said Brenda's Dad would have something. Or her brother; she had an older brother. "Let's," she said, and she closed the door and walked away, looking back and waving for Mason to come. And so he joined her and, for several hours, the time between 1:30 and 5:30 on that Saturday morning, he let the richness of Brenda Darby and her life swallow him up. He hadn't met Brenda before. Sadia had explained that she went to a private school and observing her Mason figured that she knew about things he couldn't begin to guess at, but she let him come into her house and she said, "Hi, Mason," and handed him a pair of baggy black swimming trunks and told him to change in the downstairs bathroom. He rose from the basement, walked past a pool table and a steam room, and out onto the patio, where the milky pool lights revealed Brenda and Sadia floating on their backs, bodies shimmering. The green water, the dark sky, the strange bathing suit against his skin, the humid air, Brenda's soft slow voice, Sadia's dark narrow waist; he felt, for a moment, that he was hovering above the scene and watching a boy called Mason Crowe stand at the edge of a pool in which two girls swam. A sharp quick loneliness that he shook off. The pool was a bright hole. The warm water slid over his head and he sank into the silence, hearing the occasional echo of the girls talking above him. He swam alone, near the deep end, and then joined the girls on the deck where the three of them shared a joint. Again, he thought of Lena, but then the thought of her disappeared and he lay on his back and looked up at the sky. At some point Brenda served croissants and olives and grape jelly in tiny jars that crowded the plates. There was no alcohol because Brenda's father didn't allow drinking and swimming. Brenda said this and smiled at Mason. She was wearing a green-and-white-striped two-piece and only once, when she was walking away from him towards the house to get more croissants, did Mason study her body.

She was slightly thick-waisted and she had a small bum that made her look oddly proportioned. Before Brenda came back out onto the deck, Sadia said, "Isn't she gorgeous," and Mason said, "Yes, she is," though it was not a beauty he wanted to hold in his hands. She was rich and refined and Mason saw that this was the life his mother wanted and now had. Brenda was polite, asked Mason questions, not too personal, and she paid attention to him, and when he went back into the pool he saw Brenda and Sadia sitting and talking and laughing and he knew that he was not in danger, and that the night would not end badly.

When the sky began to lighten, Mason changed back into his clothes. He said goodbye to Brenda, and Sadia walked him out to the driveway. She had put on a dark bathrobe and as she tiptoed barefoot beside him she touched his arm and said that she'd had fun and that it might be nice to see each other again. She pushed her wet hair back with one hand and said too loudly, "We could even play tennis."

Mason was standing beside his mother's car. Sadia's left foot was close to his runner. He looked at her small toes, the slim ankle. The bathrobe made her look older and more vulnerable. "Very funny," Mason said.

Her head moved sideways and she stepped backwards. "I'm very serious. I'd like that. I could play on Tuesday."

"Okay. It will have to be late, about seven o'clock. I still read to Mr. Ferry after school."

"Good. Great. I'll wait for you." She lifted a hand and then let it drop and then said goodbye.

On Tuesday he picked her up at her house and when the door opened Seeta was standing there. She looked out into the evening shadows and she said, "Mason?" She was plainer, everything about her was less defined. Mason said, "Hi, Seeta," and he held out his hand. She looked at it and leaned forward as she shook his hand lightly, limply. Her hand felt the same; a cool silkiness. Marriage hadn't killed her completely.

"Who are you looking for?" Seeta asked. She seemed worried.

"Oh, oh," Mason said. "I came here for Sadia. You thought I came to see you? God, no. I'm sorry. Sadia and I have plans."

"Do you?" Seeta studied Mason's head and his chest and his legs. She said, "You look the same." She smiled slightly as she turned away and called out for Sadia and then she looked back at Mason and said, "Well," and, "Nice to see you again." Then she walked into the other room and Mason never saw her again.

He told Sadia later, as they crossed the railroad tracks and cut down the embankment towards the tennis courts, that Seeta had seemed different. He said that it was weird and depressing to think of her as married. "Is she happy?" he asked.

"I told you the other night that she was happy," Sadia said. "Anyway, let's not talk about her. C'mon," and she pulled Mason out onto the court.

Though they played several more times over the following week, the ease of the previous Friday night at Brenda's had disappeared. Sadia seemed awkward. Once, they talked about Brenda, and Mason tried to explain how he felt, the possibility of some other life, did she ever feel that, he asked, but she didn't understand, thought that he might be saying he liked Brenda Darby. He said he didn't. He liked her but not like that. And even if he did, she was rich and she outclassed him.

It was a humid day and some thunder in the distance threatened rain so they walked up Academy towards Mason's house. A quick, hard downpour forced them to take shelter in a coffee shop. It was the same place Mason had sat and waited for Lena as she passed by on the way to voice lessons. They sat, Sadia and he, at the middle table.

Sadia prattled on about school and Brenda and how Brenda had thought Mason was great. That after Mason had left, they'd watched a Fellini film. "Brenda said Fellini was amazing. The film was called *La Strada*, and it was about a woman who joins a circus and falls in love with a tightrope walker who is murdered. The woman is very odd-looking. Not pretty at all. Almost stupid." Mason listened to Sadia and thought that she could be describing herself. Not that he minded.

Mason was facing the window. The rain had stopped and he could see the sidewalk and the people passing by and then Lena Schellendal was standing there, on the outside looking in. She was reading a poster that had been pasted against the window. Was she perhaps coming from her singing lessons? Was she going to her singing lessons again? At first Mason didn't recognize her and then he said, out loud, "Lena." Sadia turned and looked and then she faced Mason again and smiled. Out on the sidewalk, Lena swung away from the window and disappeared. Later, he left Sadia at the corner, even promised to call and arrange some more tennis, but he knew he wouldn't. Lena's shadow still fell across his world.

And then one day at school, in the hallway, Rosemary gave Mason a note. It was from Lena. She wrote that she was better. She was going to be baptized in two weeks, on a Sunday morning, and she wanted him to come. She said that this was the last thing she would ask of him. Mason read the note and then asked Rosemary if she knew what the note said. Rosemary said she didn't. "I'm just the go-between."

Mason showed it to her and asked, "What would you do? I mean, several months ago she told me it was over and now she wants me to come to her baptism. Is she okay?"

"Maybe she's worried you're in love with someone else."

They were standing in the hall between classes and there were kids flowing by on either side of them and Rosemary was looking up at Mason as if everything was absolutely clear.

"Did she tell you that?" Mason asked. "Because I'm not. I think about Lena all the time."

Rosemary said, "She saw you with Sadia Chahal. She figured things out. Or maybe she didn't. Maybe she was wrong. Anyway, you don't have to give the answer to me. Okay?" Rosemary said she had to go to class and she handed the note back to Mason and turned and walked away.

He waited to see Lena again, outside his house or walking to school, but she didn't appear. Her note, the sight of her handwriting, had left him hopeful. He was pleased that she might have suffered some pain when she saw him with Sadia. One afternoon he skipped out of school and went to her house and knocked and waited, aware of the silence in the neighbourhood and the sound of his knuckles against the door. There was no answer so he knocked again. Nobody came to the door. He walked away then, looking up at Lena's bedroom window to see if she might be watching him. The house was empty.

He called her that night and Rosemary answered and when he asked for Lena, Rosemary said, "Sure," and put the phone down. It took a long time for Lena to pick up. Mason could hear voices in the Schellendal house. Two girls and then a man and then it was quiet and then someone said, "Did he?" and a woman, Mrs. Schellendal perhaps, said, "That's not the point."

Then Lena picked up and said, "Hey."

"Hi. It's me," Mason said.

"I know. Rosemary said."

"Is this okay? That I phoned? I came by your house this afternoon but nobody answered so I thought I'd phone."

"This afternoon?" she asked. "I don't know. Really? Maybe I was out."

Mason thought that she sounded different. The words floated away from her. He said, "So, you're going to be baptized, too."

There was silence until she said, "I wasn't the best person before, was I? A change might be nice."

"I don't know," Mason said. "I liked you. I still do. I love the sound of your voice. I've told you that, haven't I? Your voice rolls and it's low and husky."

"You still do, eh?" she said. She paused, sighed, and finished, "That's really nice, Mason. I mean it. That's a terribly nice thing for you to say." Then she said she hoped she'd see him on Sunday and she said goodbye and hung up.

When the day of her baptism arrived he walked down through Lena's neighbourhood and past her house, which was quiet, and on towards the church which was on Portage Avenue, across from Rae and Jerry's Steak House, at the edge of Omand's Creek. It was a bright sunny day. Joggers and cyclists passed by. Dogs on leashes, dragging their owners. Mason entered the church and sat near the back. He saw Rosemary and Lena's parents and the other sisters, sitting near the front. Margot had her hair up in a tight bun and she kept turning to look behind her. Lena was seated along the side, with three other solemn-looking girls. The service was long, with much rising and singing and praying, and Mason kept his eye on Lena, who never once turned to survey the crowd. Her profile was sharp. Then, between the singing of two songs, Lena and the three other girls stood and left the sanctuary. They passed down the side aisle towards the back and Mason could see the shape of her head quite clearly and the outline of her jaw. She was chewing gum.

The baptism took place at the end of the service. There was a tank of water above the choir pews and a man in a black robe descended into it. The water lapped against the glass. The man turned and held out his hand and a young girl appeared from behind a curtain and stepped down into the water. It wasn't Lena. The older man held the girl as if he were whispering into her ear. He put his hand against the back of the young girl's head and asked her three questions, to all of which she said yes, and then he dunked her backwards into the water and pulled her back up and she rose, holding her nose, her hair falling behind her like a waterfall. Then it was Lena's turn and the ritual was the same but this time Mason sat up. He saw Lena's left ear, her long neck, the lack of her shape in the large gown she wore, her profile as she looked straight ahead and answered the questions, her blank face as she fell backwards and rose again, exiting the tank, the black robe clinging to her body, her ineffectual attempts to pull the wet cloth away from her body. A soloist, tall and beautiful, sang the baptismal song from the movie *O Brother, Where Art Thou?* Mason thought it was quite humorous.

After the service, Lena caught Mason just outside the door as he was leaving. They stood at the edge of the parking lot, on the grass, and looked at each other. "You came," she said.

"I said I would." He wanted to reach up and touch her wet hair. The sun fell onto the side of her head. The sounds of normal life – a dog barking, a child crying out – drifted from across the creek.

"Still, I didn't think you'd come. You didn't have to. I wasn't my best on the phone the other day." She was wearing a dress that was too big; it made her look childish. She wore no makeup and the many earrings she usually wore had been reduced to a single pair. She clutched a white purse, one of those thin vinyl handbags with a snap. She looked right at him and said, "I've missed you. There were times when I thought that I should call you." She pushed the heel of her left hand against Mason's shoulder. "That's why I sent that note with Rosemary. It seemed safe."

"Are you saying you'd like to see me again?" Mason asked. He wanted to take Lena's hand, but just then the door behind Lena opened and an old woman wobbled out on a walker. She paused, breathing hard, and studied Mason.

Lena looked down at her purse. "It's possible." Then she said, "You know what I wish? I wish you'd see the error of your ways. You could become a Christian, you know. It's for everybody." Lena looked around as if hoping someone might witness her speech. The blue-haired lady and the walker were approaching.

The old woman paused beside Lena and said, "Lena Schellendal," and she took Lena's hand and patted it with her own mottled hand and said, "Good for you," and then she looked at Mason and said, "What a good-looking boyfriend, Lena."

Lena was still attached to the old woman's hands, which were now sliding up and down her forearm. Mason saw the tendons of the old woman's hands. He was looking down onto her thin hair. "What's your name?" she asked.

Mason told her.

The woman looked at Lena and said, "Mason. That's very nice," and then she patted Lena's hand one last time and stabbed at her walker until she'd grasped it and she shuffled onwards.

"She's so sweet," Lena said.

She bit her lower lip and took Mason's hands. She said, "My problem was I was trying to forget myself. Before. So, I was defiant and desperate and lost myself in debauchery."

Mason smiled slightly. She did not sound like Lena. He said, "Was it my fault then? The debauchery?"

A brief smile, then it disappeared. "Of course not."

More people had begun to exit the church. Lena let go of Mason's hands and stepped back slightly. "So," she said.

Mason saw, just over Lena's shoulder, the Schellendal family walking towards them. Mr. Schellendal stopped to talk to someone. Rosemary stood off to the side; she gave a slight wave. Emily was clutching her mother's arm. Mr. Schellendal shook hands with the man he had been talking to, swung back towards Mason and Lena, and came up beside them. He put his arm around Lena and she looked up at him and said, "Daddy." She said, "You remember Mason, don't you?"

Mr. Schellendal nodded. Lena's mother came up and said, "Hello, Mason," and then she turned her back to him and hugged her daughter and said, "Lena, we're so proud of you." "Come," Mr. Schellendal said, and he gathered up his family. As Lena walked away, her father's arm around her, she looked back over her shoulder at Mason and it seemed, in that moment, that the baptism, the speech on debauchery and desperation, the religious bragging, all of this was Lena crying out.

One day, about three weeks after her baptism, Lena went to Mason's house and she stood and looked for signs of life, movement, perhaps Mason leaving for school or returning, but she saw nothing. She went up the walk and knocked on the door and turned to look out at the street. When the door opened Danny was standing there. Lena said, "Oh," and Danny said, "You're Lena."

Lena hesitated, and said, "How do you know?"

"I know. Mason's talked about you."

"Is he here?"

"At school," Danny said. He was wearing jeans and he had no shirt on and Lena saw his mouth, his shoulders, and the hair at his belly. He stepped backwards and told her to come in.

She hesitated and said, "I can come back. I'm not supposed to be here."

"Why shouldn't you be here?" Danny asked. "Where else could you be?"

"Out looking for work. Doing something constructive. Certainly not visiting Mason's brother." She stepped into the house and followed Danny into the kitchen.

"You want something?" he asked. "Juice? Coffee?"

Lena said that she didn't need anything, that she was just walking by and thought Mason might be there and she had to go right away, she was actually on her way to apply for a job. She paused and looked at Danny as he bent into the open fridge. He was barefoot. He reappeared holding a container of juice and poured himself a glass. He said, "I like to meet Mason's friends. I've been gone for a while, in Montreal, and I've lost touch with people, so it's nice to have someone to talk to."

He opened the patio door and stepped outside onto the deck and called back at her to follow. She did this, found herself standing beside him and stepped away and sat on a plastic chair, beside which there was a wrought-iron table with a glass top. She could see Danny's feet through the glass.

He said, "I'm supposed to cut the lawn today. That's my job. It's shitty when you're so aimless and broke that your father has to tell you what to do. I used to have a good job and a great car and now I don't. Smoke?" He pulled out a Cellophane bag and some papers and rolled himself a joint and lit up, pulled on it, and then handed it to Lena. She looked at it and said that she shouldn't really, she was working on this new life for herself. Danny grinned and said, "Up to you." Lena raised her eyebrows. She reached out, took the joint, and said, "Here we go." She took a drag and handed it back to Danny. They passed it back and forth in silence until Danny had stubbed it in the ashtray.

A bird hopped along the branches of an apple tree and Danny said, "There's a family of wrens that come back here every year. I'd like to build a house for them."

"That's so sweet," Lena said. She slipped out of her boots and removed her socks. "Hot," she said, and put her feet on a free chair. Danny looked at her, then at her feet. He said, "Does Mason ever talk about me?"

She was aware of Danny's size, the bulk of him. "My swarthy brother," Mason had said once. She giggled. Time slowed. "No," she said, "Why would he?"

"Because I'm his brother."

"What would he say?" Lena squinted into the sun. It was hotter now and she was sweating between her breasts and under her arms.

Danny shrugged. He stood and went through the patio door and when he came back he was carrying two beers and he handed one to Lena.

"I shouldn't," she said. "If I smoke and drink I get sick. Once I thought I was going to die." She opened the beer and drank and looked at Danny who was looking at her.

"You've got great feet," he said.

She looked at her feet. "Yeah," she said. "I know." She giggled again and lifted a foot and held the cool bottom of the beer bottle against her left arch. Then she said, "Does Mason ever talk about me?"

Danny said he did. "At first I thought he talked too much about you but now that you're sitting across from me I understand what there is to talk about."

"Fuck off," Lena said. "What does he say? That I'm crazy? That I tried to jump off a bridge?"

"He never told me that. Is it true?"

"It was true. Still is true, I guess. It doesn't go away. That was another life, though sometimes I think it still is my life. I woke from a dream the other night where I was sitting on the bridge again. Does life repeat itself? Can exactly the same thing happen to you today that happened a year ago?"

"A memory of something?"

"No, an actual event. Something real that happened."

"It could, but it wouldn't be the same."

"It *could* be the same."

Danny drank from his beer and studied Lena. He said, "If you say so." He leaned forward and touched Lena's instep. Ran his finger along it and then sat back.

"Don't," Lena said.

"I'm sorry," Danny said. He shrugged. Pushed a hand through his hair and puffed up his cheeks and blew out. "Jesus."

"What's with you Crowe boys, taking the Lord's name in vain?"

Danny shook his head and finished his beer. "Weird," he said.

"The thing is," Lena said, "You don't just touch someone without asking. It's pretty personal. You know?"

"Oh, may I touch your foot?"

"No," Lena said and she grinned and Danny looked at her and he began to laugh and then Lena said she was hungry so Danny took her into the kitchen and slipped her into an apron, tying it behind her, just at the small of her back where her short shirt met her jeans and she felt him fumbling with the bow. Then he stood and opened the cupboard and said, "We'll make a coconut curry. What do you think? Do you like a coconut curry?" He directed her to open the cans of coconut milk while he chopped the tenderloin. Then he spilled the milk into the wok, and mixed in the paste. Lena stood by the stove and watched while Danny moved about the kitchen. Once he brushed hips with Lena, and another time, passing by her on the way to the fridge, he touched her waist lightly with both hands and said, "Sorry," and she said nothing.

They ate out on the patio. The dish was spicy and Lena drank a lot of water as she ate. They were sitting on green plastic chairs at the glass-topped table and Lena was aware of Danny's hands and of his nipples, which were hairless and dark and small. She wanted to push a finger against his chest. She looked away and then back at Danny.

The front door banged then and, turning around, Lena said, "Who is that?"

"Somebody," Danny said.

Then Mr. Crowe walked into the kitchen, stepped out onto the patio, surveyed the scene, and said, "Hi, Lena."

"Hello, Mr. Crowe."

He looked around. "Where's Mason?"

"At school," Danny said.

Mr. Crowe looked at Danny and then over at Lena and then he nodded as if in agreement or as if he recognized the possibility of something, and he asked Lena, "How are you?"

"I'm good, Mr. Crowe. Really good." She put her feet back on the patio deck and sat up straight.

"Great," Mr. Crowe said. He lifted a hand slightly and in that motion, a polite gesture that indicated both shyness and confusion, Lena recognized Mason. Mr. Crowe turned back to Danny and suddenly became all business. He said he was leaving and wouldn't be back for a few hours and he reminded Danny to mow the lawn and clean up the kitchen and, if he had time, to paint the soffits on the garage. Then he dipped his head towards Lena and he left.

Lena waited until he was gone and then she said, "Oh, God, he thinks I'm a slut."

"Nooo, I don't think so. My dad doesn't think along those lines," Danny said.

"He thinks that, I can tell." Lena reached into her backpack and pulled out her cigarettes. She lit one and said, "Mason'll be home soon and then what? He'd be hurt if he knew we did this." She waved at the table.

Danny said, "What's so special about my brother?"

Lena did not hesitate. She tapped at her head and said, "He knows and understands me. And he's patient. For the longest time he watched me when I went to voice lessons. He didn't say anything, he didn't chase me, he just sat and watched."

"So, you like to be watched."

"I liked it that it was him watching me. If it'd been a freak like Randy Burt I would have been scared. Mason Crowe, no problem."

Danny pushed his empty bottle onto the table. Lena saw the hair under his arms.

"What about me?" he asked. "If I watched you?"

"It wouldn't be your idea, would it?" Lena said.

"So, you like enigmatic, good-looking boys spying on you?" He grunted. "Go figure." Then he stood and he said he'd be right back and he went into the house. Lena sat and watched the wrens. She heard Danny moving around in the house. When he came back he had a pencil and a sketchbook. He sat down and he opened his book and began to draw.

Lena said, "You're so obvious, Danny."

Danny paused. He should have been embarrassed but he wasn't. He said, "So are you," and then he said, "*Esse* is *percipe*."

Lena went, "Whooaaa, who's smart," but she was also content with the situation; the bit of Latin, the heat of the sun on her head, Danny's eyes studying her. A fly had found the leftover curry on the plate and it crawled about, rubbing its legs. Lena watched this for a while. Then the fly flew away and came back with a friend. Lena listened to the scratch of Danny's pencil. She saw herself as Danny would see her: the forehead, the line of the jaw, the mouth. At one point she said, "This makes me sleepy," but Danny did not answer. One fly climbed onto the other's back. They sat like that for a while and then flew off. Danny kept drawing her. When he was done he closed the sketchbook and laid it on the table. Lena waited for Danny to ask if she wanted to see what he'd drawn, so that she could say she didn't care, that she didn't like to look at drawings of herself, but he never asked and because he never asked she found herself wanting to see.

At the door later, as she was leaving, Danny said, "You can come back any time."

Lena said that she couldn't come back. "Even if I wanted to I couldn't. Not that I didn't have a good time. I did. It's just kind of odd. You're Mason's brother and I'm Mason's girl-friend, or was, and I'm sitting on the deck and we're talking and all of a sudden you're drawing me and that's way too strange. If I were a slut I'd come back and you could draw me naked or something. But I'm not."

"I wasn't suggesting anything," Danny said. He was standing too close to her.

"Yes, you were. You're probably thinking I owe you a hug or a kiss, just because you gave me lunch."

Danny raised his hands in defence. "Hey, I don't know what you want. Okay? I had fun. You're great. I certainly don't see any *madness.*"

"Don't you? Well." She hesitated and then asked, "You going to tell Mason I was here? I mean if you want to, it's fine. I was just wondering."

"No. No I'm not."

Lena turned to go, but then she faced Danny again and said, "Okay," and then she left.

*M*ason loved the Winnipeg sky. It was a wide clean blanket laid out over a flat sprawling city. There was more sky than earth, and birds overhead were smudges; jet trails appeared like chalk lines and were then erased. Mason, walking home from school on a bright day in June, was aware of the silver dome above him, but was also thinking about cake, and eggs, and if there were enough eggs in the fridge to bake a white cake for Lena, who was coming over in an hour, at 5:00 p.m. after she'd seen her doctor, and Mason was wondering if, when he got home and there weren't eggs, he'd have time to go out and buy some.

Over the last while, he had seen her several times. Once, she was sitting alone at Cousins and he had stood by her table and they had talked briefly and easily, and another time he had seen her on the street. He had been walking with a friend, it was a warm day, and he had sensed her presence and turned and there she was on the other side of the street. She saw him and waved and then she turned the corner and disappeared. Another time he'd left his house to go see his mother and suddenly she was walking beside and behind him slightly so that he had to turn and look back at her. She was wearing pants that were too short so the bottoms swung around her ankles and she was slightly stooped, as if carrying a heavy load. She wore a thick jacket, in spite of the weather. Her face was thin and pale.

"Here I am," she said.

"Hey, Lena," Mason said.

"I'm walking," she said. "My doctor says I should walk and of course I obey my doctor. She's quite smart. The other day she asked if I saw myself as an exhibitionist and I said that I didn't know. Do you think I'm an exhibitionist?" She stumbled and caught herself and giggled, "I'm clumsy. I know that."

Mason wanted to take her hand but wasn't sure if she would let him. He looked down at her arm and then at her feet and he said, "I never thought that. You're curious, that's all."

"Really? Do you think so?" They walked on and up to a park which bordered the river and they went into the park and followed the footpath. Mason said that his mother had moved out and was living with Aldous Schmidt, the man they had seen her with once in the shopping mall. He was going over there now. "Do you want to come?" he asked. "My mother's home but she wouldn't mind."

Lena said, "No, I don't want to see anyone. Not today. Maybe tomorrow." Then she said, "Rose says she sees you in school. That you seem happy."

"Sometimes," Mason said. "Yesterday afternoon I wasn't happy. Right now I am."

She lifted her face and for a moment it was radiant. She said, "Ten or twenty years from now, when you're married, you might regret doing what you did with me."

"That's stupid," Mason said.

She touched Mason's hair. "Your hair is getting longer. That's good, I don't want you to be dull." Then she said, "I have to go," and she turned and walked back along the sidewalk, her clownish pants spinning at her ankles.

The next day Mason phoned her in the evening, to ask her to come over, and she said, "The time is late," and her voice went up as if this were a question, and then she said, "How about Friday, around five?"

And so, thinking of cake, Mason boldly hurried home towards the girl who had clapped her hands over his eyes.

There were eggs. He cracked three into a bowl and added sugar and scalded milk and vanilla, and then he mixed in flour and salt and beat the batter and poured it into a pan. When the cake was in the oven he made an icing and tasted it and added more icing sugar. Then he went downstairs and took off his T-shirt. He sniffed his underarms and put on more deodorant. Looked in the mirror. There were a few hairs growing near his nipples and he wished it weren't so. In his closet he found a shirt that Lena liked and he put it on. When he came back upstairs Lena was inside the front door calling out. She lifted her nose and sniffed and said, "Cake." She was wearing corduroy pants that were the right length and a loose white top with three buttons near the neck. She was barefoot in her sandals. She had braided her hair and had pulled the braids to the back of her head and attached them there.

"I like that," Mason said and he reached out and traced one braid.

"Rose did it. It's my pulled-together look. Sort of, 'Hi, I'm a hippie and I'm earthy and grow bean sprouts in my bedroom and I'm not hard.' What kind of cake?" She went up on tiptoes and pushed her nose against Mason's ear. "Hmmm."

Mason held his hands in the air. He said, "White cake. My mother taught me how to make it." He took Lena into the kitchen and poured her tea and handed her a piece of cake on a plate and he sat across from her and said, "It's strange, kind of like we're starting all over again, you know?"

"You like that?" Lena's mouth was full of cake. "I was wondering if you'd think that or if I was thinking that. I was reading Dr. Seuss yesterday, *Oh, the Places You'll Go*, and I realized that you should read it. It's really philosophical, about being alone and choosing the right path. I'm not sure what I'm saying." She nibbled at her cake and shrugged.

Mason took her hand and asked, "Is this okay?"

Lena said that it was fine. She liked it. Then she said, "You seeing anyone?"

"No, I'm not seeing anyone." Mason thought he might have answered too quickly. Two of Lena's fingertips had Band-Aids.

"I was just wondering," Lena said.

"You saw me with Sadia Chahal, didn't you? On that rainy day. I saw you looking in through the window of the Bagel Shop and it was like I was drifting back in time. Not drifting. Flying. I saw you there. I ran into Sadia and we stopped for a drink. That's all."

"You didn't plan it?"

"Actually, we were playing tennis. I used to play with her sister, Seeta, and all of a sudden I was playing with Sadia. She asked me to. I said, Sure."

"All of a sudden." Lena was smiling. "Did she kiss you?"

"No. Why do you think that?"

"Girls like you. I know what I know and I know what girls like and they like you. It's okay if she kissed you."

Mason was about to argue but he didn't get a chance because Danny entered the kitchen at that moment and he stood near the table and said, "I'm Danny, Mason's big brother." He held out his hand.

"I'm Lena." She was looking right at Danny's face as she shook his hand. She didn't look over at Mason.

"What do you want?" Mason said.

"Just saying hi," Danny said.

"It's all right," Lena said, "I know about you. You're a chef."

"Was," Danny said. "I was in Montreal working and one night I had a sniff of my own mortality and so I thought, 'I gotta get outta here.' Now I hang around here and I draw. You want me to draw you some time, I'll do that."

Mason said, "He doesn't draw. He talks about drawing. There's a difference."

"Runs in the family," Danny said. "One of us wants to be a poet, the other an artist."

"Mason's a good poet," Lena said.

Danny looked Lena up and down. "You a fan, or are you just loyal?"

"Like Mason's dog, you mean?" Lena asked, and she went "arf arf," and Mason wasn't sure if she was mocking herself, or him, or Danny, or if she was trying to please Danny in some way. Mason put his feet on the only available chair and waited for Danny to leave. He said, "Don't you have to mow the lawn, or something?"

"Listen to him," Danny said. He nodded at Lena and then he wandered off into the living room where he turned on the TV. Mason said they should go to his bedroom. Downstairs, Lena lay on Mason's bed, her arms like wings beside her head. Mason sat on a chair, his feet against the bed, and said, "Danny's a prick."

"Forget your brother." She put her foot on top of Mason's foot. "Talk to me," she said.

Mason saw the shape of her knee through her pants. He said, "Yesterday, at school, Shauna Guard checked out my aura. She used two wire hangers and walked backwards away from me and when the hangers swung sideways that was where my happiness ended and my sadness began. I had fifty feet of happiness surrounding me. I was surprised because I've always thought I was dark and serious but now I find out I'm an optimist. I guess that's a good thing."

"Shauna Guard. I don't know her."

"She's in Grade 10 and thinks she's a radical. Wears McShit T-shirts and sticks padlocks through her earlobes."

Lena didn't seem to be listening. She sat up and touched Mason's foot, as if she were testing the temperature of an object. She was thinner now. Walking down the stairs earlier Mason had been following her and he'd noticed that her pants hung loose and her shoulders were bony. He wondered if her breasts were smaller and what they would feel like in his hands. His throat was tight.

"Things are still pretty fucked up," Lena said, holding his toe now. "I mean I don't have fifty feet of happiness like you. Maybe two feet. Some days, none. You're probably wondering, what's happening here? We gonna get naked, that sort of thing, but I'm still walking around with this big space between me and other people. I'm holding your toe but it doesn't mean anything. To me. To how I feel. It might as well be a rock or a piece of bread. Before, I would have been thrilled and I would have taken off your sock and sucked on your toe and you would have sucked on mine and I'd have had little bumps on the backs of my arms but now there's nothing." She paused, still holding Mason's toe.

He said, "You can choose. I choose you. What do you choose?"

"Aww, Mason." She let go of his toe and pulled him onto the bed with her and held his head to her chest. Mason closed his eyes and opened them again. Lena's rib cage moved up and down with her ragged breath.

"This is nice," he said, his voice muffled.

Lena let him go and he was aware of her cheek, her hair, and her ear. Neither spoke. For a long time they touched each other's faces. Once, Mason slipped a hand inside her top but Lena said, "No," and Mason said, "Okay."

Later, he walked her up to the corner by the steak house and they sat on the curb by the parking lot and they shared a cigarette. They said goodbye then, standing on the sidewalk. Mason had his hands in his pockets. Lena put her arm around his neck and tipped her forehead in against his shoulder.

"Sorry," she said.

Ms. Abendschade's pregnancy began to show. She wore longer and looser tops, though once, when she reached upwards to retrieve the string on the overhead screen, her belly flashed briefly and Mason saw the slight roundness near her navel and then it disappeared. She was suddenly less grumpy. *Crime and Punishment* was drawing to a close and the last unit of the year would be poetry, though she warned the students that it was like eating a strong cheese, you had to acquire a taste.

One afternoon, walking home from school, Mason saw Ms. Abendschade. They were both cutting through the grounds of St. Mary's and when she called out to him he stopped and waited for her. It was raining, a fine drizzle, and she carried her briefcase in her left hand, and with her right she clutched an umbrella. They walked on, side by side, and she tilted the umbrella upwards to protect half of Mason's head. She said, "I see you trespassing every day, along this path. How are you this afternoon?"

He said he was fine. He could have held out his hand to capture her breath.

"Good. Good. It's strange that I see you in the first class and then not at all for the rest of the day. The school's too big. I don't want to swell your swainish head but your class is definitely the highlight of my day. Not that *your* marks are great." She smiled. He noticed her teeth and tongue, her earlobe, and heard the rain hitting the umbrella. "But marks are so arbitrary, so necessary, which is unfortunate."

Mason said that most teachers loved marks, all those graphs and missed assignments and the median and the mean. Very black-and-white. They had reached the edge of the Academy grounds.

"Where are you going?" Ms. Abendschade asked.

Mason looked about. He said he was going up to the library, though this was not true and had just now entered his mind as an option because he knew that Ms. Abendschade lived in the Gates and the library was at the edge of the Gates and this would give him five more minutes beside her, listening to her voice rise into the afternoon air.

"Walk with me then," she said, and they crossed over the bridge and Mason waited for her to say something but she didn't and it was only when they arrived at the library that she said, "I heard about Lena Schellendal. I know you were her friend and I was wondering how she was."

They had stopped walking. She turned to face Mason. Up close like this Mason saw that her cheeks were rounder.

"She wasn't going to jump," Mason said. "I know guys who sit up there for fun."

"I don't know what she was going to do," Ms. Abendschade said. "I just heard the other day and I was shocked. Lena Schellendal was a lovely girl. So bright."

"She didn't die."

"Oh, of course not." She touched Mason's hand briefly. "Have you seen her?"

"Yes. A few times," Mason said. "She says she's better." The rain was running off the umbrella and hitting his back but he ignored it. Ms. Abendschade's stomach was a few inches from his body. Her breath mingled with his. She waved a hand out at the rain as if attempting to catch a few drops. She said, "Come to my apartment for a bit. It's just down the street in the Gates and it's wet out here. Would you like that?"

Mason said he'd be glad to come. Visions of drinks and a fireside chat about Joyce and Eliot while Ms. Abendschade touched her collarbone with a red nail, the trace of the lace of her bra, and, "So, Mason," she would say. "Sweet boy." They walked down the sidewalk to a large brick house and Ms. Abendschade showed him up the stairs to the third floor where he removed his shoes and jacket and stepped into an open space that was kitchen and bedroom and living room and den and against the far wall sat a piano and at the piano sat a tall long-haired man, fingers poised over the keys. Ms. Abendschade called out merrily to him that she had brought home a student, Mason Crowe, and she turned to Mason and said, "Meet my husband, Richard."

Richard came over and shook Mason's hand and said, "Hello, Mason, Liliane's talked about you." Mason had failed to fit his whole hand into Richard's and so the handshake was weak and sloppy and this bothered Mason.

Ms. Abendschade said, "I always talk about my favourite students." Richard kissed his wife on the cheek and lightly

touched her stomach, just below her breasts. He whispered a
few words in her ear and then excused himself and put on his
shoes and jacket and left the apartment. Mason watched him
go and heard Ms. Abendschade say that Richard played piano
in lounges late at night and so he slept in till noon and they
usually saw each other at dinner.

She crossed the hardwood floor and set a pot of milk on
the stove. The large window of the apartment looked out
across the river and Mason stood at the window and through
the clearing in the trees he could see Aldous's apartment, over
on Wellington, rising above all the others. He counted up
twelve and thought he saw his mother standing by the
window, holding a glass of something, and though he could
not be sure it did seem possible; and this possibility, the fact that
he was here and she was there at this moment, struck him as
strange, and he said to Ms. Abendschade, "My mother lives
over there. She lives with a man called Aldous Schmidt. A man
who she fell in love with."

Ms. Abendschade joined him at the window. Mason
pointed and Ms. Abendschade said, "Not your father, then."

"She left my father."

"Ohh. And your father, do you still live with him?"

Mason said that he did, though he sometimes visited his
mother and her boyfriend. "Aldous is rich," Mason said.
"My mother likes that."

Ms. Abendschade stepped away from window and walked
over to the sink. Mason moved around the apartment, looking
at the books and CDs, and the photographs that hung, framed,
on the wall. There were many shots of Ms. Abendschade and

her husband. In most of them Ms. Abendschade looked cheerful but in several she seemed pensive, almost unhappy, and he wondered about this. Ms. Abendschade called out to him and they sat at the kitchen table and drank hot chocolate. Ms. Abendschade poured cream into hers, stirred it with a spoon. She talked about Lena Schellendal again. She said she knew that Lena and Mason had been good friends. "Are you still?" she asked. Then she said, as if protecting him, "You don't have to answer."

"No, it's okay. I think we're friends, though I'm not sure. She's mixed-up these days."

"What do you mean? You're not sure about her, or you're not sure about yourself?"

"Both, I guess. I don't know. You don't want to hear about it."

"I don't mind. I wouldn't ask, otherwise. I'm not so old that I don't remember those tortured days of high school." She lifted her mug and drank and Mason was aware of her forehead and her dark eyes above the rim of her mug. She continued, "I teach Lena's sister, Rosemary. She's very bright, too. She doesn't have the same confidence that I saw in Lena when I taught her, but Rosemary sees things all in one swoop."

Mason looked at Ms. Abendschade.

Liliane.

Her hands were perfect.

She had a mole by her left eye.

She said that what she remembered about Lena Schellendal, and she didn't want this to sound like a eulogy or anything, she knew that Lena was very much alive and fine, but what she remembered was her wish to be seen. "I'm not saying that's a bad thing. We all want to be seen. It's just that some people not only want to be seen, they want to be recognized. They're afraid of anonymity. Is this too harsh?"

Mason shook his head.

As if passing a blessing over the drinks, she lifted a hand and she said, "Oh, I have something," and she stood and walked over to the bookshelf by the window. Mason watched her, saw her heels flashing. Her movements, everything about her, even the manner in which she approached a basic object like a bookshelf, exhibited boldness and certainty. She slipped a book from the shelf and walked back and handed it to Mason and said, "This is for you. I've often thought that you should have this, but I've never managed to get it to you. So here it is, finally. All writers should read it."

It was *Letters to a Young Poet*. Mason turned it over and read the back and then said, "I have nothing for you." As soon as he spoke he recognized how foolish this sounded but Ms. Abendschade seemed not to think so because she said that a gift was not given in expectation of getting something in return, a gift was simply that, a gift.

They talked some more of school and of books and Mason wanted to tell her how lucky he felt to be in her class and how he loved it when she talked about longing and regret and described the girl swinging her hair like a rope, and he wanted to ask her questions about Lena, about what Lena Schellendal might want from him and what he, Mason, should do about her, but he said none of this, and when he left her house he ended up at home by himself searching through the dictionary for the word *swainish*.

～

One Tuesday afternoon in June, as the light poured in through the south-facing windows, Mason asked Mr. Ferry about Rilke. Mr. Ferry lifted his head, as he always did when considering a question, and he said that Rilke was a melancholy boy whose mother dressed him as a girl. When he was nineteen he had an affair with a very cultured older woman who exposed him, among other things, to a Russian sentimentality that would lead to a religious vision for his poetry. Mr. Ferry paused and then he said that these days Rilke was particularly appreciated by university students, human beings who saw the world as full of opportunity and hope. "Like you, Mason."

Mason wondered how old the woman was that Rilke loved.

Mr. Ferry said, "I don't know if he loved her. That's another thing entirely. She was a libertine in her early thirties and her name was Salome and I have read that she was friends with Nietzsche and Freud." Then he said that he had a young woman, almost six feet tall, who was reading to him on Saturdays. "Her name is Cory. She studies philosophy and is very incisive and likes to argue. She took one of my books. Unamuno. But that's okay, I like the idea of her holding my book. And perhaps she will return it and it will carry her scent. She is nineteen. Almost *too* old. Do you know why Socrates loved the young? Because they smelled of eternity. Hah." He folded his hands in his lap.[17]

The calico cat, Minnie, appeared in the doorway, crossed the room and rubbed against Mr. Ferry's legs, and then disappeared. The book Mason held was a collection of letters from one obscure writer to another. When Mr. Ferry had handed him the book the previous week, they had covered, as they did every time Mason arrived, the news of the past few days. This took the form of Mr. Ferry asking questions and Mason answering. Over the year, Mason had revealed the skeleton of his life to Mr. Ferry: his mother and father; his mother's German lover; Danny leaving for Montreal; Lena's despair. Those were the larger moments. The smaller details, the secrets, he kept to himself. Not that Mr. Ferry didn't ask. When they talked about Lena, for example, he prodded Mason and asked him about Lena's voice, was it happy at the moment when she had told him, "I don't want to see you any more," or when she had met him in the street. How did he feel, talking to a girl who still, but might not have, existed. "Was that strange?" Mason didn't answer all of these questions. He felt that there was something perverted about Mr. Ferry, as if he got off on second-hand stories and the sadness

---

[17] Mr. Ferry loves the young, especially young girls, and, though he loves them as a blind voyeur and his love is unrequited and futile, it still pleases him. Mason, sitting quietly, wonders if Mr. Ferry masturbates to the smell of the book stolen and returned by the six-foot university student. He is also thinking of the books he stole, and he will, in the next month, begin to return them.

of others. Once, when Mason had mentioned to him, without intending to, that the summer before he had sat in a café and watched Lena walk to and from voice lessons, Mr. Ferry had turned excitedly and he had said, "Is that true? That's quite interesting." And then he paused and moved his head from side to side and he made a noise inside his throat and said, again, "Interesting."

When Mr. Ferry had first handed the book of letters to Mason, he said, "I've always thought that letter-writing was a skill, an art that will one day be looked upon as arcane and eccentric. Oh, I know you kids have chat rooms and e-mail and there's the immediacy of the phone, but writing letters is a lot of hard work and it's that hard work that makes them so special. They are intimate and full of useless detail. They go in circles. They beg for a response that is more than a few lines. You can draw pictures within the text of the letters. You can meander. They aren't just about information. Do you ever write letters to Lena?"

"She writes me notes," Mason said.

"That sounds like a beginning. Have you ever thought of sending her your poetry?"

"I showed her a few poems. But not any more. I don't think she likes my writing."

Mr. Ferry said that he had to feel something when he read a poem. There was no exact formula. He said that memory was involved, and experience, and language.

That had been the previous week. This week Mason confessed to Mr. Ferry that he had written a poem and that he had it with him. "It's called 'The Case of Lena S.'"

"Good, good, read it," Mr. Ferry said, and Mason, surprising himself, took the poem from his pocket and read.

In the street you come and go
Watching and
Wishing to be that woman in the grey dress
Or that girl on the black bicycle
Who carries a tennis racquet and swings her hair like a rope

Your reflection in the window
And beyond
Your lover sitting with
That girl on the black bicycle

Swinging your hair like a rope.

There was a silence and then Mr. Ferry said, "Well." He tapped his knee with one hand and said, "I like the hair and the rope. I like the 'you.'"

Mason was pleased enough with this response and that night, at home, he read the poem to Danny.

"That's a piece of shit," Danny said. "Okay, maybe the first line is nice but it's lifted out of T. S. Eliot, and so plagiarism gets you an F. Anyways, I don't know what you're talking about."

"About Lena."

"Yeah, yeah, but what if I don't know Lena? What if she's just a name?"

"I didn't write this for other people. It's for Lena."

"She'll be very happy to know that."

Mason took the poem and threw it in the garbage. The next time he saw Mr. Ferry he said that he had changed the poem because his brother Danny had thought the first draft was plagiarized.

"That's interesting that you should believe him. He's not the poet, you are."

"Yes, but he can be pretty convincing."

"Read the new version. Let's hear it."

So, Mason read.

Swings her hair
Delighted to be seen
Vain neck
The hollows at her shoulders

When Mason was finished Mr. Ferry nodded his head and said that Mason had read the poem too quickly. He took a drink from the wine glass on his side table. Mason said that it was, he knew, a completely different poem and a lot vaguer and he wasn't sure if even Lena would understand what it was about. "It's pretty," he said. "That's about it."

"Nothing wrong with pretty," Mr. Ferry said. "And it's not vaguer. You can draw the poem. I figure if you can draw the poem then it's doing a job." Then he asked, as if tired of indulging Mason, if Lena was going to come for a visit.

"I don't know. She could, if I asked her."

"Do that, ask her. Ask her if she wants to go to a movie. We'll all go. It'll be my treat."

Mason didn't think this was a great idea. He'd recently gone to a movie with Mr. Ferry, *The Deep End*, and he had spent the two hours muttering in the old man's ear, describing the images. Besides, the people around them had been fed up with the talking, even though Mason had tried to whisper. The movie had gone by in a blur and Mr. Ferry had been grumpy and demanding. "Talk to me, Mason," he had said. "What does she look like?" "She's blonde." "Short or long?" "Mid-length. It looks almost dirty. Greasy." "What's she wearing?" "A skirt. No, a dress. Red."

Then the scene had shifted, and on the descriptions went, and in the end Mr. Ferry had done amazingly well. He had kept up with the nuances and had understood when the woman seemed to be falling in love with the younger man. "She likes him," Mr. Ferry whispered. "She's getting dressed up a lot more."

After that experience Mason had avoided taking Mr. Ferry to the movies, and to go with Lena would be even more difficult. He'd have two people to care for and Mr. Ferry would be sitting there, clutching his cane and swinging his head, calling out for the two of them to explain the film to him.

"Lena is unpredictable these days," Mason said. He paused, aware that he was crossing into a dangerous space. "About two months ago she saw me sitting in a restaurant with Sadia Chahal. She walked by and looked in and there we were, the two of us. And, at that moment, everything changed. I was talking to Sadia, and then Lena showed up and immediately I wanted to be out on the street with her. I realized later that she probably wanted me to want that. She knew I was there, she followed me, and she was forcing me to think certain thoughts. You see how twisted it gets?"

Mr. Ferry spoke softly: "'Here I sat and waited; here it was I nourished my love with the longing and refreshed it with the sight. My eye could take in the street and the sidewalk on the other side where she walked. Oh, what a beautiful time.'" He paused and offered one palm to the ceiling, and the oddity of the words and the upraised hand made Mason feel exposed and strange. Mr. Ferry said, "You watched Lena. Kierkegaard watched Regine. Phaedria watched the cither player. That is a fact." His mouth worked silently, and then he said, "Lena." And he smiled.

That afternoon Mason went home, and he took a clean notebook and began to write what he would call "The Lena Poems." He wrote briskly and furiously, late into the night. And then, exhausted, he went to bed and fell asleep, dreaming of immortality.

⁊

Mason's father was usually home for breakfast. He liked to be there for Mason and he had taken to making him poached or scrambled eggs and toast and he'd serve juice and then sit with a cup of coffee and watch Mason eat and he'd talk. He had stories to tell about the night, about one fare that refused to pay or another, a young girl he picked up in the Higgins area, who at five in the morning wanted to go to Perkins and have a grilled cheese sandwich and who asked Mr. Crowe if he wanted to join her. She would buy. "She was way too young, at best eighteen, but she was done for the night and I thought she was lonely and needed something so I went into Perkins with her and I thought maybe she could pass for my daughter or something but they wouldn't let us in. They looked at her and said the place was full. It wasn't. There were empty booths everywhere but I guess they could tell what her job was. She was a prostitute."

"I know that, Dad. It's obvious," Mason said. He was eating his toast and he was aware of his father's diminished size, as if in the last while he'd been sick.

"Okay, fine, it's just it wasn't that big a deal. I mean, she was wearing a very short skirt and carrying a pink handbag and she wore those fishnet stockings but I don't think that's any reason to not let her eat a grilled cheese sandwich. I told them that. Then I said that they had just lost my business. That I wasn't about to come back to Perkins and it was a place I ate at a lot and I had a family of six children and they wouldn't be seeing any of my children there either." Here he paused and rubbed his eyes and looked down into his coffee mug. He said, "They thought I was her customer. I realized that later. Or maybe her pimp. I could've been that. It was amazing. I dropped her off on Langside. She lives in an apartment there. Her name was Barbara. She was young enough to be going to school with you." He gestured at Mason's plate and asked if he was still hungry. Mason said he wasn't. His dad needed a shave and his hair was too long and when Mason thought of him going into Perkins with the girl he was embarrassed and could only think of his father as ignorant. Or maybe he was a liar and he had known exactly who the girl was. Mason didn't want to think those thoughts. He stood, poured himself more juice, and sat down again.

Mr. Crowe said, "I've got to get your brother up. He's supposed to be out looking for work." Then he asked, "Does Lena spend time with Danny?"

Mason said that they'd only met once, just last week when Lena was over. "Why?"

Mr. Crowe lifted several fingers and made a shooing motion. "Forget it."

Mason held his glass of juice and watched his dad. He said, "What's going on? Did Danny say something?"

"No. No. Not at all." His father looked at him. Then he shrugged and said, "I saw Lena out here on the deck one day. With Danny. That's all."

Mason thought about this. He wanted to ask if Lena had looked pleased but he didn't. He said that Lena was too smart to get tricked by Danny. "She sees through people. She knows when they're fake."

"That's good," Mr. Crowe said. He got up from the table and poured himself more coffee, stood and drank, and then he said that he'd been seeing this woman, her name was Dorothy, and that he'd like Mason to meet her some time. "She's older than me, in her fifties, and she's not beautiful in the traditional sense, but *I* think she's beautiful. I don't want to do what your mom did, foist some stranger on you. She certainly isn't rich like Mr. Schmidt."

"I don't care about rich," Mason said.

"Of course you don't. She's got a daughter living in Calgary who's twenty-one. I gave Dorothy a ride home from work one afternoon and we started talking and didn't stop." He paused and drank the remainder of his coffee and then looked at Mason.

Mason said, "Great, Dad," but he didn't really think it was that great. Nor was he interested in meeting Dorothy. He was still thinking about Danny and Lena and later that day, when he got home from school and the house was empty, he went into Danny's room and he looked around. He opened drawers and looked under pillows and though he didn't know what he was looking for he thought he might find it. He came across Danny's sketchbook and sat down and opened it and near the middle he came across the sketch of Lena. Danny had done a good job. It was Lena from the waist up. She was sitting and looking straight ahead and she looked relaxed and the folds of the top she wore, near her stomach, were shaded in. Mason closed the book. Opened it and looked again. Then he ripped the page out and put the book back on the shelf and he went to his room and lay down on his bed and studied the drawing. What Danny had done was make her bigger than she actually was. Not physically. Just her presence. It may have been her eyes. She was holding a cigarette and her mouth was slightly open and it looked as if she was about to do or say something. Danny had concentrated on the straps of her tank top. She had breasts. Mason placed an index finger against the drawing, close to Lena's shoulder.

That night, when Danny came home, Mason went into his bedroom and stood in the doorway and said, "Last week, when you met Lena, you shook her hand. Do you always do that? Shake hands with people like you're an accountant or a car salesman?"

Danny looked up. "She shook *my* hand. She offered her hand and I took it. She's the weird one."

"Dad told me she was here with you."

"Dad's a loser."

"He said you were sitting out on the deck together. You shouldn't have done that."

"She came here," Danny said. "She *was* looking for you but you were off being the scholar so I invited her in. She accepted. However," and here Danny turned his face so Mason could see the wideness of his jaw, "she was perfectly chaste."

"I saw the drawing," Mason said. His brother was sitting by his barbells and Mason thought it might work to pick up a weight and drop it on Danny's head. "What did you do, bribe her to sit for you?"

"No. She was perfectly fine with letting me draw her. She's like a fucking Tinker Bell." Danny fluttered his hands like wings. "She needs people like me to tell her she exists."

"Stay away from her. She's not Seeta. Just stay away from her."

Danny waved Mason away. "She is, though. She's a girl just like Seeta and Maryann. All girls have a little secret place, a centre that you have to discover. Didn't you know that? Only Lena's centre is a little harder to find. Anyway, I haven't seen her since. She likes you. That mad mad girl likes *you*." Danny shook his head, indicating that this fact was unbelievable.

Mason walked away then. He left his brother sitting there and he went to his own room where his newborn book of poems, and the sketch of Lena, awaited him, but he found himself lying on his bed, eyes wide open, thinking about Lena and wondering if it was true that her centre needed to be discovered. He wondered if he, Mason, could ever find her secret place and save Lena Schellendal.

He did not know what he would say to her the next time they met. He imagined he might carry the sketch in his back pocket and pull it out to show her. Not say anything, just let her explain, but he pushed this idea away. The next day she phoned him and said, "I have to see you," and they met on the street outside his house. When she approached him and held his hands and said, "Take me somewhere," he was glad he didn't have the sketch to show her.

"Where do you want to go, Lena?" he said. She was wearing cut-offs and a pale-blue top with half-sleeves and rubber flip-flops. Her arms and legs were unbearably white and Mason couldn't help thinking about the way her breasts looked in Danny's drawing. He wondered if Lena liked Danny's bulk, the way his arms and shoulders were shaped.

Lena looked around and then she went up on tiptoes and held Mason's elbow and whispered in his ear, "To the beach. The big wide beach." She dropped away and looked up at him, as if he were a parent who could give her permission.

"I can't stand the city," she said. "Julianne was at Grand Beach on Sunday and she said the water was warm and everyone was out playing volleyball. She said it was perfect. I'd like to go there. Or somewhere." She was hollow; it wasn't her body, it was her voice. It exited from her mouth like an echo inside a thin tube. Mason had the urge to tap a knuckle against her skull.

He borrowed his mother's car on a Thursday when he had no school and he took Lena to Patricia Beach. They lay in amongst the dunes, out of the eye of the public, and alternately slept and read. Lena wore jean shorts and a long-sleeved white shirt. At one point she smelled the shirt and said it was her father's. When the heat overwhelmed them they went out to the edge of the lake, where Lena waded up to her ankles and Mason walked out until the water was up to his chest and then he sank beneath the surface. He swam parallel to the beach, keeping his eye on Lena.

In the afternoon they ate peanut butter sandwiches and drank warm water. Then they lay on their backs and smoked as dragonflies hovered above them. Lena kissed him. She said, "Here," and hovered above him and when he tried to touch her she pushed his hands away but kept kissing him. "Harmless," she said. "Let's pretend we just met."

"But we haven't."

"Let's pretend."

And so she asked him his name and he played along and asked about her family and her work and she said she was a bona fide genius.

"Are you in love?" he asked.

"Truly, madly, deeply," she answered. "With a boy. There is only one."

She ate a grape that was transparent and clear and the juice dribbled down her chin. She wiped it away with her wrist.

"What happened to the girl who loved God?"

"She still loves God. She just needs something else."

"You scare me. I worry that you'll kill yourself."

"Don't, Mason. Don't worry. Do I look dangerous? Come, let's go swim. I'll show you."

And so they waded out into the water until the shore had receded and they swam and Lena's head bobbed in the brown waves and her arms were thin sticks floating on the surface.

Later, on the way home, Lena sat back against the passenger door and laid her bare feet out over Mason's lap. He placed a hand on one of her ankles.

"I like that," she said. Then she asked him if he was happy.

Her window was half open and the wind snapped at her hair and he was aware of her legs against his thighs and he said, "Right now, like this, yeah. I am."

"I was thinking that we could just keep driving. You and me."

Lena was watching him. He knew that, but he didn't look at her. He said, "Is that a test question?"

"If it were, would you pass?"

He said, "My mother thinks I should stay away from you. She's never said it in those words exactly, but she worries."

"That doesn't surprise me." She sat up and tucked one leg under her and laid an arm across the back of the seat. "And your father?"

"He doesn't interfere like that. He's got this new girlfriend, Dorothy, who I've never met but he says she's nice. And older. That's what he said. My father likes you. He said once that you were special. That you needed looking after."

"He told you that? What, was he feeling sorry for me, like I was some pathetic creature lying on the sidewalk?"

"He didn't say you were pathetic, or a creature. He said something about the world being turned upside down and how the first, in the end, would be last."

"It's hard to tell what he's thinking. When he picked me up that night I didn't know what to say. At one point he said there were more important things than love. Do you think he knew about Aldous?"

"He probably suspected something, though he was gone a lot and he tends to believe people. If you say you're telling the truth, he believes you. I think if my mom told him, even today, that she still loved him, he'd believe it. He can't help it. Actually, I think he's still trying to figure out why she left him."

"That's so sad."

Mason shrugged. "There are two types in my family. My father and me, we're faithful, and then there's my mother and Danny." He watched Lena to see if Danny's name would affect her.

Lena laughed. "You? You consider yourself faithful, the guy who liked Seeta and then Sadia and then me and now Rosemary and who knows who else after that?"

"My dad said he saw you at our house."

"Yeah, I was. Remember, you made me a white cake." Her face was innocent. There was no hint of deception or malice.

"Another time, too. With Danny. I saw the sketch that he drew."

"Oh." She took her hand off his shoulder.

"You acted like you didn't know him. When he came into the kitchen. A big show of shaking hands and stuff. Was that for me?"

"I guess it was. I'm sorry."

"When he was drawing you, he was looking right at you," Mason said. "Like, for how long? Half an hour?"

"Less. Anyway, Mason, it didn't mean anything." She said that she had no interest in Danny. She had no interest in boys at all these days. Except for Mason, who was like a path she could walk down in the darkness. "I'm gonna slide over and put my head against your neck, okay?"

Mason looked at her. He nodded.

She did what she said she was going to do. He could smell the sunscreen on her face and forehead. She was wearing her bikini top and jean shorts. She'd removed her father's shirt. She said, "Now put your hand on my leg. Not on the inside, just on the top and hold it there. There."

They passed the town of Libau. Lena said she didn't want to go home yet so at a gas station they picked up a coffee to go. A few miles further on, Mason detoured onto a side road and drove until they came upon a driveway that led to a broken-down barn. Mason parked the car and Lena climbed out and went behind the barn to pee. Mason stood in the bright sunshine and stretched and, when Lena reappeared, she came up to him and stood close. "This is our place," she said. "Hang a little sign, *Home Sweet Home*, set a table with flowers. Bet we could live here for weeks and nobody'd notice." She pressed the palm of her hand against his chest. He caught her wrist and the underside of her arm flared white. The dark and heated mat of an unshaved armpit.

"You look worried," she said.

"Maybe I am. A little. I never know what's going to come next. That time when we met on the street, I saw you and you said my name and you talked to me but I wasn't sure if you were really there. Then you go and sit for my brother like he was some kind of Gauguin and when I ask you about it you say it's nothing. Nothing. Well, in my mind it's more than nothing. It might not be terribly important but it's not nothing. You know what nothing is? It's you never meeting my brother, never letting him look at you, never letting him draw your hair and mouth and breasts. That's nothing."

"Don't." She took his hand and held it and said, "I thought it might be okay, having him draw me. But then I thought sending you away would be okay, too. What I understand and what I don't understand are the same. I keep thinking I've forgotten something and then I go back and I can't remember what I've forgotten." She stopped. Her hands were at her side. "But," she said, "Right now, I feel great. Everything is clear. I've been stripped clean. Remember that day you came to my baptism? I felt something then. I wanted to be with you but my father took me away." She paused, then said, "What have I done wrong? I haven't hurt anybody."

Mason listened to her talk and he leaned against the car and drank his coffee. Lena stood close to him and smoked. Then she reached through the open car window and stuck a CD in the player and put it on and began to dance through the deep grass. She closed her eyes and threw back her head and called out, "Don't you love girls, Mason? Aren't they amazing?" She was a wraith. Her arms and legs. Her belly button like a place where you could insert a key. She came back to Mason and stood close to him and said, "I wonder sometimes if Jesus loved any girls. Like when he was a boy. Or even a man. Did he notice girls in the street? Did he want women? Did he think about them naked? It's a good question to ask. He was supposed to be perfect, but he was human. Maybe he secretly loved someone. Like Mary Magdalene. She was always hanging around stalking him. At his speeches, his crucifixion, his tomb." She looked up at Mason. Grinned. "Mary and Jesus."

Mason grinned. Lena put her fingers like a handcuff around one of his wrists and said, "I love this." Later, back in the car, she drove, the heel of her hand hitting against the wheel in time to the music. Mason slept briefly and dreamed of two blackbirds banging beaks on a wire. He woke and considered telling Lena about the dream but he didn't. She had bitten the skin at her thumb and a thin line of blood had seeped onto her cuticle. It was hot and Mason rolled down the window and watched Lena drive. She looked over at him and said, "Hey." Then she took his hand and she said, "Take me away and you can have whatever you want."

She smelled of the sun and the water. Her shoulders were slightly red from too much sun. Mason said, "Where would we go, Lena?"

"We would disappear. I was thinking that we should steal Mr. Ferry's car. It just sits in the garage out back and he can't drive. He wouldn't miss it."

"I couldn't do that to Mr. Ferry," Mason said. "It was one thing to steal his books, but I couldn't take his car."

Lena was quiet, and then she said, "That's a no, then?"

"Yeah, I guess it is."

Lena still held Mason's fingers but she'd stopped playing with them and, after a bit, she took her hand and put it on the steering wheel.

She drove to her house and got out and Mason slid over behind the wheel. Lena leaned back into the car and kissed Mason on the mouth and said, "Bye, Mason," softly in his ear, and this surprised him and he was about to say something but Lena was already running up the sidewalk, her beach bag swinging from her hand, her shorts, the sleeve of her father's shirt dragging on the ground. At the door she turned and waved and there was the wink of her belly and her face, then she was gone.

When Mason walked into his mother's apartment, she was sitting out on the balcony in the late-afternoon sun. Her legs were stretched out in front of her and she was reading a newspaper, and when she heard Mason she turned and said, "Hi," and motioned with her left hand for him to come over. He went to her and she took his arm and pulled him down and pressed her cheek against his and he saw her bare thighs and her nipples through her thin top.

He got himself a Nestea from the fridge and came back and sat and asked, "Where's Aldous?"

"Golfing. He wanted me to come but I hate golfing, and he hates it that I hate it. Your dad doesn't like golf either. That's to his credit."

"He can't afford it," Mason said.

"Is that why?" Mrs. Crowe said. She placed her palms on her thighs and studied her hands. She said, "We're going out for dinner. Very simple. And it would be nice if you'd join us. I'd really like it if you stayed the night."

Mason finished his drink. He said he had no change of clothes.

"You don't need them," his mother said. "We're going out for pasta at that new restaurant on Corydon. You can borrow some sandals from Aldous. You might even fit into his clothes."

"He doesn't like me," Mason said.

"Oh, that's not true. He thinks you don't like him. Now, see?"

"I don't."

"You can't dislike someone you don't know," she said. "That's silly. Don't be small."

They went inside where the air conditioner had kept everything cool. It was both wonderful and false to be in the apartment with his mother, who was standing in the white kitchen, her back to him, talking about the life she had and how she wanted to share it with him. She turned and said, "But you think I'm awful."

"Not awful," Mason said. He looked around the apartment. "Maybe you're lucky."

"Mothers aren't supposed to leave their children and husbands. Our duty is to nurture and if we don't, we're lousy human beings."

"I didn't say that."

"No, but your dad did." She laughed but it wasn't a cheerful laugh. She was about to say more but Aldous came in and kissed her on the cheek and when he learned that Mason was staying for the night he seemed pleased and he said that after dinner they could get a movie or something. "How about it, Mason?" he said, and Mason shrugged and said, "Okay."

So they did that and the evening was slow and easy and by the time it had passed Mason realized that he didn't mind Aldous's presence. Later, when Aldous had gone to bed, Mason and his mother sat on the balcony and looked out at the river and Mrs. Crowe said, "So, tell me about Lena."

"I don't know what to say about Lena."

"Well, why don't you start with today. How was it?"

"We sat in the dunes and she talked about me going away with her." It was dark now and the lights of a plane crossed the sky in the distance and Mason could see the outline of the trees along the river bank. The darkness was a good thing for confessions. He said, "She talks about forgetting things and not understanding and she says that she likes me but then she says she has to push me away. Everything is important to her, even the smallest bug." Mason paused and lit a cigarette. He thought about Danny and considered telling his mother but decided it wasn't worth it. Mason believed Lena's version of the story. He remembered her dancing through the long grass and calling out, "Don't you love girls, Mason?"

"You know what I think, don't you?" his mother said.

"Yeah. You told me."

"But you're not going to listen, are you?"

"No, I'm not. She wants to drive up to Edmonton to see her aunt. She wants me to go along."

"With whose car?"

"I don't know," Mason said. He looked over at the shadow of his mother. Earlier, eating supper in the restaurant, she had bent over her linguine and some sauce had remained at the corner of her mouth and Aldous had reached across and wiped it away with his finger and then put his finger in his own mouth. Mason had watched this and Mrs. Crowe had seen him watching and later, when Aldous had tried to touch her ear and her hair, she had gently pushed him away.

"You can't have mine," his mother said now.

"I know. I told Lena that."

Mrs. Crowe said, "She needs help, Mason. What would she do in another city?"

"I don't know. Maybe she'd be freer there. Away from her father."

"Does she make you happy?" his mother asked.

Mason looked out over the railing of the balcony at the lights of the city, and he said that he didn't think so but then he wasn't sure if any girl had ever made him happy.

"Not even me, I guess," his mother said, and she rose and came and stood behind him and held his head close to her chest and rocked slightly and said, "Oh, Mason," and he felt her breasts against his right ear and he heard her voice deep in her ribcage and he let her hold him until she had had enough.

He slept on the couch in the den. There was the TV and the computer and the walls full of books and there was a photograph on the desk of Aldous standing beside his new airplane and there was a Tiffany lamp that pooled light onto his own head where it lay on the pillow his mother had given him. She'd come in and handed him the blankets and then later, when he was lying on the couch, staring at the ceiling, she came back and asked if he was okay and he said he was. At night he woke and walked past the kitchen and down the hall to the bathroom. His mother's bedroom door was open and as he passed he saw her and Aldous lying beside each other and on the way back he left the bathroom light on and this allowed him to see into his mother's bedroom more clearly and there she was, sleeping beside Aldous, one arm under her head, a bare leg lying across Aldous's legs. She was naked. He went back to the couch and lay there for a long time not thinking about anything specific and finally he took off his boxers and masturbated into them and while he did this he chased Lena from his head and thought about Sarah Benoit, the big-chested girl with the dreadlocks in his Physics class.

*T*wo days after the trip to the beach with Mason, Lena went to visit Mr. Ferry. It was a Saturday morning and Wellington Crescent was full of joggers and mothers with babies in strollers. She walked up the boulevard and then crossed over to Mr. Ferry's front yard and she went around the back and saw the garage and the two swinging doors and she paused and looked around. Along the back lane everything was quiet. She went back around to the front door and she rang the doorbell and as she waited she saw herself in the glass of the door. She stuck out her tongue. Mr. Ferry opened the door and before he could speak Lena introduced herself and Mr. Ferry smiled and said that he had fond memories of Lena Schellendal. He groped for her arm and, finding it, lead her into the library and told her to sit on the couch. He sat beside her and asked if she wanted a job reading to him.

She said she didn't, that madness ran in her family and she was on a steady diet of lithium, and work wasn't something the doctor was recommending. Reading made her more depressed, she said. She spoke quickly while Mr. Ferry nodded his head and listened to her and then said that "mad" was a bit harsh, wasn't it? She said it could be and then she asked if she could have a drink and he said that he would get it but she said, "Sit, sit," and went into the kitchen and poured beer into glasses and looked for the keys. They were there, on the little hooks under the sign, KEYS, and she took the car key and slipped it into her jeans pocket and returned with the two glasses and pressed one into Mr. Ferry's hand and said, "Cheers."

"How are you, Lena?" Mr. Ferry asked.

She said she was fine. "I was with Mason the day before yesterday. We went out to the beach and he said that you'd asked about me. So, I thought I'd just come by and say hello." She was looking at Mr. Ferry's thin legs and his long feet. She wondered how Mason managed to keep coming back to this man month after month. She began to lose courage. She drank quickly and put her empty glass on the table.

"That's good. Very good," Mr. Ferry said. "Another?"

"No, I have to go."

"I've frightened you."

"No, no. Why would you say that?"

"I do that. Cory McPhail, the girl who reads to me on Saturday afternoons – in fact, she will be coming in several hours – was frightened the other day as well when I asked her to describe herself. As if I am too forceful. Or, as if I were fond of young girls."

"You're not. It's just I have to meet someone."

"Ah, yes. Good. I remember your other visit. You wandered upstairs while Mason read. We drank beer like we're doing now. You see?"

"Yes. Thank you, Mr. Ferry."

"You don't like me very much. Do you see me as a fool?"

"No, I don't." The keys pressed against Lena's thigh and if Mr. Ferry had not been blind, he could have seen the outline of them through her jeans. "I don't think that."

"I just get that impression. Most people, especially girls, they like me. They find me pleasant and approachable. You, on the other hand, seem to think I am a mountebank. Have I deceived Mason in some way?"

"No. He thinks you're amazing and smart and full of knowledge. You can do no wrong."

"Ah, so that's it. I'm perfect," Mr. Ferry said. "And you might be jealous." Then he said, "Why did you come here all by yourself? What do you want? Something for Mason? Or something for yourself? Something real, something you can touch?" He held out his hand, palm up. "Here," he said.

Lena looked at his hand and shifted on the couch. She said, "That's your hand."

"Take it," he said. "Please?"

Albert padded into the room, jumped onto Lena's lap, and pushed his nose against her chin. Lena reached out and took Mr. Ferry's hand. She laid her own palm down on Mr. Ferry's and they held hands loosely. His hand was smooth, as if he had never done anything physical, or as if he were a child. He looked straight ahead and Lena closed her eyes and nuzzled Albert, who was purring. When Mr. Ferry said, "There," and pulled his hand away, Lena placed both of her hands on Albert, who looked up sleepily.

Mr. Ferry said, "Would you take me to a movie? I'd love that. I have my car out there and you could drive, you have your licence, don't you, and we could slip over to Silver City and watch a movie. Any movie."

Lena giggled as if she had suddenly discovered something both foolish and absurd. "Like a date?" She was breathing raggedly.

Mr. Ferry's mouth went up at one corner. "Lena," he said. Then he moved his head as if searching for something and he said, "How about a kiss?" His hands were shaking.

Lena looked about. She slid over against the far edge of the couch. "No," she said.

"Just a small one. I won't hurt you."

"No," Lena said. She pulled Albert closer and stood and stepped away from Mr. Ferry and said, "I'm going to go now."

"Huh." He swung his cane in a wide arc. It passed over the spot Lena had just vacated. She stepped back. Mr. Ferry stood and stabbed his cane in her direction. He didn't speak, just took a step and stabbed and took another step. He called out, "Albert. Here, boy. Come to Daddy."

Lena reached the back door and opened it and still holding Albert she stepped outside and quietly shut the door. Down the stairs and across the large lawn towards the garage. She entered through the small side door and stood in the cool darkness. She was breathing quickly and this surprised her because she didn't imagine that there was any danger. Mr. Ferry's car was there, a large black beast whose top caught the faint light coming through a small window just above the double doors of the garage. Albert meowed. Mr. Ferry was out on the back porch now, calling for his cat. Lena listened and did not move. After Mr. Ferry had stopped calling and the back door had closed, she still waited. Then she stepped back outside and put Albert on the lawn and said, "Go. Shoo," and he made a dash for the house. Lena re-entered the garage. The double doors opened onto the back lane. She walked around to the rear of the car and reached up and undid the latch at the top of the doors and swung them open. Standing in the lane now, she could see the top of Mr. Ferry's house beyond the fence. She was hidden. The neighbourhood was silent. She went back into the garage and climbed into the car, which smelled of dust and plastic, and she turned the ignition and pressed the gas. It started. She backed the car out of the garage rubbing the front bumper against the door. The door stuttered and banged against the fence. Lena turned the wheel, put the car into drive, and followed the lane out towards the side street. Further along, she passed Mason's house and saw his backyard and the shape of someone on a lawn chair. Danny, maybe. A giddiness, a floating, a rising above the mundane, the stupidity of the world. She called out and the womb of the car received her voice.

She drove back into her own neighbourhood and parked the car several blocks from her house and walked home. Her father was outside, mowing the lawn. He waved at her and she waved back and went into the house and up to her room and packed a bag. She stood at the window and observed her father, who had stooped to dig out a cluster of dandelions. Emily came into her room and saw the bag and said, "Where are you going?"

Lena turned and looked at her sister and said, "Away, but you can't say anything."

Emily was frightened. Lena went over to her and said, "Don't worry, I'll come back." She hugged her and then picked up the bag and went downstairs and out the back door and walked up the lane and circled up towards Mr. Ferry's car and climbed in. The interior was brown and clean and the mats on the floor said Impala. The radio had only AM and Lena played with the dial until she'd found some suitable music. She turned it up loud and drove west down Portage, towards the Perimeter, the window slightly open and the hot air pushing against her head. Beyond the windshield things were happening. Two boys talking to a girl, a group of children, a dog peeing against a lamppost, the traffic flowing by.

She drove just beyond Portage la Prairie and then turned northwest. Three hours later, in Russell, she stopped at a gas station and filled the tank and, using her debit card, paid for the gas and bought herself a Fruitopia and a day-old muffin. It was suppertime when she arrived in Yorkton. She pulled into a motel parking lot. The Flamingo. She said the name to herself and then she got out of the car. She registered at the motel and was surprised at her efficiency, at her ability to pretend that she was a traveller passing through who needed a room for one night, a room to rest in. The man behind the counter was dwarfish with a flat forehead and he wanted cash up front. Lena reached into her wallet and took out the money and handed it to him. He gave her the key.

The room was airless. There was a double bed, a small wooden chair, a bureau with a mirror, a bathroom door, and, inside the bathroom, a shower with a dark-blue curtain and a small sink, and above the sink, another mirror. Everywhere she looked she found herself.

She was standing in the middle of the room. She sat down on the bed. Lay back and opened her mouth. Closed it. Opened it again, a fish pressed up against the glass of a tiny aquarium.

She stood and looked at herself in the mirror and touched her hair and her nose. "A pimple," she said, and squeezed it, and leaned into herself. She washed her face and dried herself and walked outside and saw a man and two women sitting on lawn chairs on the tarmac. They were mostly naked except for bathing suits and one of the women was quite fat. She was wearing a bikini. She looked up at Lena and said, "Hi," and Lena nodded.

"Shy," the fat woman said and the man laughed and mumbled something.

"Jesus Christ, Tray." This was the third woman. She was skinny and wearing dark glasses and Lena couldn't tell where she was looking. After Lena had passed by, this same woman laughed in a high-sustained pitch and then she said, "I didn't," and the man said, "Blanche, of course you did. With me, even."

Lena went into the lobby of the motel, which wasn't really a lobby, and she slipped a dollar into the vending machine and pressed the letter K and the silver coil holding the Aero bar spiralled obediently and was pushed out over the precipice and fell, clunk, and Lena bent to retrieve it, her hand and wrist lost briefly in the maw of the machine. She stood and unwrapped a corner of the candy bar and took a bite. She turned to her left and stopped and shivered. The dwarfish man was studying her.

He lifted his chin slightly and said, "If the three of them in Number 9 give you trouble, let me know."

Lena looked around and finally understood that the man was talking to her.

The man said, "They can be rowdy. A ménage à trois," he said, strangling the last word.

Lena shrugged and left. She passed the threesome again. The skinny woman raised an arm and waved, calling out to Lena, "You're back."

Lena halted, then walked around the three bodies.

The man said, "Wanna join us? Beer? Whisky? Gin? Coke? Tang?" He looked Lena up and down.

"Shut up, Tray," the fat one said. "Don't listen to him," she called, but Lena had passed by and gone into her room. She shut the door and placed her head against the frame and could hear, quite clearly, the man talking about her. She lay down and looked at the ceiling and thought about her mother and father and she imagined the smell of dinner cooking and her empty place at the dining-room table and her father's self-control as he pretended that her absence was both normal and forgivable. Sitting up, she opened her suitcase and removed her bottle of pills, soft silver-white, the lightest alkali metal, poured them into her hand, sniffed at them, and forced them down her throat. She gagged and swallowed. Gagged again. She ran to the bathroom and bent over the tap and drank and came up for air. After she had steadied herself, she sat on the toilet and peed. Wiped herself and pulled up her panties and left her shorts in a puddle on the floor. She put on lipstick. Checked her eye shadow and liner and found a blurred vision of herself. A crack of thunder startled her and she heard someone arguing in a nearby room. She made her way back to bed and climbed in and covered herself with the blanket. She thought she might have slept because she dreamed that she was surrounded by water and when she woke she could hear the rain. She tried to stand, to go over to the window and look outside, but her body would not move. She saw the flashing of the Flamingo sign, or it might have been lightning that had arrived with the rain. A lovely furious rain that beat away the noises in her head and flooded the streets and crept up over the sidewalk and under the crack of her motel room door and leaked into the hard-to-reach places and finally eased her loose and carried her away.

Not long after Mason started reading to Mr. Ferry, Mr. Ferry tried to explain, with many gestures and much looping logic, how to make sense of things. These were the words he used and he said them carefully, as if what he were about to say had great import. He said that in fairy tales and legends a knight perceives a rare bird and he runs after it and almost catches it, may even hold it briefly in his hand, and then it flies off again and night falls and he finds himself lost, separated from his companions, unable to find his way. The knight, Mr. Ferry said, starts out with great hope and then must resign himself to failure.

At this point, Mr. Ferry paused and touched his chin and then his head and he took a drink from his glass of water and he said that existence was an enormous risk. We can never know whether we have chosen the right path, simply because we cannot go back and try again. He said that both "double" and "doubt" spring from the same root, "duo." So, consciousness itself, the act of seeing ourselves, was a form of doubt and – here Mr. Ferry was quite emphatic – "We have the potential to doubt ourselves to pieces."

"Imagine," he said, "a man who is unhappy, standing before a mirror and not recognizing himself."

It had been early summer and one of the windows on the north side of the house was open and from the outside came the sounds of children calling and cars passing by and in the distance, up by the Misericordia perhaps, a siren started up and then stopped. Mason, whose interest in the psychology of free will was minimal, listened to Mr. Ferry because he was being paid and because it was often easier to listen than it was to read. Still, there were moments when he was aware of something fresh, as if it were a line from a poem, and he liked the sound of "doubting oneself to pieces." Mr. Ferry said that a person could choose anything. And this was crux of the matter, because when we are aware that we can choose anything, we become frightened by the magnitude of the choice and we disguise it by going about our daily lives: eating toast for breakfast, driving to work every day, cleaning the dirt out from underneath our fingernails, watching TV, listening to music, reading to old men – anything to distract us from our fear.

When Mr. Ferry said this he was smiling slightly and moving his cane in tiny circles across the floor. He turned to Mason and asked, "Does this sound right?"

Mason wasn't sure. And, because he wasn't sure, he felt that he had failed in some way, and that this bungling somehow proved his own ignorance. But the moment passed and the hours passed and the months passed and nothing, at least not in a direct way, was said of these ideas again.

Now, a year later, in the middle of summer, Mason went over to Mr. Ferry's and told him that he wouldn't be reading to him anymore. When Mr. Ferry asked him why, Mason said that he didn't really have a reason, at least not something that he would be able to explain. They were standing, the two of them, in the centre of the room where Mason had spent many hours. Mr. Ferry seemed agitated. He asked Mason if he was okay. Did he need anything?

Mason shook his head, and said, "No." He hoped that Mr. Ferry would not ask questions about Lena, and he did not. Rather, in his abstracted way, Mr. Ferry said that Mason was young and that that was good, and he said that Mason should not lay blame, either on himself or on others. He apologized for sounding trite. Then he cleared his throat and said, "Perhaps I should tell you a story. One that begins well and pulls you along and ends beautifully. That kind of story."

Mason did not answer. He looked around the room, at the bookshelves and the tiny table and the two chairs. He was aware of Mr. Ferry's head moving back and forth; he was bent forward slightly, near the shoulders, as if on the verge of stooping to retrieve something that he had dropped. Mason stepped backwards and said that he was fine, he really was, and that he had to go. Then he said, "Thank you, Mr. Ferry," and he turned and he walked out of the house.

In late August, before school started, Mason moved to his mother's apartment. She and Aldous had cleaned out a small spare room and his mother came to pick him up when his father was at work and Danny was out.

"Your father's not happy about this," Mrs. Crowe said.

"It's not because of him," Mason said. "I just need to change something."

"I told him that but he takes it personally. I'll talk to him."

Together, he and his mother carried several boxes and one suitcase out to the car. As they drove down Wellington Crescent to the condominium, neither of them spoke. The stereo was on and a woman sang in a low voice about the colour of her lover's hair.

That night for supper his mother made crepes with cream sauce and boiled asparagus and they ate by the open balcony doors. Aldous was on a business trip, so they were alone. A warm wind entered the room and lifted the corner of the tablecloth. At one point, Mrs. Crowe said, "Do you miss her?" and the question was said so easily that Mason wasn't sure if he had heard correctly. And then, before he could answer, his mother said, "It's okay to miss her."

Later, he went to unpack, laying his clothes out and placing his books on the shelf by the foot of the bed.

During the night he woke and she was standing over him. She was part of the shadows though he saw the outline of her head and shoulders and he heard her breathing. She stood and looked down at him and held a hand near his face and then left the room. After she had gone he lay awake and listened for her, but he heard nothing.

And then, one day, Mason met Mrs. Schellendal on the street. When they first saw each other they both looked away but the corner on which they stood had trapped them and so they made clumsy small talk until Mrs. Schellendal cried out, "We lost her." She leaned into Mason and he thought that she looked very much like Lena. He had not noticed this before. They shared the same paleness, the downturn of the mouth, a softness at the jaw that made them seem frail but was, Mason knew, deceiving. He felt, briefly, a sharp sadness for the woman who stood before him, but this seemed forced, as if it were expected. He hunted for some words to offer her and said, awkwardly, "I have dreams about her." Mrs. Schellendal looked at him with horror, sucked in two quick breaths, and said, "I don't hold it against you." Then she walked away and he did not see her again.

And yes, he did dream of Lena. In one recurring dream she was playing a certain piece on the piano, over and over again, and then she turned and said something but he could not understand her. When he woke from these dreams it was with a vague sense of shame and defeat, though the shame, he thought, was not a bad thing. It made him more careful.

In the fall, when school began again, he worked part-time at the local supermarket and in the evenings he went out to the neighbourhood park and watched the cyclists and the joggers and the dogs with their owners. The days grew shorter. Sometimes he sat on his mother's balcony in the late afternoons and observed the scene twelve floors below. A taxi boat moving up the river. Two men standing on the bank and fishing, their voices occasionally rising to where Mason sat. Above him, the sky was clear and deep and blue and infinite. As the weather grew colder, the leaves turned colour. Geese and ducks flew in from the north and used the river as their runway. They gathered near the bend in the river and rested in the tall grass along the banks. For several weeks they made this their home. And then they were gone.

Bob Milan

David Bergen is the author of three highly acclaimed novels: *A Year of Lesser* (1996), a *New York Times* Notable Book and winner of the McNally Robinson Book of the Year Award; *See the Child* (1999); and, most recently, *The Case of Lena S.* (2002), winner of the Carol Shields Winnipeg Book Award, and a finalist for the Governor General's Award for Fiction, the McNally Robinson Book of the Year Award, and the Margaret Laurence Award for Fiction. He is also the author of a collection of short fiction, *Sitting Opposite My Brother* (1993), which was a finalist for the Manitoba Book of the Year Award. A section from *The Case of Lena S.* was chosen for *Toronto Life's* Summer Fiction issue in 2000. Bergen won the CBC Literary Prize for Fiction the same year.

David Bergen lives in Winnipeg.